MORE BURGLAR DIARIES
THIEVES LIKE US

Danny King

BYKER BOOKS

MORE BURGLAR DIARIES: THIEVES LIKE US

Copyright © Danny King 2009

All Rights Reserved

Second edition

First Published 2007 by
DMKing Publishing

www.bykerbooks.co.uk

ISBN 978-0-9560788-4-1

Printed in Great Britain by Lightning Source, Milton Keynes

THE WAREHOUSE JOB

1. Avoiding the enemy

What is it about seeing a bloke reading in a pub that's like a magnet to other blokes? Four different no-mates have wandered over and asked me how it's going in the space of the last half hour despite the fact that I've got a book in front of my face. I tell you, if I was sat here staring at the wall or crying my fucking eyes out, no one would give me a second look. Open a book, a newspaper or a packet of peanuts and suddenly I can't beat 'em away.

"What's it like?" Norris asks me, eyeing the front cover of my book as he takes the seat opposite me.

"What, being continually interrupted by a load of illiterates while I'm trying to read? Fucking annoying now that you come to ask," I reply without looking up.

Norris misses the sarcasm. He flies right under it, evading my words like a Stealth fighter pilot evading Akak flak. This is something Norris is particularly adept at; a self-preservation skill that he's honed after a lifetime of opening doors to the sounds of, "oh for fuck's sake, it's fucking Norris".

"No, your book I mean," he says, reading the title. "*Harry Potter*, huh? What's it about?"

"You don't read much, do you Norris?" I suggest, going out on a limb.

"What, books? No, boring in't they?" he reckons, before cutting the small talk and going straight to the favour. "Anyway look, you know that bird you're going out with?"

"Vaguely," I reply.

"You know that tart she works with, that skinny thing with the eyebrows?"

I reluctantly pull my mind's-eye away from Hogwarts and take it over to Mel's office for a quick gander at Rachel before confirming I know who he's talking about. "Yeah, go on."

"Well, you know they work together?" Norris continues.

"Is it a tank?" I guess.

"What?" Norris says, looking confused.

"Oh I'm sorry, I thought we were playing twenty questions." I say.

"No, I'm just asking you about her, that's all," Wing Commander Norris tells me, evading a fresh barrage of sarcasm in order to get past my defences and annoy me at close-quarters.

I drop my book on the table and throw in the towel when I realise the only way I'm gonna get rid of Norris is either to meet him head on or take off a sock and borrow a couple of reds from the pool table.

"What d'you want Norris? You thinking of doing her place over? Cos' if you are, I wouldn't bother if I was you, she ain't got nothing..."

"No no, it's nothing like that," he protests. Was ever a man so banged to rights? "I was just wondering if anyone was knobbing her, that's all."

"Why?" I ask, cautiously.

"Why? Why d'you think why? That I'm concerned about her happiness or something? No, I want to steam in there myself if the coast's all clear. Do her, you know. I mean, she's alright and all, but let's face it, she can't be getting too many requests, not with those caterpillars crawling across her glasses, know what I mean?" Norris says, smacking his lips at the thought of an easy meal.

"I ain't read nothing on the bog wall about it," I assure him.

"Well d'you reckon she's up for it then?"

"How would I know? I only say hello to her when I go into the office. I don't sit around watching *Bridget Jones* and moaning about geezers with her now do I."

"Oh yeah, but you know her a bit," Norris insisted. "So what d'you reckon my chances are?"

"You? Slim to comical."

"Well look, put in a good word for us and there'll be a drink in it for you," he finally offers. I decide to bite.

"What like, fifty quid?"

"Fifty quid! What are you pimping for her all of a sudden? No, I mean a drink, from the bar, you know."

"All right, I'll have a pint of Bollinger '78 and a packet of pork scratchings," I tell him. "Actually, make that '76. The '78 never goes down well with pork scratchings."

"Bex, I'm serious..." Norris starts until I hold up my hands.

"Alright, look, I'll tell you what I'll do. I'll finish my drink, get back to my book and ignore you until you go away."

Norris glares at me for a moment before folding his arms and sinking back into his chair.

"Oh cheers. Nice one. Do the same for you some time," he threatens.

"What, ignore me in the boozer? You don't frighten me, Norris," I reply.

Norris thinks about this for a second and is just about to tell me that's not what he meant when Ollie finally turns up and cuts him off with an enthusiastic, "Bexy boy!" like this'll somehow gloss over the fact that the big doughnut's half an hour late.

"Alright Ol," Norris smiles.

"Urgh," Ollie replies on contact.

"What time d'you call this?" I demand. "You were meant to be here half hour ago. Half hour. All the while I've been stuck here getting both barrels off Captain Charisma. Where were you?"

"Honestly Bex, I got here as soon as I could... be arsed," Ollie chuckles. "Nah, I'm only kidding." A thought then occurs to him. "Who's

6

Captain Christmas?"

"No you're not only kidding Ol, you did only get here when you could be arsed. Nine o'clock we said. Nine o-fucking-clock. How is it that we can both agree to meet at nine o'clock but then you don't get here until half nine? You only live ten minutes down the road so that means you were still at home picking your feet or juggling oranges twenty minutes after you were supposed to be here."

Ollie rolls his eyes and sags his shoulders in an effort to help me understand just how boring and uncool I can be some times.

"Christ, you sound just like my Probation Officer. He's always moaning his guts out like a good 'un an' all. I don't know what his problem is," Ollie sighs.

"By crikey yeah, what a puzzler!" I proffer, standing up to pull my coat on.

Norris senses a second-chance to get to grips with Lurch and asks Ollie if he knows that bird Mel works with.

"Which one, the one with the teeth or the one with the hair?" Ollie asks, sorting Mel's work colleagues in terms *Mr Potato Head's* Marketing Manager would approve of.

"No, the one with neither," Norris corrects him.

"Don't know her, but she sounds like a stunner, hey," I nudge Ollie.

"Hang on a minute, I know who you mean, in't she the one with the eyebrows?" Ollie suddenly twigs.

"Yeah, it's her turn," I tell him, drawing a line under their conversation and stuffing my book into my coat pocket. "Right, let's get going. You did bring the van, didn't you?"

"Of course," Ollie says. "You told me to bring it so I brung it."

"Yeah, I also told you to get here for nine o'clock if you remember, so pardon me if I don't go putting your name forward should reliability become an Olympic event."

"I brung it. Fuck me, I brung it!" Ollie sighs, shaking his head.

"And the stuff's in the van?" I double-check.

"What's in the van?" Norris butts in, ears suddenly hot and twitching.

"Some rope and a hammer," I tell him, in no uncertain terms. "Wanna have a look?"

Norris retreats his interest. Sarcasm might not penetrate his armour, but full-blown threats of violence still have some effect.

"Right, come on then," I tell Ollie, draining the last of my pint.

"Here Bex, hold up," Norris objects. "You going to see that bird or not?" he tries one last time.

"See her and warn her Norris mate. See her and warn her." I plonk my empty pint glass down in front of him. "No charge."

Norris swears somewhere off behind me, but he's missed his target with me and is left to fly around in circles until his fuel runs out over the

7

black abyss of his own shortcomings.

Obviously, it would be better if it was the actual sea, but there you go.

"I did try ringing you," Ollie tells me when we get outside.

"I've got my phone off. Mel's on the war path so I can't risk turning it on," I explain, following Ollie round the corner, up the alleyway and back to the van.

"What's she want?"

"I don't know, but she's had murder in her eyes for the last couple of days over something," I reply, then tell Ollie about how I came home with a Chinese take-away tonight and it couldn't have gone down worse had I come home with a Chinese bird.

"What d'you have?"

"That's not important. What is important is that she's got the raging arsehole with me and no mistake and I haven't got a clue what about. So I wolfed down me dinner like a hippo in a hurry and got out of there sharpish before I ended up decorated in chop suey."

"You must've done something to upset her," Ollie tells me.

"I swear, I haven't. I mean, I normally have, but seriously this time I haven't done a thing, the big moody cow."

"What d'you reckon it is then?"

"Phhp, I haven't got a Scooby mate. Ain't Christmas is it?"

"I hope not, otherwise we're all in trouble," Ollie replies.

"Dunno then. Anyway, halfway down the road, I get a right old fatwa on the mobile from her, so I turned it off a bit lively."

"You could always ask her," the big naïve dimbo suggests.

"What, and admit I don't know what she's upset about? Not tempting. No, better to slap on the emotional blinkers and drop off the radar for a few days until it's all blown over. That's how I prefer to deal with these things."

"Hmm, good plan," Ollie complements.

"Thanks. I came up with it myself."

Thinking about it though, what was it with girls? (and by girls, what I actually mean is Mel, but I like to generalise whenever possible in order to open up the debate and be as inclusive as I can in the name of political correctness, especially when it comes to dealing with such socially sensitive questions such as, what is it with fucking girls?) Why can't they just come out with it and say what's on their minds, rather than resorting to the usual moody, sulky, cupboard door-slamming bollocks that makes us rack our consciences and accidentally apologise for half a dozen things they didn't even know about? Mel's a right one for this. Every few months she slams up tighter than a clam's backside and I never know what it is I've done. And it don't matter how nice I've been to her or how much I've gone out of my way to make her happy, once

8

she gets a mood on, that's it. There are no other mitigating circumstances.

Take a few months back; me and her family don't really see eye-to-eye. In fact, it's fairly safe to say that they hate me right down to the bone marrow, but I always try to make a big effort with them for the sake of Mel and even went along to her stupid dad's annual family summer barbecue last July. Now, you would've thought that this would've earned me a few Brownie points and stood me in good stead the next time something pissed Mel off, but oh no, no such clemency. For almost a week afterwards, Mel wouldn't even talk to me after I supposedly somehow embarrassed her in front of her whole family and still refuses to tell me what I did to this day. Christ only knows what it was. I can't remember as I was far too pissed at the time.

Still, that was then and this is now and I've got a whole new case of slamming doors to deal with, so I figure it's probably best to deal with them from the safety of Ollie's sofa for a few nights until I'm sure she's taken the worst of it out on that big bar of Dairy Milk I've left in the fridge (which is actually mine - or more accurately, Sainsbury's - but you could bet your bottom dollar Mel won't take any notice of the Post-It note I've stuck on it when she finds it).

2. The Price is always wrong

I'm mulling these thoughts over as we walk back to the van, partly to try to sift through the events of the last couple of days and partly to try to block out Ollie's latest "I never done it" story, when I notice a bulge in his jacket.

"… so I said to the bloke, 'I don't know what you're talking about, mate, what would I want with your phone?' So he goes…"

"Hold on, stop a minute," I tell him.

"What?"

"Have you got a pub ashtray in your pocket?"

"What?" Ollie repeats.

"For crying out loud, you big clepto. What's the matter with you? Can't you give it a rest for five minutes? The stuff we've got in the van and you're risking drawing attention to yourself by nicking a poxy pub ashtray."

"Well I needed one didn't I," he tells me, which is his stock response whenever someone loses something of theirs in his pocket.

"Why, your other one full or something? What if the landlord had seen you and phoned the Old Bill? He's had 'em down there for less the miserable old bastard and you're only parked around the corner," I point out.

"Oh leave it out, the Old Bill wouldn't give a monkey's about an old pub ashtray," he says.

"No, but they might give a monkey's about the twenty-five brand spanking new fan heaters we've got in the van," I say, which would be enough to see us both go down for a nice little stretch. See, the Old Bill around this way know us. And they know our van. But they can't stop and search us every five minutes for no good reason, otherwise we'd grow fat on compensation claims for harassment and victimisation. Given just cause though and Weasel and his mates would have our floor-boards up and our windscreen wipers in bits before we could even report our van stolen. And a half-inched pub ashtray, as petty, cheap and trivial as it was, would give them just such cause.

I'm just waiting for Ollie to come out with the usual old flannel about how it was fine because no one had seen him and how I shouldn't worry because he's such a great thief, when the criminal genius goes and says something that makes me realise it ain't just pub ashtrays he's been help-ing himself to tonight.

"No, I don't think there were twenty-five fan heaters."

I stop dead in my tracks and roll my eyes.

"Oh for God's sake, how many you had?"

Ollie comes storming back.

"I ain't had none. What a terrible thing to say," he protests.

"Then there should be twenty-five in the van. I counted them."

"You probably just miscounted them or something."

"What's more likely, you've had a couple away to stand your collection of pub memorabilia on or I can't count up to twenty-five?" I ask.

"What am I, Professor of Sums at Oxbridge University? How should I know what you can or can't count up to?" he asks, but Ollie's a great bloke to play cards against because he has trouble bluffing and smoking at the same time. Ollie knows I know this, so whenever we're playing poker together, he always stubs his fag out when he's got a load of crap in his hand. And while Ollie doesn't stub his fag out here, I can read him like a health warning all the same.

I decide not to bother quibbling any more about who's had what, as Ollie knows he's been rumbled, I just tell him how it is.

"Well I'm telling you this, any missing fans are coming out of your cut."

Ollie sees my rumble and raises it a grumble.

"Well why don't you tell us what happened to that car alarm last week then while you're telling us things?" he says, spying the moral high ground in the distance, admittedly a long, long way from either of us.

"I told you, it was nicked," I tell him again.

"I know it was nicked, I helped you nick it. What I want to know is what happened to it after we nicked it."

"I don't know, maybe it wandered off with that same mysterious bloke who had my good torch away. You remember him? Broke into the van one night and had it away from underneath the seat, then locked the van up again after himself leaving no visible signs of breaking in?"

"Nah," Ollie muses, picturing that self-same bloke. "I'm pretty sure he wasn't involved."

At that moment, a set of headlights sweeps across the car park and Electric's van circles around ours like a shark circling its prey, before stopping just behind ours, fin to fin.

"Look out, Electric's here. Hand on your wallet and let me do the talking," I say.

"What, for a change like?" Ollie continues to grumble, before finally finding enough spit to take a pull on his cigarette.

Electric slides from his van and lands on his arthritis. He winces, slams the door behind him and makes his way around the back to meet us.

"How do boys, lovely evening," he nods.

This is remarkable for so many reasons that I can't even begin to explain, most notably that Electric simply doesn't do small talk. Small talk for Electric is like anaesthetic at a stoning. It's somewhat besides the fucking point. The only reason Electric ever asks me how I am or points out how inclement the weather's been this week is usually because he's trying to lull me into a false sense of security so that he can suggest paying by cheque.

I decide if it's small talk Electric wants, it's small talk he can have.

"Yes, yes I was just saying that to Ollie in fact, that it's very mild for the time of year. Very mild indeed. Reminds me in many ways of those long Indian summers of my youth when the curtain of night wouldn't necessarily spell the end of play and the air would be tinged with the aroma of a thousand sticky marshmallows roasting on the end of a thousand bobbing sticks."

I look at Electric and await his response.

Electric frowns.

"Got the fans?"

There we go, that's the Electric I know and am comfortable around.

"In the van," I tell him.

"How many d'you get?" he asks.

I look to Ollie for the answer.

"Er, eighteen," he sheepishly replies.

"Eighteen? You greedy fucker. One or two I could've just about understood but you've had seven fans away!"

"Is it?" Ollie ponders. "Oh, er seventeen then."

It doesn't do to argue in front of business acquaintances, so I make do with a scowl and tell Ollie we'll be talking about this after we clock off tonight.

"You going out again then boys?" Electric dilates.

"Yeah, big warehouse on the trading estate. We've got it all lined up. Should have some tellies for you tomorrow. Widescreen and everything."

"Nice, I can do things with tellies I can," Electric nods confidently.

"Yeah I know, like rip us off for 'em," I tell him. Electric winces, like a dagger's been plunged into his heart at the very thought, but he doesn't get time to air his pain as Brain-Donor of the Year's suddenly at it again.

"Here, you never said nothing about this to me," Ollie objects.

"Ollie mate, you do this every time. I told you about it at the weekend and even texted you a reminder yesterday."

"Did you?" he says pulling out his phone and having a look at it. "I never got nothing."

"Which is coincidentally the title of your autobiography," I chuckle, congratulating myself on a first-class piece of joined-up piss-taking.

Ollie stares at me blankly.

"What?"

"Oh never mind," I sigh.

"But I'm meant to be seeing Belinda in twenty minutes," Ollie protests.

"Well you'll just have to take a cold shower and think about the time your dog got run over then won't you, because you and Belinda are going to have to put it on hold for the evening, aren't you?" I say.

"But Belinda doesn't like putting it on hold for the evening," Ollie says, which is an understatement to say the least.

Belinda (or Bell-end-her, as she was previously known before Ollie went all soft in the head for her) has been around the block more times than an Egyptian stone mason. Which is no bad thing, by the way. I'm not passing judgement on her here. In fact, if push came to shove, I'd much rather live in the world full of Belinda's and spend my days tripping up on their discarded knickers, than retire my nuts on Planet of the Librarians. Electric's somewhat more judgemental, but then that's probably just his generation and the fact it was quite normal tarring and feathering your old lady of a morning if she so much as blinked at the coalman.

"Bit of a bike is she?" he scowls.

"Not many Benny," I tell Electric, possibly as part of some petty pique to pay Ollie back for being half an hour late this evening. "You know, her number's been on permanent display of The Badger's bog for about five years, despite that place getting renovated twice in that time. All the builders are under strict instructions from the regulars not to paint over it."

"Load-bearing phone number, was it?" Electric smirks.

"You're not wrong mate. In fact, we even had blokes down from English Heritage to have a look at it, didn't we Ol?"

"She's not like that no more," Ollie flim-flams, like Sir Galahad on the occasion of his joyous union to Abi Titmuss.

"Oh don't ruin it, do the joke," I nudge Ollie, prompting him again. "Go on, we even had blokes down from English Heritage to have a look at it, didn't we Ol?"

Ollie sighs reluctantly.

"Yeah, they all banged her," he mutters, putting absolutely no effort into the punchline.

"I don't know what's up with you, that used to be your favourite joke, that did," I say, shaking my head with disappointment.

"Yeah, but that was before I started going out with her, weren't it," Ollie snaps back.

"Get shot of her son, she sounds like a wrong 'un," Electric - the wrong 'un's wrong 'un - advises.

"Oh yeah, and what would you know about it?" Ollie glares.

"I know, believe me, I know," Electric tells us with the look of a man who's been there, caught it, got it taken care of, caught it again and given it to his missus. "A few years back, I used to know this old sort. Fantastic she was. Dead dirty and horrible and everything, but at the end of the days I never trusted her, not an inch, because birds like that they have no morals. They're just not decent. I mean, how can you trust a bird who goes running around behind her husband's back with his own brother?"

Me and Ollie blink a few times.

"Very enlightening," I say. "Anyway, you want these fans or not?"

"Oh yeah, I'll take 'em all. What did we say, fiver a fan, was it?"

"Hold your horses Kane and Abel," I stop him. Blimey, they're all at it tonight, aren't they? "Where d'you get a fiver a fan from? You said a tenner the other day, remember?"

"Tenner? God no, a tenner. I'd be cutting my own throat for a tenner," Electric hams.

"I'd pay a tenner to see that," Ollie quips.

"Your shoes on the right feet?" Electric barks in response, but I'm not prepared to let this go.

"You said a tenner, the other day. When your mate with the spots gave us the tip. You also said there'd be at least fifty fans in the wagon an' all, not bleeding twenty-five."

"Seventeen," Ollie corrects me.

"Oh yeah, seventeen!"

"Supply and demand, my friend. Supply and demand. Price goes up. Price goes down," Electric explains.

"That's funny, ever since I've been dealing with you, I've never once known the price to go up. Have you Ol?"

Ollie looks at me, his mind still on lower things, evidently.

"With what?"

"Jesus, it's like talking to my socks some times," I complain to Electric. Electric gives me a nod of solidarity. "Just tell me this, when does the price ever go up?"

"When stuff's in demand. This stuff's not in demand."

"What are you talking about, it's the start of winter. These are fan heaters. I expect you can't get your hands on enough ice creamer makers, hey?"

Electric decides negotiations have gone on long enough and tries to distract me with a flash of cash.

"Hundred quid, take it or leave it," he says, separating ten tenners from a load of their mates in front of me.

I realise we could be here all night haggling over brass tacks, so I cut to the chase and name a realistic price that I know Electric'll go for.

"A hundred and twenty-five otherwise we will leave it," I say, splitting the difference between a fiver and a tenner and vowing to chuck the lot in the canal rather than compromise further.

Electric bites.

"A hundred and twenty-five, you say," he muses, fingering a couple more notes into my bundle.

At least, that's until *The Apprentice* sticks his fucking oar in.

"Yeah, or a hundred and ten, at a push," Ollie tells Electric in no uncertain terms.

My eyes roll shut in disbelief, so Electric snatches two notes back and takes the opportunity to stuff the lot into Ollie's top pocket.

"Done," he eagerly agrees.

"Hold on, let's count it first shall we?" I say, fishing the cash straight back out. "Just in case you've given us too much."

I count through the notes with Ollie at my shoulder. When I'm done, he looks at me and asks the inevitable.

"Has he?"

"They're cute when they're this young, aren't they?" I tell Electric.

*

As a rule, I generally prefer to conduct my affairs away from prying eyes. Hence the deserted car parks, the clandestine meetings and the black woolly hats. It's all part and parcel of the game I'm in. Some industries do their business in board rooms and on golf courses with blokes called Gerald, I do most of mine in empty lay-bys with blokes called Electric, Greg the Cunt and Freddie Three-Teeth. But our intention are the same as the blokes on the golf course. We all just want to make money and get by. Now, I freely admit, I'm hardly the squeakiest of blokes, but then a standard night's business for me usually involves the liberation of a couple of dozen electrical appliances and their release onto the black market. I make money, Electric makes money, and the eventual appliance buyer gets brand a new must-have consumable for a fraction of its market value - though knowing Electric, that fraction's probably 9/10ths - everyone's a winner. Except the bloke who's appliances they originally were, obviously. But even he's prepared for this and takes out insurance and ups his prices accordingly so that the burden is soaked up by the masses, the supposed "honest law-abiding citizens".

Now, I don't know about you, but knowing all this is going on, which side would you rather be on - the doers or the losers?

It's not a nice state-of-affairs by any stretch of the imagination, but them's the facts, and I've just got too much self-respect to line up with the suckers. I mean, we're all being fleeced on a daily basis you know, by breweries, tobacco companies, the government and internet pay-as-you-view sites. My job simply allows me to claw back a little self-esteem so that I don't end the day feeling like a victim too. It's a strike for the little guy, against the big conglomerates, though I'm not averse to doing over little guys too if they leave their back doors unlocked. But never fear, I've got a whole load of other bullshit excuses to justify that sort of behaviour that I've worked out on beer mats while the rest of the world's been at work.

I don't know, at the end of the day, I guess I'm just pro-active.

You'd think that this sort of get-up-and-go would be well regarded in a capitalist market-place like ours, but it's not. Very much the opposite in fact, hence the need to conduct business away from prying eyes.

However some times, no matter how secluded your car park is, or how carefully you've watched your back, a snooping set of prying eyes occasionally falls upon you all the same.

You never know it at the time, but the consequences always make a loud clatter before the night's out.

Just as they would this night.

3. The high wire act

"Dud-der-li-dum, dud-der-li-dum, dud-der-li-dum, dum-dum-dum-dum, dud-der-li-dum, dud-der-li-dum," my care-in-the-community mate taps on the steering wheel next to me, before asking, "see *Doctor Who* last night?"

I'd been wondering what the tune had been but I hadn't wanted to ask in case it accidentally ignited a whole night of "name that dud-der-li-dum".

"No, I got out when Peter Davidson got out," I reply.

"Load of bollocks it was. Good, but bollocks, if you know what I mean. That stuff would never happen in real life," Ollie shakes his head, then starts up again, this time murdering the *"Ooo-ooo-ooooh"* bit.

I tell you, the sooner we get something to attach to those red wires hanging out the front of our dash board where our stereo used to be the better.

Ollie ups the *"Ooo-ooo-ooooh"* and brings in a little accompanying honking, which is when I finally crack.

"Ollie, for fuck's sake!"

"What?" he honestly asks.

"What? What d'you mean what? What d'you think? Do us a tape will ya, this is great."

"Really?" Ollie asks suspiciously, knowing I'm taking the piss but unable to pick up on exactly what.

"Of course not. Shut your cake hole will ya, I've got to phone Roland," I say, pulling out my mobile and switching it on.

Ollie screws his face into a frown.

"Oh, we're not doing it with Roland, are we?"

"You know we are. We've been through this already," I tell him. "Anyway, what's wrong with Rollo? He's alright, ain't he?"

"To you maybe, but you're not the one he's always trying to cuddle and smell," Ollie objects.

I have to admit, Roland does have an unhealthy fascination for Ollie. I don't think there's anything sinister to it, more just a deep-rooted, instinctive longing that occasionally grips big dummies like Roland, causing them to wander around after the object of their affection and sit next to them whenever possible for reasons they're unable to even understand themselves. Though that said, I'm not sure I'd ever want to pass out face down on Roland's bed if I was Ollie. Especially not with a bottle of baby oil sticking out of my back pocket. Still, no need to burden Ollie with such concerns, not when we've got a job to do and need Roland to get in, so I tell him it's all in his imagination and that Roland's cool.

"No Bex, he's a weirdo," he insists.

At that moment, my phone suddenly starts ringing in my hand and for a moment I half-expect to see Roland's name appear on screen, saving me a phone bill entry, but no such luck.

It's Mel.

"Oh bollocks. Suspicious old cow must've had us on call-back or something. Quick, answer it for us will you?" I say, giving my phone to Ollie.

Ollie answers.

"Hello? Oh hey Mel, how are you? Hmm, what? Oh right, yeah he's right here," he says, then hands the phone straight back to me. "It's for you."

I stare at Ollie with incredulity and fingers flexing inside my gloves before taking the phone.

"Hello?" I cautiously say.

"WHERE THE BLOODY HELL ARE YOU, YOU SELFISH GIT!" the phone asks my left ear'ole.

"How is she, alright?" Ollie smiles, leaving me in no doubt that this was payback for me scuppering his evening with Belinda.

"I don't know. I'll ask her when she stops screaming at me, shall I?" I scowl, before returning to Mel. "Sorry luv, you're gonna have to speak up, it's a terrible line."

"Yeah, they all usually are coming from you, you big scumbag!" she replies, bang on form tonight.

I rack my brains for a response and am rewarded with a flash of inspiration in the shape of the OFF button on the top of my phone.

"I think we'll deal with that one later," I tell Ollie, mortgaging next week's peace and quiet in order to concentrate on the task in hand.

Somewhere across town, cupboard doors start furiously slamming.

"So what are we going to do about Roland?" Ollie asks. "Aren't you gonna phone him?" But there's no need.

"He ain't you Ollie. He said he'd be there, so he'll be there. Roland, if nothing else, is at least professional," I reassure him.

*

Twenty minutes later we're standing outside two suspiciously-locked-looking vehicle gates with no sign of tonight's special guest star.

"Where the hell is this big idiot? These fuckers are meant to be open. Have I died and gone to unreliable arsehole heaven or something?" I moan, pushing against the gates.

"Do you want me to give him a bell?" Ollie offers, reluctantly confessing that he's got his number too.

"Just tell him to shake a leg and get himself over here. I seem to spend my life hanging around on street corners waiting for you lot," I fizzle.

"Jesus, not this record again. Ain't you got nothing else on your play list?" Ollie asks. "Here we go, it's ringing. Nah, it's just gone to voicemail. I'll leave a message. Hello Roland, d'you wanna get your leg over? Only we're hanging about on the street corner."

Ollie blinks a couple of times when he sees me shaking my head.

"Hang on, what was it again?"

"No, that sounded fine to me," I tell him.

"So what d'you want to do?" Ollie asks.

"Well it would've been easier if Roland had been here, but we can still do it without him. I know where everything is. Okay?"

"S'pose," Ollie mopes, looking miserably disinterested.

"You remember the wire cutters?" I ask.

"Yeah."

"Give 'em here then."

"Oh right, yeah I see what you mean now. No, I ain't got 'em," Ollie shrugs.

"Well why not?"

"Because you said Roland would open up for us," Ollie explains, catching himself out.

"Ah, so you remember all of this now," I pounce.

"What?" Ollie replies blankly.

"This. You did remember about this tonight then?" I point out.

"What?" Ollie repeats.

"Oh whatever," I frown. "You did bring the blanket though? You did remember that, didn't you?"

"The blanket," Ollie asks, furrowing his brow. "Oh, you know what I did?"

"Was it not bring the blanket?" I guess.

"Sort of. I slung it out to make room for the fans."

"Well this is fantastic. How are we meant to get over the barbed wire without the blanket without cutting ourselves to ribbons?"

"We could always give up," Ollie suggests.

"That's hardly the attitude that's made this country great, is it now?" I lecture him. "No, we'll just have to go over the top then, won't we, like my granddad and his brother did in the Great War."

"Did they?" Ollie asks. "And did they survive?"

"Yeah, of course. It was only a low barracks wall wasn't it. And they spent the next three years hiding under my great nan's stairs. Not too many bullets whizzing about under there. "

"So who goes over?" Ollie asks, nervously eyeing the vicious steel barbs.

"I'll tell you what, we'll flip for it," I tell him, pulling a coin from my pocket and tossing it into the air. "What d'you want?"

"To give up," Ollie replies.

"Tails it is," I confirm, catching the coin and turning it over on the back of my glove.

I can't decide which hurts more; the dozens of razor-sharp barbs that are slashing my shoulder blades or that lone spike that's pierced the front of my jeans and is skewering my scrotum. Possibly the scrotum one, but not by much.

I hate picking my way through barbed wire, which is one of the hazards of my job and the reason I invested a good few hours sewing a load of blankets together to create a thick protective carpet for laying over the top of wire. It's not so thick that it's able protect you from every single barb, but it does keep the other fifty that spring up and whip around behind you off your back as you crawl through each coil.

No such luck today.

The barbs slash me from every angle; across the shoulders, down the sides, up the legs and all along the arms until all my arse needs is a cellophane wrapper and it wouldn't have looked out of place in a butcher's shop window.

Mercifully, my jacket's padded and my jeans almost new, so the damage to my poor old worthless hide could've been so much worse, but by the time I'm through the wire and lowering myself down the other side, I'm ready for a tetanus shot, hug and happy finish off the school nurse.

I cling to the top of the wall and prepare to let go and plunge into the blackness of the compound when I feel a pair of hands reach up and grab my waist.

"There you go, I got you," Ollie reassures me, as he guides me down to the ground safe and sound, and brushes some of the crud from my jacket.

I stare at him with complete and utter disbelief and wonder where I've gone wrong. Have I got lost halfway through the wire and ended up doing a total one-eighty or have I simply got straight over the corner? Have they moved the warehouse in the time it's taken me to get across the wire or has Ollie waited all these years before deciding to introduce me to his twin brother?

Ollie (or his brother) sees me pondering this and explains.

"The little door was open," he says, flicking a thumb over his shoulder.

I look back at the gates, the ones that are locked, and see a little latchkey door inset in the gates, swinging open.

I then look at my arms and legs and wonder when those lazy fuckers at Microsoft are going to pull their fingers out and come up with a Control Alt Z button for real life.

"Oh, let's just get this done, shall we?" I grumble, and walk around Ollie to take a look at the gates.

A chunky padlock hangs onto the back of the main gates and smiles back at me.

"You've at least got the hacksaw? You did bring that, didn't you?" I implore Ollie.

"Of course I have, it's under the driver's seat. I'm not an idiot you know," he retorts all hurt.

There's a saying in life that if you want something done properly, do it yourself. Admittedly this hadn't quite worked out with the gates and the barbed wire, but then that was just because I hadn't spent the day shadowing Roland and checking the van every five minutes to make sure it still held the equipment we needed before setting off. And knowing what Roland and Ollie were like, technically I was as much to blame as they were because I'd trusted them to do a job - though this wasn't something I'd be admitting any time soon. Still, how many of the King's ships had been lost because the Captain had sent a fuckwit like Ollie up to the crow's nest to get a good suntan when he should've been looking out for the Spanish fleet?

With this in mind, I decide to take no further risks and go and get the hacksaw out of the van myself.

"Fine, you stay here and don't touch anything," I warn him. "I'll go and get it."

I stagger through the inset door and wobble back to the driver's seat.

Incredibly, I find the hacksaw exactly where Ollie tells me it is and I'm about to relax into a false sense of optimism when I hear Ollie shouting at me to bring his fags and all.

I turn around just in time to see him giving me the thumbs-up as the latchkey door swings shut behind him.

Ollie turns to go back inside, but is confused by the door he's suddenly confronted with. He tries pushing on it, but the door's in no mood to do anyone any favours and all at once we're outside the fucking compound again.

How did that happen?

Ollie looks at me rather sheepishly.

"I'll tell you what, I'll have heads this time if you want to flip for it again," he generously offers.

"Oh will you now?" I reply, dropping the hacksaw and rolling up my shredded sleeves.

4. Strangers in the night

As we're thrashing out the ins and outs of our working relationship over a fag and a slap, back across town, my exuberant young girlfriend is just entering The Badger, whence we came, and asking after my whereabouts.

"Has that thieving scumbag been in here tonight?" she shouts at the barman.

"Give us half a chance luv, that's all we get in here most nights," Keith later tells me he told her.

"Bex, my boyfriend. Rat-faced, back-stabbing, light-fingers bucket of sick that thinks it can pass itself off as a man," Mel says, giving Keith a brief run-down of my finer points, though seeing as I heard all this through Keith, I suspect he may have added a couple of those adverbs himself for a laugh. Well, I would've.

"Oh for God's sake, Adrian Beckinsale," Mel spells out.

"Don't know him, but please pass on my sympathies when you see him next luv," Keith replies, to which Mel's eyes melt into Keith's face. "Oh please, excuse me, I mean your Royal Highness."

"You do know him pump monkey, I've seen you talking to him loads of times before, thick as thieves," Mel retorts.

"I talk to lots of blokes darling, even thick thieves. And it's my job not to know where any of them, are at any time, other than when they want a drink or are trying to leave with the fag machine," Keith grins.

"Sarcastic twat," Mel hisses, spinning on a heel and stomping off.

Now, this could've happened, but knowing Keith as I do, I suspect the conversation probably went something more like this:

Mel: "Has Bex been in tonight."

Keith: "Dunno."

Because in all the years I've been drinking in The Badger I've never known Keith to be as witty as he always is in his stories, so the chances are he probably worked on that one for a bit before it evolved into the form I heard it in. I'm sure given another ten years and a bit more fleshing out, it'll be Keith who went over the wire at the warehouse this particular night, not me. And it'll probably turn out that it was also Keith who Mel was looking for too. Because she was gagging for it.

I spoke to Dirty Dan who was in all that night and he reckons he can't even remember seeing Mel talking to Keith, though he did say he saw her pop in briefly and talk to Norris. And this much I know to be true, because of what happened later on.

Norris, it seems, had earwigged us in the car park this evening, particularly taking note of the fact that Belinda was all dressed up with nothing to sit on, because he swooped like a Knight in stolen armour and whisked her out to The Badger for a dozen Bacardi and bendy straws.

Well, if *she* had nothing to do and *he* had nothing to do, they might as well do nothing *together*, mightn't they? So Norris had combed his hair, nipped into the bog, scribbled down her number off the wall and phoned Belinda.

"Looking for Bex, are you?" Norris asks Mel when she catches up with the pair of them.

"Why, think there's room on your lap for both of us," Mel replies.

Norris chuckles at that one. Belinda shuffles over a little.

"No, it's just, I do believe I overheard where he'll be tonight, if you're interested," Norris winks.

"Where?"

"Well, normally I'd want something for this information, but let's just say I owe Bex a favour, shall we?" Norris grins, this particular favour in question no doubt being my refusal to put in a word on his account with Mel's eyebrowed mate.

"Oh, in't he nice," Belinda coos.

"Well, you gotta be really ain'tcha! Heh-heh-heh!" Norris cackles.

*

I wait by the little latchkey door for the groaning to stop, then the latch twists and Ollie opens it up from the other side.

"Nice jacket," I chuckle, looking at the catalogue of gouges and rips across his sleeves and back. "I've got one just like it."

"You bring my fags?"

"You can have one after you saw that padlock off," I say, handing him the hacksaw.

"Oh, I'm no good with the saw. You're better at it than me. You wanna flip for it?"

"How you gonna flip a coin with ten broken fingers?" I ask.

"Alright, don't get in a boo."

I leave him to it and go and take a closer look at the warehouse. Everything's closed up and there's still no sign of Roland. I'm guessing it was him who opened the latchkey door the first time around before disappearing, but he's done us no such favours as far as the actual warehouse goes.

I circle the place a couple of times before finding an open window twenty feet up. I never brought the ladder or the grappling hook with me today (though I'm sure even if I had, Ollie would've probably swapped them for magic beans by now) because Roland had assured us everything would be open. Drive in, load up, drive out. Ten minutes at max. Yet here we are almost half an hour later and we still haven't even backed the van through the gates.

So, I see this open window above, right next to a drainpipe that has a generous window sill for me to stand on, and figure getting in should-n't be too much of a challenge. I grip the drainpipe, plant my foot against the wall and start to haul myself up...

... only for the pipe to snap at the joint and a torrent of shitty water to soak my shredded jeans.

"Oh, for crying-out-loud!" I yell.

Ollie appears at my elbow almost instantaneously.

"What are you doing?"

"I'm trying to get into the warehouse. What d'you think I'm doing?"

Ollie looks at the end of the broken pipe.

"Well you ain't gonna fit up there," he chuckles.

"Have you got that padlock off yet?" I snap, shining my torch in his face.

"Weren't locked, just resting shut," he says, showing me the lock.

We eventually try our crow bars out on a couple of side doors and find a winner. After yet another scoot about, there's still no sign of Roland, but the alarm's also been dismantled, so he's here in spirit if not in actual body mass index, which is fine as far as Ollie's concerned. He's desperate for us to get loaded up and get out of here before Roland can turn up and start walking around on his shadow.

The tellies are big. Thirty-two inch, surround sound, flat-screen, high definition, digital sets. Who wouldn't want one of these? They'd look great in the corner of any living room and really set a place off, right up until you turned the bastard on and found there was nothing on but celebrity lifestyle consultants lining up to tell you how shit the rest of your house looked.

Still, that ain't my job, I'm just the middle man, in charge of diverting stuff from A to Q.

"... so matey goes, 'fifty quid for a second-hand set of golf clubs? It ain't even got a number five in there'. So I tell him, 'well maybe if you try hitting the thing a bit further when you're driving off mate, you wouldn't need a five, you could use the seven, you big monkey'," Ollie is telling me as we're loading up. I wasn't quite sure where this story had started. As far as I could remember, two minutes earlier, I'd asked Ollie how his God Father was getting on in the hospital. As it turns out, not so good.

"And did he buy 'em?"

"Nah, had to chuck 'em in the canal in the end," Ollie says.

"Quite right, best place for 'em."

"Why couldn't he have left me something decent. Like that leather arm chair. I could've shifted that, I could."

All at once a torch light falls on us and big guy in a security guard's uniform asks us what the hell we think we're doing.

We freeze.

"You lift with the legs, not the back, you'll do yourself a mischief," the guard tells us, dropping the light from our faces and stuffing a fag into his own.

"Rollo, where the hell you been? Why aren't you answering your phone?"

"I left it on the desk when I had to sprint for the bog. Been glued to it for the last half an hour. I tell you, never go to that kebab place on Moulsham Lane, not unless you wanna know what having kids is like," Roland says, then elaborates. "Little, hot, skinny ones."

"Trouble with the old number twos, hey Rollo?" Ollie asks, seemingly taking pleasure in Roland's discomfort.

"You're not wrong, Big Guy. I don't think I got much past number one-and-a-halves, Ol. Anyway," Roland now says, taking an enormous stride towards Ollie, so that he's suddenly towering over him, "how are you?"

"Fine thank you, Rollo. And how are you?" Ollie shifts uncomfortably, backing off a step, though he and Roland might as well have been standing in a pantomime horse together for all the distance he manages to put between himself and his self-appointed best-mate.

"Super Ol, terrific. Here, we should go out for a beer some time soon, just you and me, you know?" Roland suggests.

"Yeah, that'd be great," Ollie says, sidling around the crate and past me, with Roland right on his heels. "I'll give you a bell about it this weekend."

"Will ya?" Roland asks, stepping on the backs on Ollie's shoes.

"No."

I decide to throw Ollie a bone and get Roland off his back, literally.

"Anyway, before you two go opening a laundrette together, let's get this stuff loaded up and get out of here shall we, before my night fills up with Old Bill."

Ollie takes the opportunity to put a few more feet between himself and the Honey Monster, as Roland stoops to pick up one of the tellies.

"No problem. Here Ol, you get one side of this big box and I'll get the other," Roland suggests.

Ollie looks at me.

"What's he think I've been trying to do?" he says quietly.

The three of us start making good time and filling up the van. We've got quite a sizeable van, but it's not big enough to get the lot in, which means we're going to have to leave some tellies behind, which is an incredibly difficult thing to do. I mean, here we are, the kings of all we survey and not a genuine security guard to ask us what we're doing, but still we've got to leave a good portion of the gear because we haven't got space for it in the van. Still, that's just part and parcel of being a professional unfortunately. We've just got to make hay while the sun shines, get what we can and try not to look back at the free £700 widescreen tellies we're leaving behind.

You have no idea how many times I've found myself in this position (you would've thought I would've bought a bigger van by now, wouldn't you?) but more often than not the ability to leave stuff behind is the thing that marks a person out as a good thief over someone who tries to have the lot away.

See, it's not the breaking in and getting your hands on the stuff that's the tricky bit - anyone can do that - it's the getting away with it at the other end. That's the mark of a good thief. I mean seriously, anyone can walk into M&S, put on a big overcoat and start filling the pockets with socks. This isn't a terribly difficult thing to do. Making it out to the car and driving off without paying for it all, that's where you start getting problems.

So, there's a dividing line between getting enough to make it all worth while and not getting so greedy that the warehouse staff come into work the next day to find you standing on a step ladder next to a big pile of light bulbs.

Mind you, they'd still find they had more missing than we're able to take this evening.

"I tell you, four pound an hour don't buy you much peace of mind these days, does it?" I say, watching Roland help Ollie lift another telly into our van.

"You're not wrong. I've been pilfering their gear for weeks now just to make ends meet," Roland agrees. "I tell you, this is why we've had to do this tonight. They're having a stock-take on Friday and if that goes ahead without us faking this break-in, they're going to find out that it ain't just Asda who's been doing some really great deals on their tellies."

"Yeah, but what I don't get is how someone with your record gets a security job with this firm in the first place, Rollo," Ollie says.

"Simple, the bloke in the office who checks the records only gets four pound fifty an hour," he shrugs all matter-of-fact. "And you don't exactly get Eliot Ness for four pound fifty an hour. I swear this country's going to the fucking dogs."

I chuckle at this, but stop chuckling when I look up and see a CCTV camera pointing directly at me. If there's one sure-fire cure for laughing at the stupidity of others, it's realising you're doing something even stupider yourself.

"Er, Rollo, you did turn that thing off didn't you?" I ask uncomfortably.

"Of course I did. Turned it off in the office before you got here. Stop and Start, that's all there is to it. I tell you, a banana could do my job," he reassures us. "Here, just make sure you take the tape with you when you go, otherwise they might wonder why it got paused."

"Don't worry, we will. Right, now let's get a shift on."

I'm inside the truck, packing the tellies away to fit as many as I can in, while Bill and Ben are passing them to me, when all at once a torch beam illuminates the three of us.

"What the..."

"You lot are so nicked it's unbelievable," a voice behind the torch beam delights in telling us. The beam drops and we see fourteen stone of supreme smugness squeezed into a navy blue security uniform. "Bob Shaw, Head of Security. Surprise inspection," the uniform tells us, then adds presumably for his own amusement, "Surprise!"

There are times in a thief's life when all that's left to do is hold up your hands, admit it's a fair cop and start working on your mitigating circumstances (ie. temporary insanity, sick family members in need of operations, society's to blame, that sort of thing) but I guess Roland has less pride than me because he starts jabbering on like a five-year-old with his hand stuck in the biscuit jar.

"Mr Shaw, it's not what it looks like," he explains.

"No, I didn't think it would be," Bob guesses right.

"We're just stock-taking, you remember?"

"What, as in taking our stock?" Bob simplifies.

Roland now realises he's chasing a lost cause and changes tack.

"We can put it all back," he offers.

"Well that would certainly make the paperwork a lot easier, but I'm not sure how it's going to help you lot out," Bob says.

Roland's brow creases.

"Well, because if we'd put it all back..." he tries explaining, "then nobody needs know about anything and if nobody knows then... er," he tails off with a smile, willing Bob to fill in the blanks for himself.

"That's it boy, keep thinking, keep thinking, you'll get there in the end, I have every confidence in you," Bob says, his grin widening as his eyes narrow, and suddenly I realise what he's getting at.

"Well, how about we cut you in then?" I offer, jumping down from the back of the van.

"Bex!" Roland coughs, but Bob likes the sound of the idea and asks me to expand upon it.

"Four ways sound good to you?"

"Well no, not as good as one way, if I'm perfectly honest," Bob replies.

"What?" Ollie explodes.

"No, hang on, play the game. You can't do that. We might as well just leave the stuff then. I mean, what's in it for us?" I fume.

"Well, you don't go to prison for one thing. Quite a bargain if you ask me. So you'll either flog the stuff and give me all the money or I'll spill my guts to the Old Bill. Now there's a word for this, isn't there? What is it again?" Bob ponders. "Oh yes, that's it, blackmail."

"There's a few words for you an' all I reckon," I tell him.

Bob smiles. "Well, I wouldn't spend too long trying to think of 'em if I was you Raffles because you've got tellies to sell. And you'd better get a bloody good price for 'em an' all because if you don't, you're going to be making up the difference out of your own pocket," he warns us.

Ollie decides to come back with a counter-offer.

"Well, why don't we just smash you in the chops and kick you up the arse while we're at it?"

"Because I've already taken a picture of you and your van on my phone and sent it back to the missus," Bob informs us, holding up his camera phone to underline the point. "How d'you like those apples, tough guy?"

"Not much to be honest," Ollie admits.

"No, I didn't think you would. So, now that we're all best mates again, put your brains away and let's get these tellies loaded. We haven't got all night you know." Bob flicks his torch light directly in Roland's face. "Oi you, George Clooney, give us a hand with this big one, will you?"

And so that was it. Old Bob had us. Like I say, some times you just have to hold your hands up and admit it's a fair cop, but I had more than a sneaking feeling this wouldn't be the end of it. Not by a long shot. See, you should never give in to blackmailers, because blackmailers are rarely satisfied with one-off rewards and almost always come back for more when they see you're willing to cough up to keep them quiet. The only thing you can ever really do when you find yourself in a blackmailer's sights is to fall on your sword and take him (or her, as they're often disgruntled ex-girlfriends) down with you. Why do you think all these actors and politicians keep outing themselves at short notice? It's not because they think it's some shrewd career move, that's for sure. No, it's usually because they're two days away from bankruptcy and ruin after a new pen pal's emptied their bank accounts with pictures of them befriending lorry drivers in lay-bys.

So, you can't give in to blackmailers. Admittedly, by keeping schtum, loading up the van and agreeing to Bob's terms, it probably looks like I am, but there's really very little else I can do about it at the moment. He has us over a barrel, so all we can do is play along and bide our time. Sooner or later he'll drop his guard. They always do. And when that happens, I'll have him. Of that you can be sure.

And talking of dropping your guard, a fresh set of headlights suddenly lights up the compound as a little Peugeot skids in and stops just short of our van.

"Blimey, what now? Who else we expecting?" I exclaim in disbelief.

"Right scumbag, get out here NOW!" I hear an all-too familiar voice shout, causing me to drop the telly I'm holding and flee.

"Shit it's Mel. Quick, cover me," I tell Ollie as I leg-it into the depths of the warehouse in search of a place to hide.

Back here in the darkness, I find a door leading to Roland's little security office, so I duck inside and flick off the lights. I can't even begin to imagine how Mel's tracked me down, but I'll find out in due course. Still, for the moment, that's the least of my concerns. All I can do is stay out of sight, bolt the door and hope to fuck Ollie does the business for me out front.

As luck would have it, I'm able to watch the whole thing unfold on Roland's CCTV monitors. The picture's blurry and grainy and there's no sound, but I'm about to make out Mel's expressions nevertheless and it's clear she's definitely upset about something.

If I'd had sound, I would've found out what.

And if I'd had sound, I would've also discovered that my best mate's covering-up skills were on a par with his time-keeping.

"I know you're in here, so just get out here!" Mel's shouting.

"Excuse me miss, but do you know you're trespassing," Bob tries, having first go.

"Do you know you're nicking tellies?" Mel responds, flicking her eyes towards to the telly Bob's just loaded into the back of our van, before turning her attention back to locating her errant boyfriend. "Right, I'm going to count to three. One…"

"I'm sorry miss, but I'm going to have to escort you from the premises," Bob tries again, grabbing Mel by the elbow and wheeling her round to her car. Big mistake.

Mel whips her arm free of Bob's grip and pulls out her mobile.

"Oi, watch yourself rent-a-flop, you seem to keep knocking the nine button on my phone and I get a brilliant reception outside. Shall we test it and see?" she warns him.

Bob gives up and takes a step back, confused as to how poetic justice could've caught up with him quite so quickly.

"Right now, where was I? Oh yes, that was it; TWO! "

Ollie now jumps in with both feet and tries his luck.

"Mel. Mel luv. Honestly, Bex ain't here."

"Don't give me that you great big dummy, you and that rodent are joined at the hip. And besides, you answered his phone earlier on, remember?"

Ollie suddenly remembers.

"Er, oh yeah, but he had to shoot off," he reaches, uncomfortable at finding his brain in uncharted waters. Mel's not buying it.

"Get out here Adrian and show some backbone for once!" she screams into the darkness at the wrong person.

"Mel, Melsy, honestly, cross my heart and hope to die, Bex ain't here. He's gone," Ollie insists, trying his best to usher her out of the warehouse.

"I don't believe you," Mel insists right back.

"Please, Mel, you have to go otherwise you're gonna get us all nicked," Ollie pleads with her.

"Oh, and wouldn't that be a shame," Mel scoffs, like this is the least of her concerns.

"Seriously, Mel, I promise he's not here!"

"He's here somewhere and I ain't leaving until I see him," Mel tells Ollie in no uncertain terms, then starts screaming at a volume that could wake up every security guard on this trading estate; "GET OUT HERE, ADRIAN AND SHOW YOURSELF YOU PIECE OF..."

It's at this point that a splendid moment of inspiration strikes Ollie and he quickly blurts out; "He's with another girl."

Unsurprisingly, this catches Mel's attention and finally plugs her hole.

"You what?"

"Straight up, that's the God's honest truth," Ollie continues, sensing victory is within his grasp. "That's why I didn't want to say anything."

"He's with another girl?" Mel double-checks, hardly daring to believe she's heard right.

"That's why he couldn't make the job. Bit annoying really. Seriously, he ain't here," Ollie promises her and Mel buys it completely. Well why wouldn't she? Ollie, the big doughnut, had stumbled upon the perfect formula for lying. Get one accusation quashed by coughing to an alternative offence that's a hundred times worse. eg: "Honestly officer, I couldn't have stolen that Pot Noodle as I was far too busy killing my wife and kids at the time."

"He's with another girl..." Mel chokes, "... on my birthday?"

"Oh, is it your birthday? Happy birthday!" Brains congratulates her.

"WHERE IS HE?" Mel explodes.

"In the Anchor, on the other side of town. That's where you'll find him," Ollie snitches.

"Right, he's a dead man!" Mel does a handbrake turn and storms back to her car, leaving Ollie sighing with relief.

She opens the driver's side door and is about to get in when a final thought occurs to her.

"Oh, one last thing," Mel tells Ollie. "I bumped into Belinda tonight."

"Oh yeah, how was she? Alright? " Ollie asks optimistically.

"Oh yes, she was being very well taken care of by a friend of yours. A Mr Norris, is it? Well, one good turn deserves another," she winks, before screeching out of the compound to tear the heads off me and my fictional bit-on-the-side.

This last bit of news stuns Ollie like a blow to the head. Belinda and Norris? That was like leaving your dog in charge of your Sunday roast.

And a Sunday roast that was only too willing to jump into the dog's gob after a skinful of basting, come to that.

Ollie turns, cocooned in a trance of miserable helplessness, and almost stumbles over Roland who's standing two inches behind him.

"Get the fuck off me for fuck's sake," Ollie snaps.

Sensing the coast is clear, I make my way down from the security office and find Ollie leaning against a big telly in a coma.

"She gone?" I ask, and have to repeat the question several times and burn a match in front of Ollie's eyes before I finally get a response out of him.

"What? Yeah."

"What did she want? What's the matter with her?" I ask.

Ollie shakes his head in despair.

"She says Belinda's with Norris," he mutters.

"Urgh, there's one keyhole I won't be peeking through tonight," I puff, finally catching some vital signs off Ollie. "Nah, I'm only joking, she ain't like that no more. I know."

Roland casts me a glance that I can read like a book. I skip to the back page and see Belinda and some wheelie-bins rolling out from behind The Badger full of dents. Still, nothing anybody can do about that now. The dice had been thrown. And so had the pants probably. Ollie just had to get a grip and turn his mind to matters in hand.

"So what's d'you tell her?" I press.

Ollie shakes his head.

"I don't know, some old nonsense," he mumbles.

"Well done. Top man. See, you can use your smarts sometimes," I praise him, though I'd later come to retract this praise when I arrived home the next morning to a volley of plates and all my Arsenal strips in just that. I turn to Bob and Roland. "Right then, let's get on with this and get you two tied up shall we?"

"Here, hold on. Tied up? What are you tying us up for?" Bob objects.

"Well I don't know. I just thought it might look a little less suspicious if your governors didn't find you two standing around in the middle of a half-empty warehouse with a couple of hernias. What d'you reckon?" I point out.

"Fine, but you just remember my old lady's got a picture of you two, so don't go trying anything comical otherwise my price goes up a few hundred per cent, you got it?" he warns us.

"I tell you, everything's good news tonight. Have you noticed?" I remark to Ollie.

Ollie frowns in agreement.

*

The next morning the police find Bob and Roland right where we left them, tied to a couple of chairs by the front doors. Bob's still fresh from having spent the night discussing Roland's wages and exactly how much he'll be taking as his cut from now on, so he spots them first as they climb over the gates.

"Oi you awake? Well look sharp cos they're here. Just follow my lead and stick to the story, yeah?" Bob tells Roland, as Weasel and PC Bennett pull up. Bob goes straight into it, Oscar-winning performance an' all. "Oh God, thank you, thank you, you've saved our lives, thank you. It was terrible. They were Chinese and there was six of them. We thought we was gonna die," he hams, cueing his fellow performer to contribute. "Didn't we?"

Roland thinks about this, then agrees. "Er, yeah."

Weasel's not quite sure what to make of them, but he figures it's his turn to say something police-like all the same.

"Well Constable, what do you reckon? Looks like the work of baddies, I'd say," is Weasel's best guess.

5. Paying Bob

Well, we got rid of the tellies. Electric took the lot, as he always does, for a whopping great knock-down discount, as again, he always does. But then that's just business for you. Electric has a right to make a profit as much as the next bloke, though that next bloke does seem to be Mohamed Al-Fayed. I mean, take those fan heaters we sold him. I think it worked out that we got a little over seven quid for each fan heater, yet there they were in his shop the very next day for forty-five. Evidentially market prices had shot through the fucking roof in the twelve hours since we'd sold them to him - way past the RRP and beyond, by all accounts. And it weren't just us who noticed. While we're doing the business in the back of his shop, some bloke comes in and has a look around.

"Forty-five quid for a fan heater?" we hear him say when he clocks one of the offending appliances.

"Yeah, I need the space, that's why they're so cheap," Electric tells him, somehow without bursting out laughing. "Just got some tellies in see. Widescreen they are. Big. Didn't have to pay the duty on them so I'm giving them out at cost too," Electric says, underlining this point with a wink and a tap to the nose.

Matey's eyes narrow with suspicion.

"Why didn't you have to pay the duty on them?" he asks, not unreasonably in my opinion.

Electric doesn't know. "Oh it's some Common Market legal loophole thing that a smart young fella like yourself would understand but I can't get me head around," he shrugs. "Anyway, if you want one, bring your car round the back and I'll fetch you one out."

"Round the back?" matey asks, raising an eyebrow, presumably to try and get it away from the stench of metaphorical rat that's almost making his eyes water.

"Better for parking out the back," Electric winks. "You don't have to worry about... about..." Electric's smile finally tails off. "Look, d'you want one or not?"

"They're not hooky by any chance, are they?" matey surmises.

Electric's stunned. "Of course they're not. How dare you! What sort of a person do you think I am. I run a respectable establishment and all the stock I get in is legitimate and one hundred per cent above board, I'll thank you very much. I've never been so insulted in all my life."

Matey backtracks a little. "I'm sorry, I didn't mean any offence," he apologises.

"I should think not an' all, a man of my standing," Electric fumes, his lip wobbling with indignation.

"No, anyway I'm not after a telly," matey tells Electric. "Actually, I just wondered if you might be interested in buying some guns?"

Electric looks at the heavy brown canvas bag that matey dumps on the counter in front of him and peers inside.

"Yeah, I would," he agrees without further consideration.

*

You know what I would've loved? I would've loved to have been a fly on old Bob Shaw's wall the next day shortly after our jiffy envelope dropped through his letter box.

If I had've been, I would've seen Bob pick it up and rip into it excitedly, only to find an old VHS video tape in place of the big bundle of tenners he'd been hoping to find.

"What the…" he would've mumbled, before hurrying through to his living room.

"What was that Bob?" Mrs Bob would've called after him from the kitchen.

"Nothing luv, just junk," he would've told her, unsure of the tape's contents. Mind you, I reckon he would've probably told her this had a big bundle of tenners dropped through his letterbox too. Come to think of it, I reckon I would've probably told Mel the same too.

Anyway, Bob would've slapped the tape in, switched his box on and settled back to watch mine and Ollie's little co-production, the first star of which was Bob himself, grainy, blurry and in black & white, but Bob nevertheless - loading tellies into the back of our van.

You may remember I said I'd been waiting for Bob to let his guard down. Well I never expected him to do it that very night, but that's exactly what he did when Mel turned up and screamed the place down.

See, I legged it out of there and hid in the security office, while Ollie ushered Mel out of the warehouse and back to her car. Roland, being attached to Ollie by an invisible length of cord, had naturally been impelled to follow, which left just Bob, all by himself, directly beneath the CCTV camera.

Keen to get a shift on, Bob had continued loading some of the smaller tellies into the van while my love life was taking an hammering off-camera. I could scarcely believe my eyes as I watched the pictures that were coming into the security office and found that Roland had been right, a banana could do his job, because I got one to restart the video for me, capturing Bob's huffing and puffing for posterity. Or should that be, prosperity?

God, I would've loved to have seen Bob's face as he watched himself - and himself alone - nicking his governor's tellies. I would've given anything to see that, anything. Well, almost anything. I'm not sure I would've given over the money we made from the tellies. I weren't that bothered.

We spliced a little homemade footage of our own on the back of the CCTV shots, so that Bob was left in no doubt as to our intentions.

34

There I was (minus face of course. I'm not that telegenic when it comes to incriminating videos) with several hand-written cards that read in turn:

'THE END'

'PS. STILL WANT THAT 100%?'

'PPS. HOW D'YOU LIKE THESE APPLES?'

I nicked the idea off Bob Dylan, but the apples were all my own work and I gave Bob good close-up look at them, pips an' all, as my belt and pants went the same way as the hand-written cards.

I like to think that Mrs Bob walked in on him around about this time with a couple of Findus Crispy Pancakes on a plate and an look of utter dismay on her chops.

"No dear, it's not what it looks like," Bob would've quickly tried to explain, as he frantically hit the stop button.

Well, it's the sort of thing one says when one's caught with one's hand in the biscuit jar, isn't it?

Of course, I have no evidence that this actually happened, just Ollie's word that he heard shouting and what sounded like a plate of Findus Crispy Pancakes hitting a telly shortly after he posted the jiffy through Bob's door.

Cheers Bob.

*

"Ahhhh!" I yelp, as Mel gets a bit rough with the Dettol and cotton wall.

"Well, whoever this other girl was, she wants to cut her nails I reckon," she quips, admiring my tattered and torn back as I soak in ten inches of milky warm bath water. "Who was she, Freddy Kruger?"

"I'm telling you, there was no other woman. That was Ollie thinking on his feet," I insist, flinching again as she starts on a fresh welt.

"Yeah, unlike you, you little rabbit, who let yours do the thinking for you," Mel needles, dispensing with the cotton wall and reaching for the sandpaper. At least, that's what it felt like, the careless great cow.

"Again, I was out the back, I didn't hear you come in, honestly" I repeat for the umpteenth time.

"Oh really, perhaps I should've tried shouting," Mel ponders.

"Well yeah, might've helped," I agree. "And also, I didn't want to come out because I thought it might spoil the surprise of what I'd got you for your birthday," I add, nodding my head in the direction of the enormous widescreen plasma telly just outside the bathroom door I'd been forced to part with by way of a peace offering. "I mean, I know how much you like your surprises."

"Oh, so now you're saying you did hear me?" Mel's ears prick up.

"What?" I blink, suddenly realising what I've just said.

"You did hear me in the warehouse? You did know I was there?"

I weigh up my options and decide the only way out of this is to hit her with a classic double Ollie.

"What?" I blink again.

I feel Mel's shoulder sag behind me and breath a sigh of relief as another bullet pings by.

"Anyway, stop changing the subject. Nice telly in' it? Are you pleased with it?" I ask her as she continues cleaning up my back.

"I am, but really, you didn't have to go to all that trouble for me; barbed wire, walls and fences and all. You could've just - oh I don't know - actually bought something like normal people do," Mel suggests, a little ungratefully in my opinion.

"How the hell am I going to afford a brand new widescreen telly?" I point out.

"You didn't have to get me a telly Bex. Anything would've done. Even something small," she says.

I ponder this for a moment.

"Hmm, I did have some fan heaters..."

I'm just wondering if it's too late to swap her telly for one of Electric's forty-five quid heaters and pocket the difference when my poor old back bursts into flames of pain as Mel tips an entire bottle of neat Dettol straight onto it.

"Ah fuck me no!" I screech, desperately trying to douse the worst of the pain in the soothing bath waters.

"Sting a bit, does it?" Mel asks casually.

THE ALARM JOB

1. No sleep for the wicked

I don't know if I've ever told you this - I'm sure I have, I've told everyone else - but my favourite film is *Aliens*. Or is it *Alien*? I can't decide between the two of them to be honest, but I reckon *Aliens* has just about got the edge over *Alien* simply because of the number of *aliens*. Anyway, I've lost count of the amount of times I've seen that film. Must be three or four dozen at least so I know it inside and out. I've got the limited special-edition collectors funky box set with all the behind-the-scenes DVD and plastic *alien* figure and everything, but oddly enough, the only time I ever watch it is when it comes on the telly. I'm never in the mood any other time, probably because I've seen it three or four dozen times, but if I happen to stumble across it on ITV or something, I can't help but watch it through. Only, I have to stick on the DVD come the first set of adverts because I can't watch a film I've seen three or four dozen times before when it's broken up with adverts I've seen a million times before. I mean, what a fucking waste of a life. Seriously.

Funnily enough, the bloke in Mr Video was saying the same thing. Whenever ITV or Channel Four show some big Hollywood blockbuster movie on the telly, the fella who lives in the flat just along the way from him always comes in shortly after the first advert break and gets the DVD out so that he can watch it without all the interruptions. Incredible ain't it, that me and him come from the same species that landed on the moon?

Anyway, a rather unfortunate side effect of having *Aliens* as a favourite film is that I can hardly make it through a night's sleep without having terrible nightmares about *Aliens*. And this is precisely what's chasing me around inside my head at around half midnight one sleepy Tuesday morning when a set of razor sharp talons streaks me across the ribs.

"Bex!"

"Oh God, no!" I'm crying, flinging crates, boxes and all sorts over my shoulder in an effort to put some distance between myself and those terrible slashing jaws.

"Bex!"

The ship's already set for self-destruct and the count-down has almost reached its fiery conclusion, but I'm still several decks from the escape capsule and both stairwells are swarming with alien warriors. Christ only knows where Ollie's got to with my flame thrower. I haven't seen that Judas since I gave him it to hang on to for two seconds and now, when I really need it, the bastard's nowhere to be seen.

"Bex!"

"I know!" I reply, desperately pushing every button on the computer console in order to buy myself a little more time, but the alarm's signalling the ship's final countdown and I'm going to find myself in a couple of million pieces floating through eternity in less than twenty seconds if I don't make a break for it right now.

Oh God, here goes!

"BEX!"

I roll over and look at Mel's anxious face. Shit, I'd forgotten about Mel. And the escape pod only holds one. Oh well, hopefully I'd learn to love again some day.

"Bex," she repeats, finally getting some joy out of me.

"What?" I groggily respond.

I look around the ship and see that it's been decked out by Ikea and Habitat and breathe a sigh of relief when I remember that the only terrible things waiting for me around here are the four sacks of plaster Mel brought home from B&Q six weeks ago.

"There's a burglar alarm going off across the road," she complains.

I open an ear and realise the ship's alarm has followed me from my dream and is now rattling away like a good 'un somewhere outside the curtains.

"I didn't do it," I reply instinctively, before I've had a chance to think whether I did or not.

"I realise that, but it's been ringing for half an hour," Mel moans, before noticing that I've slipped back to sleep, which wasn't surprising really when you consider that I'd been running around a spaceship terrified out of my wits for half the night. "Oi, have you gone back to sleep?" she gripes, shaking me awake again.

"What? Wasn't I supposed to?"

"Bex, I can't get to sleep," she insists.

"Why not?" I ask.

"Because of the alarm," she replies, incredulous. "I can't get to sleep with that thing ringing all night."

"Of course you can, it's easy. Here watch," I demonstrate.

"Adrian, please," she pleads. "I've got a really important meeting first thing in the morning and I can't go into it if I haven't had any sleep."

"Well why don't you drink half a bottle of scotch then? That should get you to sleep," I suggest.

"You haven't had many important meetings first thing in the morning, have you?" Mel guesses.

"And I never made the ones I did," I tell her. Mel groans next to me, so I turn over and loop an arm around her. "Oh what d'you want luv, a bit of solidarity? No problem. Just let me rest my eyes while I'm doing it."

"Can't you do something about it?" she pleads.

"About what? The alarm? What can I do?" I shrug, though I have a horrible notion that me and my Arsenal pyjamas are going to be feeling the cold night's air before this one's run its course.

"Adrian, there aren't many perks to going out with a burglar, but this should definitely be one of them," she reckons. "Can't you knobble it or something? You must know how."

"Knobble it?" I toy. "And you used to be such a nice girl an' all."

"Adrian, do you know why I love you?" she simpers, forcing me to throw in the towel.

"Oh put your big guns away, I'm on my way," I cave in, before stopping at the edge of the bed. "Why do you love me?"

"Because you're one of life's tryers. Admittedly, you're usually trying to do the wrong thing but in these circumstances, I think it's what's called for."

"Oh," I muse to myself, a tad disappointed, then counter, "d'you know why I love you?"

Mel thinks for a moment. "My tits?"

I pick up the phone.

"Who are you calling?" she asks.

"Your mum. She told me to give her a bell if you ever started talking like a tramp," I reply.

"Bex, who are you calling?" Mel repeats.

"Who you're meant to call at times like these," I tell her, dialling the number for the local cop shop. "I mean blimey, I don't wear my black hat the whole time, you know?"

After a dozen rings, a sleepy, disinterested voice comes on the other end.

"Night desk, Sergeant Atwell speaking," he grudgingly acknowledges.

"Are you having trouble finding your car keys or something?" I ask him.

"Er," Atwell grunts, suddenly wishing he'd let it ring. "Can I take your name please, sir?"

"No you cannot," I tell him. "This is, what we call in the trade, an anonymous phone call."

"Anonymous huh?" he muses. "Well I'll still have to take your name I'm afraid."

I'm almost tempted to laugh. "Do people actually fall for that one?"

"Occasionally," he reckons. "Go on then, what's upsetting you tonight?"

"What, other than Mrs Johnson's foul-mouthed daughter, you mean? Try this big noise outside my window," I say, holding the phone in the direction of the alarm.

"I see," Atwell says, when I come back on the line. "And how are you spelling Johnson?"

"What? Never mind about that, someone's burglar alarm's been ringing across the road for the last hour," I exaggerate.

"Have you seen anyone entering or loitering about the property," Atwell asks, listing the least of my concerns.

"What? Who cares about that? We can't get to sleep over here," I moan down the phone.

"So you're not reporting a burglary then?" he clarifies.

"No, I'm reporting a burglar alarm."

"What's the address?" he asks.

Pleased that we finally seem to be making some progress, I tell him it's on Monteagle Lane.

"What number?" the daft fucker then asks.

"Mate, it's eighty decibels out there. Don't worry, you'll find it without the house number just so long as you don't dispatch Eric Sykes," I remind him.

"Hmm, yeah, see the problem is, without your details, I can't very well dispatch anyone as this could be a crank call," Atwell informs me.

"Hang on a minute, I'm reporting a burglary and you're telling me you can't dispatch anyone?" I ask, incredulously.

"I thought you were reporting a burglar alarm?" Atwell corrects me.

"Never mind about that, for all I know people could be being killed across the road this very minute," I plead.

"Oh yeah, I can see why you're having trouble sleeping now," Atwell sympathises.

"Oh you're hilarious you are mate. I'm so glad I stayed up to have this conversation," I congratulate.

Before I can say anything more, Atwell asks me if there's anything else he can help me with.

"What d'you mean anything else? You make it sound like you've actually done something for me. The alarm across the road is still ringing."

"Well," Atwell mulls, "we haven't had anything reported from the area."

"What the hell d'you think I'm trying to do, win a holiday to Barbados? I'm reporting it. And this is the sound of me reporting it," I bark, then have a sudden flash of inspiration. "And actually, now that you come to mention it, I think I do see someone trying to break in."

Atwell's got a ready-prepared answer for that one though.

"Can I have your name please sir?" he asks.

"I give up," I say in disgust, slamming down the phone and looking at Mel. "Unbelievable in' it? I tell you, I've only got to park on a double yellow for five minutes to summon a dozen Special Branch, yet the first time I actually want something and you wouldn't knock a copper's hat off if you carpet-bombed this estate with nuclear missiles."

"Why didn't you give him your name?" Mel wants to know.

"I generally prefer to keep my name away from police reports if I can help it luv, as you never know which box it's going to end up in," I tell her.

Mel thumps the pillow a couple of times and chews on her lip. Outside, the noise seems to have got even louder, though this could just be because I'm now wide awake. What I want to know is where is everyone else? Why haven't my neighbours phoned in to complain too or started running across the road with ladders? Is it just me and Mel who've got working eardrums in this street, though admittedly I'd been happily out of it too until Mel had jabbed me awake so that I wouldn't miss out on the fun.

"So what are we going to do about the alarm?" Mel asks me miserably.

As much as I could've happily screwed in a couple of earplugs and rejoined my aliens, I can't go back to sleep now that I know Mel can't - not least of all because there's no way the selfish cow will let me, so I let out a groan and slide into my slippers.

"Oh alright," I concede. "But this gets written up in the plusses column, to be drawn on any time I see fit. Meaning I can get absolutely annihilated at the next wedding we go to and have a punch-up with a vicar if I like, and you're only allowed hold my coat, look on and laugh. Deal?"

"I don't know about having a punch-up with the vicar," Mel objects.

"I only mean if he starts it," I explain.

"Oh, go on then, deal," she reluctantly agrees.

"Right, where's my tools?"

The din outside in the street's even louder than it was in the bedroom, obviously. Yet the only person I can see at any window is Mel. Incredible huh? The deaf aid shop down the road must be making a fucking fortune.

I grab my ladder and my tools from the garage and quick step it across the street.

The house with the alarm is a big five or six bed fully detached job with its own gravel drive and swimming pool out back. It looks pretty old too. Turn of the century I reckon, either Edwardian or maybe even Victorian. Certainly older than the scores of shitty little three-bed terraces that the owners must've watched springing up all around their land with dismay. But then, that's urban sprawl for you. One minute, Lord and Lady Tweed have got a lovely redbrick manor house on the outskirts of London, the next they've got a load of little ASBO scumbags for neighbours hanging around on their stone lions waiting for them to work up the courage to go and collect their pensions.

I lean my ladder up against the front of the house and give whoever lives here one last chance to make their presence known.

"Oi Beethoven! You alive in there?" I shout through the letterbox. "D'you know your latest symphony's annoying half the street?"

There's no response.

"Anyone?" I try again. "Last chance?"

Still nothing.

"Right."

I stuff some cotton wool in my ears and head up the ladder with my tools. The alarm's directly above the front door, so I'm able to stand on the protruding porch and take a proper look at it. It's in good nick, only a couple of years old, so it probably hasn't short-circuited. I run my fingers down the back of it, feeling for the box's catch and locate it at the bottom. This is the alarm's Achilles Heel and I'm able to tickle the protective casing off with a five pound lump hammer and smash everything I find inside back to sand until the ringing finally stops. Of course, it goes without saying that there are quieter ways to disable an alarm, but if the alarm itself hasn't roused anyone else up until this point, then nothing was, so why miss any more sleep twisting wires together?

"Okay then," I tell the alarm, then drop the hammer back into my bag and start back down the ladder.

Waiting for me at the bottom is a luminous jacket and a pair of size ten boots containing one of Tatley's finest.

I recognise him as PC Terry Bennett, a somewhat hopeless mass of insecurity who'd joined the Force as soon as he was able to in order to compensate for a childhood spent watching toilet bowls flush at close quarters and shinning up trees to collect his school satchel. And it weren't just me and Ol who used to throw it up there either. Lots of blokes did. It was a game at our school.

He stares at me for a moment, a smug smile dancing across his bumfluff-thatched top lip, then looks up the ladder towards the alarm, and finally back at me.

"You're getting a bit complacent in your old age, aren't you Bex?" he chuckles, but I miss this as I've still got my ears packed with cotton wool.

"Uh? Oh hang on a minute," I tell him, remembering the wool and pulling it out. "What? Say again?"

Bennett looks at me with utter incredulity and snatches the bag off my shoulder - a bit of ironic payback no doubt.

"Oh come on, you're nicked," he snaps, grabbing me by the arm and leading me off towards his mate who's holding their jam jar's back door open.

2. A brief stopover

"Not keeping you up, are we?" Weasel asks, when he sees me yawning across the interview table from him. He starts the tape player and does the introductions.

"The date is January 29th, 2007 and the time 1.28am. Present are myself, Detective Sergeant Haynes and..."

"418 PC Bennett," Bennett says for himself, grateful for a couple of lines.

"And..." Weasel says, looking at me.

"What?" I reply.

"Say your name," he tells me.

"You say it you lazy bastard. You're the ones getting paid for this, not me. Why don't I just interview myself an' all while I'm at it and let you two get back to bed?"

Weasel shakes his head, then fills in the blanks. "... Adrian Beckinsale, otherwise known as Bex. The offer of legal assistance was refused," he tells the tape.

"Well I ain't getting Charlie out of bed for this, am I? Some of us have got to get some kip otherwise this town'll fall to bits tomorrow," I point out.

Weasel continues to ignore me, preferring instead to talk to his tape recorder.

"Mr Beckinsale was arrested by 418 PC Bennett at 12.53am on sus-picion of breaking and entering after being discovered in the garden of a private residence, number 27 Monteagle Lane," Weasel says, eye-balling me for signs of stress, though the only stress I'm suffering is hav-ing to sit through a shit episode of The Bill when I should've been in bed legging it from Aliens.

"Are you doing a phone-in or something? I'm right here you know," I finally snap, annoyed at being blanked in favour of Wooden Top FM. "And what's all this cobblers about me breaking and entering? There was a spot of breaking, I'll give you that, but there weren't even a whiff of entering. I was just trying to shut the fucker's alarm up so I could get back to sleep."

I'm half-tempted to enlarge Mel's part in this evening's events but I think better of it. The more people you drag into any given mess, the messier it always becomes. There's still a chance I can talk my way out of this on my own, but bring Mel into it and suddenly they've got to go and collect her, interview her, reinterview me, stare at the pair of us, lose our details, find our details, then start all over again when they find they've spelt my name wrong, so I keep Mel in reserve for the time being and make up my mind only to call on her if they look like charging me with something.

"You were found, up a ladder, in the middle of the night, against a property which doesn't belong to you," Weasel reminds me.

"You also want to mention, for the benefit of our listeners, that I was found in my pyjamas. Who goes running around the streets in their pyjamas other than Ninjas and my eight-year-old nephew?"

"Well you, obviously," Weasel answers.

"Look, I went across the road to shut the alarm off. If you want to arrest someone you should arrest the bloke who's alarm it is." I vent, then notice Weasel's eyebrows tilting and concede, "alright, was."

"We received a phone call from a neighbour who reported seeing someone trying to break in," Weasel says, reading from his notepad.

Suddenly, it all becomes clear. "Hang on a minute, that was me," I tell him.

"Ah, so you admit the charges?" Weasel misunderstands.

"No, not me breaking in. That was me who phoned up. I was the anonymous caller."

Weasel's face turns a shade of confusion. "You tipped us off, that you were breaking in across the road," he says, then turns to Bennett and laughs. "Forget complacent, that's just plain showboating."

I sink my face into the table. "Oh, this is going to annoy me for years."

*

Unbeknown to me, Mel has taken it upon herself to get involved in this whole sorry mess without waiting for an invitation, though she's having about as much success getting past that wooden door stop on the front desk as I'd had earlier. I mean, seriously, I'm all for equal opportunities and everything, but I draw the line at brain dead coma cases who are only able to blink, do crosswords and eat bacon sandwiches through tubes.

"Er hello, you've got my boyfriend in custody," Mel tells Atwell.

Atwell drags his eyes away from four across and points them at Mel. "I see miss," he sighs, his mind still searching for a three-lettered animal that sits on, and rhymes with, 'Mat'; first letter K (apparently). "It is miss, isn't it? Or is it ms?" Atwell double-checks. "Can't be too careful these days."

"Ms is fine," Mel replies.

"Really? Okay then ms, it is," Atwell frowns, unsettled at having to deal with yet another nut-job feminist. "Hmm, ms? Never sounds right does it?"

Atwell tests the word out on several sentences and film titles before Mel brings him back to reality.

"My boyfriend?"

"Oh yes, right. I just need your name ms."

"You're joking aren't you?" Mel asks. Atwell stares at her blankly. "I

46

was in here only two weeks ago," Mel reminds him. "And three weeks before that." Atwell continues to stare. "I must've been in here at least half a dozen times before." Still no flicker of recognition from Atwell. "Oh for God's sake, it's Melanie Johnson. My boyfriend's..."

"And how are you spelling Johnson?" Atwell interrupts.

"The same way everyone else in the country spells it. J-O-H..."

"Hold on, that's odd, there's not box for ms on this form," Atwell says, turning over the form to quickly scan the back. "Would you rather be a miss or a mrs?"

"Does it matter?"

"Oh yes," he assures her. "Got to get the paperwork right. Very important."

"Just put me down as anything."

Atwell laughs, his world turned upside down by such a ludicrous notion. "We don't have a box for anything," he grins down at her from his high horse.

"Go on then, let's see the choices," Mel finally bites. Atwell turns the form around and Mel looks down the boxes. "Okay, I'll be that one."

Atwell studies her choice.

"Reverend!" he reads, saddened but hardly surprised. Well it is 2007 after all, and there are lots of strange and frightening things in the world these days. Blokes dressing up as women, women dressing up as blokes, special ramps for spastics everywhere and Negroes working in banks. So why not women vicars? The more the merrier, Atwell sighs inwardly, before conceding; "Well, you do get them these days I suppose. And such pretty ones too," he adds, to show Mel just how open-minded he is as he ticks her box. "Right now, Reverend Johnson, what was it you had stolen again? Purse was it?"

*

Some time later, Weasel opens my cell door and tells me I'm free to go. This comes as something of a surprise to me.

"Really? But you haven't even planted any drugs on me yet."

"No, we've run out. You think you've ordered enough, but you never have."

"So what's up?"

"Perhaps you should try not looking so surprised when your story checks out, just for future reference like," he advises. "Come on."

Weasel leads me through to custody and hands me a clipboard to sign in return for my suspiciously empty tool bag.

"Of course, there's still the question of the damage to the alarm. Once we locate the owner of the property, he may wish to press charges," he says, clearing up the mystery of why all my tools are still being held as evidence.

"True, though he may also wish not to have dog shit posted through

47

his letter box every few days for the rest of his life," I agree.

Weasel just glances, but doesn't rise to it. "And we may also have to look into the matter of the crank phone call."

"You what?" I ask, wondering if I've heard him right.

"You reported seeing someone breaking into a property when there wasn't anyone. In its strictest sense, that's Wasting Police Time. We may have to talk to the CPS," he says, in all seriousness.

"Our brave boys in blue. And they wonder why their takeaways always taste funny?" I say, shaking my head in disbelief, though this is fairly typical of Weasel. He wasn't about to put in half a night's work in without having something to show for it now, was he?

I swing my empty tool bag over my shoulder and follow him out to the front office.

"You know what I don't get though," I tell him. "I don't get why you're letting us go after only an hour. You could've had us banged up all night if you'd wanted to."

Weasel stops and asks; "You know what I love about this job the most?"

I think on this. "The big hats?"

"It's bringing loved ones together."

I find my own particular loved one waiting for me in the station's reception and the moment I step through the door she leaps to her feet and starts yelling at me like we're both on Big Brother.

"You inconsiderate sod! Just how many night's sleep do I have to miss bailing your arse out of the cells?" she rants, grabbing me by the arm and dragging me off towards the car park.

Behind me, I hear Weasel chuckle and tell me to have a pleasant trip home and I'm about to chuck the waste paper bin through the police station window so that they'll lock me up again when Mel whispers under her breath; "Play along, I don't want anyone knowing this was all my fault." She then ups the volume for the final beat; "You dickhead!" but I rest easy knowing that this is for the benefit of the audience rather than mine.

"Night Reverend," Sergeant Atwell chips in somewhere to the rear.

"Yes, night Sergeant," Mel replies, crossing herself theatrically. "Live long and prosper."

I decide not to ask.

*

"Thanks for that luv, I do appreciate it," Mel tells me when we get home.

"No problem," I tell her, with a benign waft of the wrist. "You know me, anything for the woman I love."

"Really? Well that kitchen still needs plastering if you really want to sweep me off my feet," she says, nodding at the bags of plaster cluttering our hall.

"I said I loved you, I didn't say I worked for you," I point out.

"Oh come on, let's go to bed. Nothing to keep us up any more," Mel says, but I stop dead.

"Oh bollocks!"

"What?"

"My ladder," I tell her. "It's still out there leaning up against that bloody house. I'd better go and grab it."

"Okay, but don't make too much noise," she yawns. "I'm so tired I'll probably be asleep when you come back in." Which worked out nicely in the event, because there might not have been anything more to keep Mel up this night, but there was definitely something to keep me up.

Namely, a big posho house across the road with a busted alarm.

3. Reinforcements

Ollie arrives in the van twenty minutes later and jumps out looking less than impressed.

"Quarter to three in the morning? What's so urgent that it couldn't wait until quarter to three in the afternoon when I normally get up?" Ollie grumbles.

"Sorry, but an opportunity like this don't come around that often and I'm not one to look a gift-house in the front door, particularly when the inconsiderate cunt who lives there owes me a modicum of compensation," I tell him.

"You what?"

"Big drum over there, nobody's home and the alarm's developed a short circuit thanks to me and MC Lump Hammer," I explain.

"A house? I thought you had an office or a factory sorted. You never said it was a house. I thought we'd given up houses."

"Hey Ol, this isn't some little old lady's retirement bungalow, this is a great big five-bed detached job. Besides, the bloke owes me for fines pending and the loss of a night's sleep. I think the very least he can do is let me have his DVD player.

"Hang on a minute, have I missed a couple of episodes here? Who owes you for what?" Ollie squints, desperately trying to keep up with the conversation. I figure it's best just to cut to the chase as it's generally a pointless waste of life trying to ensure Ollie's up to speed.

"Look, we can spend all night discussing this and voting ourselves pay rises or we can just go and do it. So are you in or what?"

"Oh well gee, when you put it like that, then obviously I'm in," Ollie lips.

"Smart, come on then," I tell him, before he can find something else to drag his heels over.

"Oh but Bex, I was all tucked up in bed with Belinda when you rang," he continues to complain as we cross the road.

"Huh, your turn was it?" I quip.

Ollie grabs me by the arm, pulls me back and sticks a finger in my face. "Oi, don't be horrible about her, alright. She ain't like that no more," he warns me.

"When did you start getting so defensive about Belinda? I've heard you laugh at worse before," I tell him, recalling his reaction to my observation in the pub the other day that Belinda had seen more cocks than the Oxford Cambridge boat race.

"Yeah, but I don't laugh about that sort of thing when she's sat behind me," he says, and I look over his shoulder to the van and see Belinda in all her gory glory wiggling her fingers to give me a little wave through the side window.

"What the hell's she doing here?"

"She wanted to come, what was I supposed to do, tell her this was a lads only burglary?"

"She's going to get us all nicked, you big rocking horse," I tell him.

"No she won't, she'll be fine, she's cool," Ollie simpers. "Besides, we're stuck with her now, so what d'you wanna do?"

I can tell you what I wanted to do, but that would've woken up my neighbours again and got blood and teeth all over my slippers, so I'm forced to do the only thing I can and agree to let Belinda be a part of it.

"Oh fine. But she stays in the van and her cut comes out of yours."

"Fine," he agrees.

"And no sneaking off to bang her for kinky danger kicks when I'm not looking," I warn him.

"Well I won't if you don't," he tells me.

"I thought you said she weren't like that no more?"

"She ain't," he says.

"Well then."

"Yeah, well then," he echoes, before turning serious. "But don't alright."

Belinda shuffles over to the driver's seat and unwinds the window as we approach. In the time me and Ollie have been talking, she's managed to make herself up like Coco the Clown and replace the air in the cab with Estee Lauder.

"Hi Bex," she creams. "Oooh, this is so exciting. Are we gonna do a job?"

"Yes, and you've got the most important job of all, the job of look-out," I tell her.

"I can do that. I'll be great," she promises. "What do I do?"

"Just stay here, in the van, and keep your eyes peeled."

Belinda nods vigorously, accepting her assignment, then thinks. "What do I do if somebody comes?"

"Don't do nothing, just be quiet," I tell her.

"But what if it's the police and they surround the house?" she continues fretting.

I can see she's fishing for some mission specifics, so I tell her if that happens, she's to beep the horn three times and quickly drive away.

Belinda agrees, then starts jabbing the horn to get a bit of practice in. I frantically slap her hand away and ask her what the fuck she's doing.

"Just checking it works," she tells me, as if I've asked some sort of daft question.

"It works! For crying-out-loud, it works alright. Look, just sit here and do nothing, okay?" I order her, before bundling Ollie off in the direction of the house. "Jesus Christ, what a divvy!"

"Oi, don't talk about her like that," Ollie once again complains.

I'm about to tell him he can drop the Sir Galahad act, the old bike's out of earshot now, when I pull up sharply and stare at the front of the house.

"Oh fantastic!"

"What's up?" Ollie asks.

"My ladder's gone."

"It's terrible, isn't it, you can't leave nothing out these days," Ollie says sadly.

"Come on, let's have a look around the back."

The side of the house is shrouded in darkness, so we break our little torches out. Ollie stops to point his at the bottom of his shoes.

"Oh what is this I've stepped in?" he complains.

"Quiet you big spanner. Between you and Belinda, you're gonna wake the whole fucking neighbourhood up," I growl at him. "Now, did you bring the glass cutter?"

Ollie looks at me as if I've asked him if he brought his bowler hat. "No. Was I meant to?"

"Not if you can melt holes in windows with lasers from your eyes. Why didn't you bring it?"

"I didn't know I had to."

"Why do we have to have a bloody inventory of all the stuff you didn't bring every time we're out on the job? Why can't you pre-empt our needs and bring the whole fucking lot for once?"

"Oh just do the French windows, that's what they're there for," Ollie tells me, testing the door handle. "They're locked," he diagnoses.

"Really? What at this time of night, when he's not in? He's a bit anal, in't he?" I reply, but Ollie's too pre-occupied shining his torch through the glass to hear me.

"He's left the key in the lock," Ollie grins. "Classic mistake. Here, watch this."

Ollie pulls a thin flat-headed screwdriver from his bag and feeds it into the keyhole. After a couple of feeler wiggles, he jabs the screwdriver and the key drops out of the lock and plops onto the carpet below.

"Very nice," I tell him. "Is there any more to this trick or is that it?"

My flat-headed partner's in full-on demonstration-mode though and pulls a sheet of newspaper from his inside pocket.

"No, now we just slide this under the door and pull the key towards us," he says triumphantly.

I spot a tiny flaw in Ollie's otherwise flaw-filled plan, but decide rather than point it out, to let Ollie stumble upon it for himself. After all, it's the only way he'll learn.

"Right, I'm going to time this and see how long it takes you to figure out what you've done wrong," I say, shining my torch on my watch and counting the ticks of my second hand.

Ollie creases his eyebrows in confusion, then gets down on his knees and starts feeding the newspaper underneath the door. After a few seconds, I hear the sound of a penny plopping between Ollie's ears.

"Oh bollocks, I should've fed the paper underneath first," he tuts, straightening up and looking to me to make it all better.

"Four seconds. You're actually getting quicker you know. Right, come on," I tell him, and turn around only to almost tumble arse-over-tit over Belinda.

"Alright?" she squawks.

The sudden shock sends me leaping back almost five feet and without meaning too, I plant an elbow straight through one of the French window panels with a deafening crack. All three of us immediately leg it over the back fence as glass tinkles onto the concrete patio slabs and we keep on legging it for several dozen yards until we find a discreet back alleyway to duck inside.

Once we're safe, I shine the torch into Belinda's face accusingly and ask her what the hell's she's doing.

"I thought I told you to stay in the van."

"I got bored," she shrugs.

"How d'you get bored? You weren't in there five minutes. My dog could keep himself amused in the van for longer than that!" I hiss, prompting Ollie to come to his fair maiden's defence.

"Oi, I ain't telling you again…" he threatens, but there's no way I'm tolerating being the one in the wrong here so I tell him how it is, Belinda or no Belinda.

"See, this is why we don't bring girls on jobs Ol, all the trouble they cause and everything."

"I don't want to be no trouble or nothing, I just want to come in the house with Ol," Belinda explains.

"But you're being trouble right now," I tell her.

Belinda looks at me blankly. "No I'm not," she corrects.

"Oh come on Bex, let's just take her. Three pairs of hands and all that. We'll get done quicker," Ollie pleads, putting me in an impossible position. See I could just tell him "no" and order Belinda back to the van, but I'd end up standing here all on my own and have no one to go drinking with for the next six months while I wait for Ollie to forget what he's in a boo with me about, so I throw him a bone and make up my mind to have him neutered next time we're passing the vets.

"Have it your way then, but don't say I didn't tell you so when we're sharing a cell with some sexually ambiguous bare-knuckle boxer."

"No skin off my nose," Ollie shrugs.

"It ain't our noses we'll be worrying about mate," I point out, then lead the way back to the house.

Unbelievably, my neighbours still haven't stirred. What is it with this lot? Has everyone died in their beds tonight or have I been fitted with bionic hearing or something? Fucking lazy cunts. Still, somewhat convenient for me, so why am I complaining?

I pick the last splinters of the glass out of the French window frame and reach through. I grab the door handle and give it a wiggle, but the doors are just as locked that side as they are this.

"Bit of a shame we pushed that key through now, isn't it?" Ollie says.

"Yes it is a bit, isn't it?" I reply sarcastically, not appreciating the "we" portion of his last sentence.

"Hey, come quick. I've found an open window!" Belinda belts out at the top of her voice.

"For crying-out-loud you big foghorn, what's the matter with you?" I frantically shush her.

"Uh? Oh sorry," she apologises, turning down a volume a touch. "But look, someone's left a window open," she urges, flapping her hand at us and disappearing round the corner. Me and Ol follow and find she's right. A little side window is hanging open, but judging by the gouge marks made around the latch, it hadn't been blown open by the wind.

"That's been jemmied open. Look there," I point out.

"Maybe that's why the alarm went off," Ollie ponders.

"Nah, if Bennett had seen this when he nabbed me, I would've definitely got charged with 'entering' too. Some budding entrepreneur's been at this place since."

"Maybe they're still in there," Belinda says cautiously.

"Well if they are, they've just taken on three partners. Come on, give us a bunk up."

Ollie makes a rung with his hands, but no sooner do I step into it than Ollie whips it away again to leave me flailing and smacking face first into the brickwork.

"What are you doing you fucking arsehole?" I demand.

"Ow, you've gone and stepped in it too," Ollie complains, sniffing his fingers and wiping them across his jeans.

"Look, stop dicking about and give me a bunk up, will you?" I tell him, waving a fist under his nose.

"Well wipe your feet first," he insists.

I wipe them on the grass as Ollie sniffs his fingers again and announces he thinks it's slugs we've both been walking through.

"I'm gonna slug you in a minute if you don't put your fucking job head on."

We resume the position and this time my step ladder stays where he is and heaves me through the opening. It's pitch dark inside the house and my torch is in my pocket, so I have to feel for a safe landing with my feet. All at once the toes of my left foot go cold and I realise with a heavy heart that I'm standing in the toilet.

"Oh bollocks!" I moan.

"Bex! Bex, what are you doing?" Ollie calls through the window.

"I'm washing me, socks, what d'you think I'm doing? Now when you're quite finished shouting my name about, meet me by the French windows."

I shake the worst of the water (at least, I hope it's water) from my slipper and go and unlock the French windows. Ollie and Belinda are patiently waiting for me outside like I've invited them over to dinner.

"We came about your ad in the paper for a couple of burglars," Ollie quips when I open the doors.

"Just get inside will you?"

"Moody," he grins.

"Right, let's see what's on offer shall we?" I say, pulling my torch from my pocket and setting to work.

4. Hardly a stick

I have to say, our initial scout about doesn't fill me with confidence. The living room has a chair, a decorative cabinet and a TV stand, but there's no TV to sit on it, no ornaments to decorate the decorative cabinet and no sofa to go with the chair. The place is about as empty as a place can be without actually being empty.

"Where's his telly?" Belinda asks.

"Where's his anything?" I trump her.

"Your DVD player's gone an' all. You think this is down to our partner, old Alice through the bog window?" Ollie suggests.

"No I don't. Someone ain't done this in the last hour. Look, no stereo, no pictures, no video tapes, DVDs or books," I point out, trailing my torch light across a row of empty shelves before taking it on a tour of the hall and kitchen. "No phone, no microwave, kettle or toaster." I open a couple of the cupboards and look inside. "A couple of plates and a few pots and pans, but that's about it."

"Well he must have something," Ollie reasons.

"Imagine if he had a safe and there was like, a million pounds in it," Belinda froths with misplaced excitement.

"Yeah, that would be good, wouldn't it?" I agree, rolling my eyes in the darkness and checking my pockets for sugar cubes to reward her with.

"We sometimes come across safes you know," Ollie invents. "I get into them, I do. I'm a safe cracker see."

"Are you?" Belinda bites. "Oh, this is so exciting. Do you think there are any safes in here?"

"A few safe bets perhaps," I weigh up.

"I'll find you a safe Ollie," Belinda promises, starting her search by looking behind three postcard-sized pictures on the far wall that seemed to be having trouble hiding their own picture hooks, let alone any safes.

"Have you tried looking under that ant over there?" I suggest, pointing my torch at the floor.

"Oi, you leave her alone," Ollie glares.

I'm two seconds away from leaving this whole night alone when Belinda suddenly announces that she's found one.

"I've found one. Ollie look, I've found one. This drawer's locked," she demonstrates, tugging on the drawer handle with all her might.

"Stand back, this is my area of expertise," he announces, dropping to his knees for a close-up look.

He runs his fingers along the edge of the drawer, compares it to a couple of its open neighbours, and locates what he thinks is its weak spot.

"Okay, step aside a little bit further will you?" he tells Belinda, then slides the blade of his crowbar into the gap and wrenches the whole lot open.

"What's in there?" Belinda orgasms.

"Is it the bottom of the sink, by any chance?" I hedge, having noticed the taps and basin above the drawer front the moment Belinda stepped to one side. Ollie studies the white plastic pipes inside his 'safe' and confirms my suspicions.

"Er, yeah."

"This place has been cleaned out," I conclude.

"Well what's he got his alarm on for then?" Ollie asks.

"To protect the house itself probably, from squatters you know. Or maybe just to wind me up for giggles."

"Or maybe it's something else!" an altogether different voice behind us suggests, frightening the fuck of me. We spin around to see Norris leaning against the woodwork grinning to himself like it's Christmas all over again.

"Christ almighty Norris! What are you doing sneaking up on people like that?" I say, when I catch my breath.

"The same as you, looking for something to nick. You found anything?"

"Only that shitting your pants isn't just an expression. Was that you who did the bog window?"

"In like Gunga Flynn I was," he winks. "Here, hang on a minute, I thought the Old Bill carted you away hours ago."

"You were watching?"

"Better than that, it was me who tripped the alarm in the first place," he declares, fishing for either a rosette or a smack in the mouth. "Didn't half go on, didn't it?"

"Oh cheers mate, I got nicked for that."

"No no, that weren't my fault. I thought the Old Bill would just come round and dismantle it if they got enough complaints, then I could get busy when they were gone," he explains.

"What a fantastic plan. You not only turn someone over, you also manage to wind up an entire street in the process."

"I guess I'm just one of life's doers," Norris shrugs.

"You know, it's a good job none of us have got work in the morning," Ollie says, checking his watch.

"That's true," Belinda agrees, catching Norris's attention.

"Hello Belinda, how's it going?" he asks her, flicking his torch beam across her tits as if it were his fingers.

"Oi, do you mind?" Ollie enquires, stepping in front of Belinda in an effort to preserve her honour - too little and way too late in mine and the bog wall's opinion.

Something suddenly occurs to me. "Here Norris, what do you mean, 'or maybe it's something else'?"

"I've found a door. It's locked."

"If it's in the side of the bath, I think I know what's behind it."

We follow Norris all the same, out the front, past the empty living room and come to a rest next to a little door in the hallway near the front door.

"There you go, one locked door," Norris congratulates himself.

"Marvellous, how much you think we'll get for it?" Ollie sarcs, but Norris has his patter already prepared and he's not deviating from the script.

"So, you have to ask yourself, why lock a door in a house that's already been cleaned out and protected with an alarm?"

It's way too early in the morning for Cluedo so I bite and tell Norris to get on with it and open the fucking thing then.

"Okay, give us a credit card then."

"On your bike! You think I'd let you thieving paws anywhere near my plastic?"

"I'm gonna be standing right here, ain't I?" Norris asserts, offended that I should even question the wisdom of leaving the key to my cheese larder with such an honest and upstanding rat. "Fine, Ollie?"

"What's wrong with your credit cards?" Ollie replies.

"Do I look like someone the bank would give a card to?" Norris points out.

"You don't have to use your platinum Diner's Club card. Your Mr Video card should do, you know?"

Norris screws up his face bitterly. "Mr Video wouldn't give me a card either. Besides, if I had a card, I would've opened it already, wouldn't I?"

"Oh this is hopeless," I quickly realise. "Go on Ol, just give him a card will ya?"

"I can't, I came out without my wallet," Ollie shrugs, his wallet almost certainly nestling in his back pocket.

"Belinda?" I nudge. "What about you, have you got anything on you?"

"Only cash," she replies. "Will that do?"

I temporarily lose the will to live, but thoughts of state-of-the-art DVDs, home computers and rare antique porcelain ducks on the wall behind this door steel my resolve and override the remnants of my common sense. I pull my wallet from my jacket pocket, take out my cashpoint card (Mr Video wouldn't give me a card either see) and hand it to Norris.

"This, comes back to me, you hear?" I tell him in no uncertain terms.

"Of course. What sort of a bloke d'you take me for?" Norris simpers. "Right, check this out."

He drops to his knees and carefully feeds the card into the door jamb next to the lock. I keep my torch on him at all times to make sure he's not scribbling down my card number and expiry date and after a few seconds of wiggling there's a little click and Norris "ah-ha"s triumphantly before handing me back my plastic. I can't help but notice that while the door's still firmly closed my card's now at some sort of right-angle to itself.

"They make it look so easy on the telly, don't they?" Norris frowns.

"Wait a minute, you can't even do it?" I despair. Norris shrugs by way of an explanation. "I thought you could do it, that's why I..." I tail off, before deciding I've seriously had enough of my mates and their Ocean's 11 tricks, so I take a step forward and put a slipper straight through the door, flinging it back on its hinges.

Unfortunately, there are no DVD players waiting to be collected in this room either. Nor are there are any tellies, computers or porcelain ducks. In fact, there's not much of anything; a desk, a chair, some ugly pictures and another great big enormous chunk of fuck all.

"Somewhat disappointing," Norris reckons.

"You can say that again. This is rapidly turning into one of those days and it hasn't even hardly started yet."

"This one's empty an' all!" Ollie spots.

"Oh not much gets past you does it Ol? You ever thought about setting yourself up as a supersleuth?"

It's at this point, just as the towel's leaving my fingertips, that Belinda saves the entire evening from being a complete and utter washout by turning over a picture to find a safe. Now, I don't want you to go thinking that we'd struck it rich or something, because we hadn't. The only glimmer of compensation this safe offered us was the chance to see Ollie swing in the wind as his earlier *Jackanory* was called.

"Ollie, I've found a safe," Belinda yaps, then gets a teensy bit more specific. "I've found you a safe."

Ollie freezes and hardly dares to turn around, so I help the situation along a little.

"Oh fantastic. Off you go then fingers. Show us your stuff," I invite.

Ollie immediately starts twisting. "Oh well, you know, I don't normally..."

But he ain't getting off the hook that easily. "No no no, no false modesty. I'm sure we all want to see the great Dynamite Joe in action."

"The what?" Norris asks, somewhere off behind me in the darkness.

"Ollie's a brilliant safe cracker," Belinda tells Norris proudly. "He's going to crack this safe, he is."

"What with, his head?" Norris dismisses.

Ollie finally gives into peer pressure and takes a peek at the patient. He twiddles its dial and tweaks its handle, but this model's obviously been fitted with a child-lock because it doesn't seem to want to open.

"No joy?" I ask.

"No, it looks like one of the new ones," Ollie explains with a sigh. "Might be a bit tricky."

But this is defeatist talk and Belinda won't hear a word of it. She puts an arm around her own personal Great Train Robber and angles her big, brown, hope-filled eyes up at him.

"Don't be like that, Ollie. You can do it, I know you can. I believe in you," she tells him, making me chuckle with delight.

My chuckling ends abruptly though when Ollie pulls out his phone and starts dialling.

"Here, hold on Ollie. Who you calling? You ain't calling a locksmith or no one daft are you?

"No, I'm calling Electric. He knows a bit about safes."

"Ollie, it's three in the morning. You can't just go phoning someone up at three in the morning," I tell him.

"Why not? You phoned me at half-two."

Ten miles away, a phone springs to life on an overcrowded bedside chest of drawers and Electric is rudely plucked from his dreams. He stares into the blackness, sleepy confusion still clouding his mind and instinctively thrusts a hand into the epicentre of the ringing. A dull thud sounds somewhere on the carpet beneath him and he tastes cigarette ash in the air. When he finally finds the light switch, he sees a grey mushroom cloud hanging over the bed and a month's worth of bed-time fag butts decorating his slippers below.

"Oh sod it!" he grumbles into the phone.

"Hello, Electric?" Ollie double-checks.

"Who the bloody hell's this?" Electric wants to know.

"It's me. Ollie."

"Well what the hell you phoning me at this time of night for? It's gone three o'clock," Electric says examining his clock.

"I wanted to ask you something, didn't I?" Ollie simply replies, like this is normal behaviour.

"Couldn't it wait? Is your bed on fire or something?" Electric barks, slamming his clock back down and sending a glass of Steradent containing his false choppers off the side of the chest of drawers to join the fag ash in his slippers. "Oh for crying-out-loud!"

"No no, it's nothing like that. It's just I'm with Bex and..." Ollie starts, but almost in unison, me and Norris frantically flap our arms at him to keep our names and any other irrelevant details out of this particular phone call. Ollie cottons on. "... and anyway, we've found a safe."

I can practically hear Electric's brain ignite from where I'm standing and sure enough, on the other side of town an old fella with cigarette-filled slippers is suddenly very wide awake indeed.

"I see. Bring it down here then and I'll open it up for you."

"No, it's fixed to the wall, I can't get it out," Ollie explains.

"Where are you?" Electric then asks.

"Hold on, I'll ask. Here Bex, where are we?" I wave my fist under his nose until he finally gets the message. "Er, nowhere special. Here look, d'you know how to get into these things or not?"

Electric growls when he realises he's not going to be party to any grand opening and sets about making the best deal he can for himself.

"Maybe, but what's in it for me?"

"A hundred quid?" Ollie offers.

"Two hundred?" Electric counters.

"A hundred and fifty?" Ollie compromises.

"Two hundred and fifty?" Electric recompromises.

"Here hang on a minute, that's not how it works."

"Take it or leave it, you know there'll be more in the safe," Electric teases and eventually Ollie bites.

"Oh go on then, two hundred, but we'd better get into it."

Electric thinks where to start and decides some specifics are in order.

"Okay, now tell me, are there any numbers on the safe?" he asks, slipping the phone under his chin as he scrapes the fag butts out of slippers.

"Er yeah, ten, twenty, thirty, forty…"

"Hold on Ollie, are you just reading me the dial?" Electric demands. Ollie wonders what the problem is. "Er, yeah?"

"No, I mean serial numbers. What's the serial number of the safe?"

"Oh, it doesn't seem to have one. So what now?"

"Okay, let me think, let me think." Electric mulls, lean back for a stretch. "Okay, have you got a drill with a diamond bit?"

"Have we got a drill with a diamond bit?" Ollie checks with us.

"Yeah, I have, as it happens," Norris volunteers.

"Yeah, we have as it happens," Ollie repeats, parrot-like into his phone.

"Okay, now listen very carefully. You're going to need to drill a precise series of holes. Do you know what an isosceles triangle is?"

Ollie decides he needs to write some of this down and starts scribbling on a near-by scrap of paper.

"Say again, a sausage what?"

The line goes quiet at the other end and Ollie is forced to ask "hello" a couple of times before Electric speaks again.

"Ollie, keep your money. You're not getting into that safe," Electric tells him, dropping the phone back onto its cradle and lying back into one of several enormous filthy ash hand prints that now adorn his duvet and pillow. "Oh what is all of this?"

"Have we given up yet?" I ask when Ollie finally admits to himself that Electric's hung up.

"No. I'm not giving up. I know I can do this," Ollie insists, falling for his own misplaced self-belief.

"Oh what, just like that Open University course in Mechanical Engineering you did?" I remind him. "You said the same thing back then and look what happened? One morning you record the Telly Tubbies by mistake and you ain't missed an episode since."

"Oh don't exaggerate or nothing, it was Bargain Hunt and you know it," Ollie puts me straight.

"Either way, don't be offended if I don't wait up will you, because you've got about as much chance of getting into that safe as I have of getting into the Brownies."

"I used to be a Brownie," Belinda tells me.

"Still are, aren't you luv?" Norris chuckles to himself.

All of a sudden, there's a clunk over near Ollie and he turns to me in triumph and gives me a sampler of his best Cheshire grin.

"What was that?" I ask.

"That was the sound of Brown Owl falling off her perch because you just made it into the movement."

"What?" I ask, scarcely believing what I'm hearing.

"Look, I've done it, I've got it open!" Ollie gleams.

"I don't believe it."

"Oh Ollie, you're a genius. I knew you could do it," Belinda whoops, skipping past my shoulder to plant a well-earned kiss on the hero of the moment.

"Well I didn't. How d'you get it open?" I demand.

"Pure skill won through."

"Ollie, how d'you get it open?"

"It's these magic fingers man," Ollie assures me, cracking his knuckles in triumph.

"Just tell me will you, before I sort it so that your magic fingers are able to scratch the backs of their own magic hands!" I warn him.

Ollie shines his torch at a yellow Post-It stuck to the back of the picture.

"I found this with the combination on it," he admits.

"Brilliant."

"Never mind about that, what's in there?" Norris says impatiently, barging past me in an effort to jump the queue. I haul him back and Ollie holds him at bay while I have a quick shufty through the contents, but there's not much in here either. No gold necklaces, no bundles of cash or atomic secrets to be sold. Nothing. Nothing that is, except for a note and a photograph. I turn the photograph over in my hand and we all crowd around to have a look at it. Ollie's eyes widen and he quickly bundles Belinda away.

"What is it? Ollie, what's there?" she pleads, but Ollie's not letting her anywhere near the picture. "Please Ollie, what is it?"

"Nothing, just step back a moment," Ollie tells her, but Belinda just tells him to stop being silly. "No, I mean it," Ollie insists, getting stern with her. "Go and wait over there a moment."

Belinda comes over all hurt at being excluded, so Ollie offers her a few gentler words of reassurance and asks her to trust him. Eventually she does as he asks and goes and waits over to the corner, without fully understanding why.

I can see from his face that Norris doesn't understand why Ollie's done this either. He's looking at the picture and simply concentrating on the bloke in the back of the limo with the champagne flute to his lips and the three scantily-clad tarts climbing all over his lap. He hasn't looked at any of their faces yet.

"Blimey, have some of that mate," Norris chuckles with approval and it's only now that he lifts his eyes from the trio of bare backsides and gives the girls' faces a quick once over. "Hang on a minute, I know that one!" he blinks, looking up Ollie and me. Belinda's still quietly waiting over in the corner and asks once again what it is. Norris looks her way and a grin breaks out across his face and sprints for his ears. "Heh-heh-heh, nice!" he clucks.

"Not a word of this to her, alright? I don't want her knowing about this," Ollie whispers aggressively, staring down at the love-of-his-life as she straddles some pin-striped city boy and felates a bottle of champagne. "She ain't like this no more. It must be an old picture."

"Looks pretty recent to me," Norris says.

"It's old!" I insist.

"Oh yeah, I see that now. Very nostalgic. Were we ever that young?" Norris quips.

"What's the note say?" Ollie asks.

"*Dear Richard,*" I read. "*You pathetic two-timing dirty son-of-a...*"

"Yeah, just the highlights please Bex," Ollie prods. "Where's their stuff."

I skim past the descriptive prose and pluck what info I can from the sea of abuse. "Blahdy-blahdy-blah, he's away on another of his business trips. She's moved out and taken everything. Pictures with the lawyers. Dinner's in the oven. Hope the weather was nice. Your soon-to-be ex, etc."

"Ha, busted!" Norris laughs joyously.

"Well what's the door locked for then?"

"*PS. I locked the office in case Harriet came home from university unexpectedly. No need to expose her to your failings as a husband and a man too, you rotten pile of...* blimey, look at that language. I never even knew you could put those two words together."

I put the note back in the safe and look around the empty room.

"All this for nothing," I grumble, then notice Ollie staring miserably at Richard's picture. "Worse than nothing, even."

"What? Ah no, she ain't like that no more. That was probably just back in the day when she was hanging out in Caesar's with Karen and her mates," he tells himself.

"I know mate, I know," I say, relieving Ollie of the picture and locking it back in the safe. "Right, well if there's nothing else, I'm off."

"Where you going?" Norris asks off-key, sounding like a man who's got nowhere better to be himself.

"Home. Back to bed. I'm gonna write off this day and start again tomorrow," I tell him, heading for the door.

Ollie's close on my heel. "Yeah, I know what he means. Wish I'd never bloody left mine. Come on luv, let's go home."

"Okee-dokee Ollie-polly," Belinda chirps, her earlier disappointment already a distant memory. "Bye Mr Norris."

"Yeah, cheerio gorgeous," Norris winks, twiddling his fingers at her and dancing his torch beam across her arse.

"Yeah, cheerio to you too. And please, do give my regards to the next bloke who's kicking your head in," Ollie bids, before following me out the front door.

Norris stays in the darkness for a moment, savouring Ollie's misfortune and enjoying a rare moment of moral superiority himself, before remembering his car's a dozen streets away, which is the closest he can ever park his memorably familiar clapped-out Ford Escort Estate to any given scene of crime.

"Here, hold on Ol, you got the van with you?" he calls out, running after us all.

Outside, in the cool night's air, I take stock of the early morning's events and don't much like what they all add up to.

"I can't believe I went through all that, and all I've got to show for it is having my ladder nicked."

"What? Hey no, that weren't nicked. I chucked it in the bushes behind the wall," Norris tells me.

"What d'you do that for?"

"Well I didn't want someone seeing it and thinking there was someone breaking in, now did I?" Norris explains.

"Fantastic. Well that's something at least," I say, the first bit of good news I've had since going to bed last night. "Come on then, give us a hand with it."

Norris steps into the bushes and starts dancing around one end of the ladder while I hang on patiently to the other.

"In your own time Norris. Come on pass it out then, will you?" I tell him.

"I will if you give me a second, I've got a bleeding tree in my face, ain't I?" he grumbles, muttering and moaning for all he's worth as he tries to untangle my ladder from an over-amorous Triffid.

"Norris, are you gonna pass it out or hang around in the bushes all night?"

Five feet of ladder suddenly surges my way, rocking me backwards in my slippers and thrusting me against an adjacent parked motor. I catch my elbow smartly against the paintwork, but my ladder fares less well and plants itself straight through the driver's side window, setting off an orchestra of horns and beeps as the car alarm starts singing.

"Oh you clumsy great Jonah!" I shout after Norris, but he's already halfway down the road and showing few signs of slowing. Ollie and Belinda have likewise disappeared, leaving me on my tod to extract my ladder from my next door neighbour's VW.

Well, almost on my tod.

"Evening Bex. Well, I must say this is a new one on me. I've never seen anyone use a ladder to break into a car before. I mean, it's not even a particularly tall car," an unwelcomingly familiar voice says behind me.

I turn and see Weasel and Bennett standing behind me, wearing the sorts of shit-eating grins you rarely see outside of Corn Flake adverts and special-needs bus tours these days.

"Where d'you come from?" I ask.

"Let's just say I didn't think I'd heard the last of you tonight, so we've been circling the area," Weasel nods officiously, then puffs out his cheeks at the din. "Crikey, what a racket! You're going to wake up the entire neighbourhood if you're not careful."

"What, this lot? You must be joking. A fucking lorry load of smelling salts blowing up in the middle of skip full of bells wouldn't wake this lot of bone idle cunts up," I put him straight.

"Very colourful Bex. Why don't you put the ladder down and step away from the vehicle?" Weasel invites.

"What, so you can nick me? What sort of incentive's that?"

"Now look, don't you get smart with me, sunshine. Terry, give Bex a hand finding the back seat of our car, will you?" Weasel suggests.

"Gladly," Bennett replies, slipping the cuffs off his belt and taking the first few cautious steps towards me.

"I don't believe this," I bleat miserably. "I shouldn't even be awake. I was happily tucked up asleep in bed I was."

"Well you should've stayed there then, shouldn't you?" Weasel points out.

I look up at my bedroom window and catch a glimpse of the curtains twitching as Mel quickly jumps out of sight, followed two seconds later by the lights going out.

"You ain't wrong, Sergeant," I wholeheartedly agree, as I feel the cold steel snapping around my wrist. "You ain't fucking wrong."

65

THE JACKETS JOB

1. The usual suspects

Once upon a time, in a land not so far away, some nosey old biddy with nothing better to do was pressing her face against the glass of her kitchen window when she happened to spy something she shouldn't have.

"Ohhh! Ooahhh!" I imagine she frothed, snatching up the phone and pressing her one and only preset quick-dial number.

"Police please," she tells the operator all urgently. "Yes, hello, come quick, there's some men breaking into the shops across the way from me."

The operator on the other end of the line however, is an experienced despatch Sergeant, so he asks his excited elderly caller to look again and just confirm for him that she isn't looking at a plastic bag caught in a tree.

"No, no, it's some men in a van," she insists, so the Sergeant puts down his Ginsters chicken & bacon slice and starts searching his desk for a pen.

"Can I have your name and address please madam?"

"Yes, it's Alice Springer. Number... oohh, hold on, I think they're going," she cardiacs, as she watches a set of rear view lights speed off into the night. "Oh you've missed them. Do you still want to come over anyway?"

The Sergeant thinks, looks at his half-eaten Ginsters and figures if she lives near some shops, he might as well kill two birds with one stone and get someone to pick him up a big bottle of Lucozade while they're there.

"Okay, what's the address?"

*

Twelve hours later, Sergeant Atwell is struggling with a crossword clue. He needs the name of an African country that has E as its second letter, but the only one he can think of is Bengali and he's not sure that one's in Africa or actually exists, so he goes next door to the drink-tank to brain storm the great minds currently in residence.

"You awake?" he asks contestant number one through the cell flap.

"What is it? My brief here?" the resident responds miserably.

"No not yet. D'you know what African country's capital is Dakar?"

Contestant number one thinks about this. "I ain't saying nothing till my brief gets here."

Atwell slams his flap shut and goes across to try contestant number two, who happens to be a mate of mine, which is how I know all of this.

"Here Roland, d'you know what African country's capital is Dakar? It's for the crossword."

Roland comes to the door and looks through the flap. "How many letters?"

"Seven."

"You got any of them yet?"

"Yeah, something - E - something - something - something - something - something," replies Atwell. Roland struggles to lay these letters out in his brain, so Atwell holds the newspaper up against his flap.

"Hmm, dunno, but thirteen down's hat," Roland spots.

"Oi, don't do the easy ones," Atwell says, ripping the paper away. "I can do them myself, I don't need you for them. Now d'you know who's capital is Dakar or not?

"Let's have another look?"

Atwell holds the paper up to the flap for Roland again. "Is it Egypt?" Roland suggests.

Atwell gives up. "You're an idiot," he tells Roland, slamming the flap on his face.

This is the part of the story where I come in. Me and Ollie are next door in the box office with Weasel when Atwell returns.

"Oh, hello Bex. Ollie. Your usual suite?" Atwell 'quips'.

"Oh not this routine again. Why can't you book us in normally for once without the stand-up?" I ask.

"Someone's a bit grumpy this afternoon, aren't they?" Atwell observes, like a particularly clucky mother hen.

"I can't think why."

"Right now, did you phone ahead and make a booking, only we're usually pretty busy this time of year?" Atwell keeps it going.

"You know what, I bet your neighbours get sick of listening to *The Laughing Policeman* blaring through their walls all hours don't they?"

Atwell grins, enjoying my irritation, so I stick my brain into neutral to take away his kicks.

"Tom?" he asks Weasel, flopping open the custody book.

"Two on suspicion of burglary. Both were picked up at home and neither gave any statement when arrested - well, nothing you'd repeat in front of your granny anyway."

"She not into that sort of thing then, no?" Ollie asks.

"Bung 'em into the cells while I sort out an interview room, will ya?" Weasel says all officiously, then heads off to spend some quality time with the coffee machine.

"Okay chaps, you know the drill. Pockets and belts please?" Atwell orders. "Oh and Ollie, d'you know what African country's capital is Dakar?"

Ollie stares at Atwell blankly. "No. Why would I?" Atwell tuts and shoves his paper to one side, and it's now that something occurs to Ollie. "Why d'you ask me that question and not him?"

Atwell glances at my white face, then back again at Ollie's black face.

"No reason," he says quietly. "No honestly, I just thought..."

"What?" Ollie asks.

"Nothing. Just, you know..." Atwell splutters, wondering how he could've allowed himself to stray into such treacherous waters.

"No I don't. What?" Ollie insists, daring him to say it.

As enjoyable as it is to see Atwell on the back foot, I realise that no good's going to come of making the bloke who's in charge of our cells' central heating feel like a complete and utter chump so I pluck the bone from Ollie's nose and toss it across the custody desk. "He just thought you looked like someone who looked good at geography," I tell Ollie, then do my bit for the Sergeant's education by informing him that Dakar is the capital of Senegal.

"Ooh, ta," Atwell quickly scribbles, relieved to have come away from this particular crossword clue with stripes still on his arm.

*

Just along the corridor, past the coffee machine, Charlie Taylor is sitting in an interview room across the table from PC Bennett and hanging his head in shame. He's doing his best to justify a rare 'lapse in judgement' but it's cutting little mustard with Bennett.

"... so that was all there was to it. I mean, thirty grand for a swimming pool. I had no idea they cost that much and it just wiped me out," Charlie's explaining.

"I see," Bennett says, but he's heard it all before.

"Yeah, I mean it wasn't even me who wanted it in the first place, it was the wife, but I've never been able to say no to her so I had to get the money somehow."

"You were desperate?" Bennett suggests.

"Yeah, desperate. And desperate men do desperate things I'm afraid. It ain't an excuse or something I'm proud of, it's just the way it is," he shrugs sadly, barely able to look at the plastic Scope charity box that's shaped like a little girl and sitting in the seat next to Bennett.

Bennett too looks at the charity box, then leans across the table towards Charlie. "So this is why you agreed to represent Norris in this matter is it?"

"It was a case of needs must I'm afraid," Charlie concurs.

Norris has finally had enough and decides it's time he speaks up for himself.

"Can I say something at this point?"

Bennett rolls his eyes and wonders how, in a town full of no-goods, he's got lumbered with the ultimate *Crackerjack* cabbage for the entire afternoon. "Go on," he reluctantly agrees.

"I never took it, honest I never."

"My client insists he never took it, honest, he never," Charlie then says, sticking the words "my client" on the front of Norris's sentence to

71

justify his Legal Aid.

"It was found in your client's car," Bennett points out.

"Well someone must've put it there then, because I never took it," Norris replies.

Bennett sags wearily into his seat, drained at having to go through this pantomime when almost every other suspect would have the good sense to simply put their hands up and let everyone else get on with their lives.

"Norris, why would anyone put this in your car?" Bennett asks.

"I don't know. This town's got it in for me, don't it Charlie?" Norris replies.

Charlie confirms this. "My client does have a disproportionate amount of local ill-will, it's true. It could've been planted by someone with a grudge," he says, then sticks out his bottom lip and shrugs. "I mean, you never know."

"Charlie, your client has three priors for stealing charity boxes and this afternoon he bought seventy-eight scratchcards with loose change," Bennett implores.

"No, I won that on the fruity. Honest. I swear on me mum's life," Norris insists.

"It was your mum who turned you in," Bennett points out.

"Was it? That snitching old cow! She's always had it in for me," Norris fumes, but his protestations are cut short when Weasel knocks on the door and sticks his snout inside for a snoop.

"Interview suspended. Oh, hey Sarge," Bennett greets Weasel."

"Hey," Weasel responds, before noticing Norris. "Oh, not him again?"

"I never done it, honest I never," Norris repeats for the benefit of late-comers.

"Are you gonna be long? Only I've got two waiting," Weasel asks Bennett.

"How long's a piece of string? And I haven't even had me tea yet. Are there any bacon rolls left?"

"I just had the last one," Weasel confirms.

Norris senses an opportunity to divide and conquer and points out to Weasel that Bennett's got it in for him.

"Oh give it a rest Norris, the tape's off," Bennett points out.

Weasel takes a step further into the interview room. "Actually Charlie, it's two more of yours I've got in; Bex and Ollie."

"Oh really?" Charlie cheers up, quickly checking his folder to make sure he's brought enough Legal Aid forms. "Fantastic, that should keep the swimming pool heated a couple more days," he calculates.

"Yes well quite," Weasel responds, running his eyes down Charlie's hand-stitched lapels, down past his silk handkerchief, to the immaculately manicured fingers that are already guiding the nib of his gold fountain pen across two fresh Legal Aid forms. "Feels good to know I'm making a difference," he sighs to himself.

*

Now, I mentioned earlier that Ollie has a black face, but this isn't entirely true. In fact, his face is really only a tinge darker than mine, but then it's not really the shade of a person's skin that matters these days but how that person wears it. See, when I first met Ollie when we were kids, I didn't even realise he was black. And in fact, for several months after that, every time I went back to his house after school (or often during it) to play Monopoly and spell out rude words on the Scrabble board, I just thought his dad had a live-in servant, you know, like in those old Tom & Jerry cartoons. I didn't know she was his mum, did I? Still, it's a sweet old hand that life has dealt Ollie and he knows how to play it for all it's worth to suit any given situation. Most of the time, he's as white as the whitest bloke I know, but get him down the cells or tell him he can't get on the bus because the bus is already full and see what colour he is then. Norris calls Ollie a human chameleon, and as loathe as I am to agree with anything Norris says, he's not wrong. Ollie does have the ability to turn blacker before your very eyes and it's this outraged hue he's wearing as Atwell leads us to the cells.

"I was born in Reading. Why would I know where Dakar is? This is institutional racism this is. Sweeping assumptions about me just because I'm black," Ollie rants, up the corridor, round the corner and into the holding cells. "We don't all dance around in top hats cooking vicars, you know. It's discrimination, plain and simple. The whole force is awash with it."

Atwell opens the door to cell four and invites me to step inside. As I walk in, I catch his eye and give him a wink. Atwell just frowns in return and slams the door behind me while Ollie continues taking civil liberties.

"In fact, I shouldn't even be here. It's only 'cos I'm black that I was even arrested. I bet if I was white I'd be…"

Ollie's voice tails off and from inside my cell I can't help but wonder if he's accidentally strangled himself while in custody, but then I hear him again.

"Alright brother?" he asks.

"Get in there and shut up," Weasel replies, his deep, husky West Indian tones devoid of any sympathy for Ollie or his plight.

The door slams shut a second later and Atwell sighs wearily. "People from Reading, huh!"

73

2. Cell mates

I'm in my cell no more than a couple of minutes when it suddenly occurs to me that I'm not going to be at home tonight for this programme I'd been looking forward to all week. It's annoying at the best of times when you miss something on the telly because you've forgotten it's on, but remembering it with time to spare, but unable to do anything about it just twists the knife. It's not unlike standing in a queue at a cashpoint watching your last bus home come and go without you. Or worse still, sitting on the last bus home watching someone walk away from a cashpoint without picking up their money. I've been there before.

Still, that's what emergency stop buttons are for I guess.

I approach the cell door and shout across to Ollie.

"Here Ol, did you set the video for *Tonight with Trevor McDonald*? It was that one about the burglars, remember?"

"Ah no, I forgot. When's it on?" he calls back.

I take a moment to try and work out if he's being funny or not before reminding him, "Tonight".

"Ah, no I didn't then. Typical in' it. Six months of single mums and NHS reports, then he finally does something good and we're both out."

But all's not lost. An idea strikes me, so I ask him if he can get Belinda to record it.

"Well she probably could if I asked her but she ain't in the cell with me you know," the little comedian replies.

"I know that you donkey, but we're both entitled to phone calls aren't we, so I'll use mine to rouse Charlie if you use yours to phone Belinda and get Trevor recorded," I tell him. Ollie agrees, but then a third voice suddenly pipes up.

"Here Ol, is that you Big Guy?"

"Who's that?" Ollie calls back.

"It's me, Roland," Roland tells us.

"Oh alright Rollo, how's it going?" I shout across from my cell.

"Yeah, pretty sweet, can't complain, you know. Here, funny bumping into you here Ol, cos..." Roland's just saying when a fourth, rather less welcome voice joins in with the conversation.

"Oi, what's all this jabbering about?" Atwell demands, banging on our cell doors.

"We're just having a chat," I explain, prompting my cell flap to drop open and Atwell to fix me with his beadies.

"Well don't. I can hear you all the way down in bloody custody."

"Stick us in the same cell then. We're all mates," Ollie suggests.

"What d'you think this is, *Big Brother*?" Atwell scoffs.

"But it's boring just sat in here on our own," Ollie complains.

"Huh, you've only been in two minutes. You're not exactly Nelson

Mandela are you, Ol?" Atwell laughs, ill-advisedly.

"And what's that suppose to mean?" comes back Ollie's outraged reply. I grin with delight when I see Atwell realise what he's said and he immediately starts back-peddling as if his career depends upon it.

"No, I didn't mean like that. I just meant he was in prison a long time," he explains.

"Yeah, he was also President of South Africa you know, but how's it you remember him? As an old jailbird with a thirty stretch under his belt. I wonder why?" Ollie speculates.

*

Meanwhile, unbeknown to me, Mel wanders into the front office and has a go on the "ring for attention" bell. Weasel pops his head out the door to see who's using up his electricity and frowns when he sees it's my missus.

"Oh, hey Mel. What can I do for you?" he asks, like he doesn't know what she's come in for.

"What d'you think? A pound of apples please," Mel says, pitting one stupid question against another.

"How d'you know we had Bex?"

"I work for Charlie, don't I? He texted us. What are the charges?"

"No charges. He's just helping us with our enquiries," Weasel smiles generously.

"Oh really? That's very public spirited of him. How he hasn't got a medal off the Mayor by now is a mystery to me because hardly a week goes by when he's not down here helping you lot out," Mel says.

"Yeah, he's a real pillar of the community isn't he?" Weasel agrees.

"Can I see him?"

"Of course…" Weasel smiles, "… you can't."

Mel scowls. "Well can I speak to Charlie then?"

"Sure, if you've got your mobile. Technology's amazing these days, isn't it?" Weasel nods enthusiastically.

This really gets Mel's goat and she lets her mask slip a little. "God, you love it, don't you? You think it's one big game. Well it's not you know, it's our bloody lives you're playing with."

It's odd but Weasel genuinely dislikes Mel, probably even more than he dislikes me. I can understand this I guess. I mean, with me and Weasel, it is a bit of a game and we've spent the last few years staring across the board at each other. I'm not making excuses here, quite the opposite in fact. I know exactly what I'm doing and I also know the consequences of being caught. I might not like it. I might even do everything in my power to try and wriggle out of it, but when all's said and done, I won't bear Weasel any malice if I get sent down because I won't have anyone to blame but myself (or more likely Ollie). That said, I'll go fucking spare if the bastard fills my shed up with stock from his evidence locker then knocks on my door with half a dozen of his mates, but then again it's still all part and parcel of the game we choose to play.

It's different with our WAGs though (or SLAGs, as he prefers to call them) as they're somewhat prone to outbursts of righteous indignation in our defence, even when we fully deserve everything that's coming to us. And it's this blind loyalty that gets up Weasel's hooter most of all, because he knows that Mel is no fan of the game and in fact, leads an upstanding and law-abiding life herself. In fact, it's the hypocrisy he really can't abide and he cringes every time he has to take down some iffy alibi from Mel when he knows she'd be the first on the phone to *Crimestoppers* if it was anyone but me.

I think this underlying bitterness probably stems from his wife walking out on him, a hard-working servant of Her Majesty, for some soapy used-car dealer with form for clocking and a four-bed villa on the Algarve. I don't think he ever really saw the funny side of that, which is weird because me and the boys all thought it was fucking hilarious. Perhaps I'll ask him about it next time I get the chance. We haven't spoken about it for a couple of weeks so I reckon he could probably do with a little reminder.

Weasel leans towards Mel and fixes her in the eye. "Anyone listening in could be forgiven for thinking it's me who keeps turning over shops at night."

"Well if it ain't you doing it, then it must be Bex. Well done Holmes, another case cracked. And just in time for tea an' all," Mel theatrically quips.

Weasel scratches his brain trying to place the "tea" reference then gets it. "That weren't *Sherlock Holmes*, that was the *Famous Five*."

"Yeah, and look how long they all ended up doing."

"Mel, just go home," he warns her, almost at the end of his tether.

"No way, I'm staying right here and ringing this bell every half hour until you either charge Bex or let him go," Mel says, dinking the bell to demonstrate.

"Fabulous," Weasel grimaces.

*

"… and it's attitudes like this that the black man has been fighting since the sixties," Ollie continues to rant from inside his cell. He's been going strong for almost ten minutes now and has barely paused for breath, which ain't bad in any currency. He should go on *Beat The Gong*. Atwell's leaning against the door and staring at his shoes wishing he was anywhere but here at the moment, while I'm watching the fun through my open flap and enjoying myself immensely. "I mean, what was the name of that film Denzel Washington was in?" Ollie asks.

"*X-Men*," I tell him.

Atwell glances my way as Ollie picks up the baton and runs with it.

"That was it, *X-Men*. Just how more of us have to take a stand before these barriers come down?"

Atwell's finally had enough and decides to take drastic action. "Ollie?"

"What?"

"You want my newspaper?"

"Yeah alright," Ollie readily agrees, so Atwell flips open his flap and posts it through.

"Blimey, look at that, more asylum seekers," Ollie says, reading the front page. "Who's bloody country is this anyway?"

Atwell senses this is a trick question and wisely keeps his gob shut.

"Here, what about me?" I ask Atwell through my flap. "Don't I get nothing to read?"

"I'm not doing a paper-round here, you know," Atwell complains, but Ollie's kneaded him for so long that he's a little more susceptible to reasonable requests than usual.

"Give us back my book then," I suggest.

"Will you be quiet if I do?"

"It's my preferred way of reading," I assure him.

"Alright," he agrees, then hits me with the stock custody Sergeant gag, "Wait here."

"Oh, alright. As long as you're quick though," I play along.

"Hey neighbour. How's it going?" Ollie says from across the hall. I look over and see that Atwell's left his flap open as well as mine, and Ollie's currently staring out into freedom. "Wanna quick game of eye spy?" he asks.

"Go on then."

"Okay, eye spy with my little eye..." Ollie begins, looking around the completely barren corridor for inspiration. Unfortunately, he takes a little too long and Atwell returns to slam the flap on his face and finish the game for him.

"... something beginning with belt up."

Atwell then crosses the corridor and passes me my book through the flap. "Here you go. *A History of Britain*? What you reading that for?"

I think about this before answering, just to make sure I've heard the question correctly.

"Because I want to find out about Poland of course. I thought they might mention something about it in here."

"No smart arse, I mean are you into history or something?"

"No, not really," I shrug, so Atwell frowns and closes the flap. I look at the book and finish my sentence. "But I think the bloke who's bag I found it in was."

Outside, Atwell's barely made it three yards before he's been clobbered again. This time by Roland.

"Here, Sergeant! Sergeant Atwell!"

Atwell drops his flap open and snaps, "What now?"

"Can I have some dinner?"

"Oh for crying-out-loud!" Atwell grumbles.

"Oh go on, please, I'm starving. I've been in here all day without nothing," Roland pleads.

In the next cell, Ollie rallies to Roland's assistance and starts quoting Codes of Practice at Atwell.

"He is entitled. All prisoners, by law, must be offered two light meals and one main meal every twenty-four..."

"I know the rules Ollie, you don't have to remind me," Atwell barks, then turns back to Roland who's staring out of his door with hope-filled eyes. "Alright, I'll get you something from the canteen, if I get five minutes," he tells us all.

"Oh great. Here, what's for grub?" Roland asks.

"The usual; turkey steaks, smash and peas," Atwell tells him.

Roland frowns. "Can I swap my peas for another turkey steak?"

"No you cannot. You eat your veg' while you're in here."

"But I don't like peas," Roland insists.

"Well what do you like then?"

"Turkey steaks," Roland reminds him.

"No, I mean what veg' do you like?" Atwell asks.

Roland cocks his head and stares back at Atwell. "Do I look like a bloke who likes veg'?"

3. Cats and dogs on my parade

I tell you, it's all kicking off today. While we're enjoying ourselves in the back of the police station, some sour-faced, nosey old busy-body's being wheeled in through the front by a couple of Sergeant Atwell's slightly less-well-paid mates.

Mel watches the old dear stumble, bumble and make a general meal out of a set of twin doors and shudders at the thought that mine and the old Post Office clogger's paths have crossed.

She leaps to her feet, approaches the front desk and leans on the "ring for attention" bell for a bit before Weasel finally reappears checking his watch.

"That was never half an hour," he moans.

"Who was that old lady you just brought in?"

Weasel straightens his eyebrows at this question. "That's police business."

"Then tell me what you're holding Bex for," Mel sighs helplessly.

"Enquiries," Weasel repeats.

"I can't get hold of Charlie. Have you told him I'm here?"

"I'll tell him when he's free, so just lay off, will you?" Weasel snaps, losing the last of his patience in the face of a lot of unwelcome questions, which is a bit rich if you ask me. I mean, how does he think me and Ollie like it? Weasel tries again to free his front reception of my girlfriend by pointing out that they've got half a dozen regulars in today all giving them grief. "And they all want their five minutes on the soap box, you know."

"Don't you mean the soapy step?" Mel baits him.

"Oh yeah, right-on sister," Weasel scoffs, clenching his fist and holding it aloft to salute her. "Down with the pigs!"

*

Just when I thought my situation couldn't get any more grim, Atwell and Charlie return, followed by some new company for us all.

"Honest Charlie, I never done it. I swear I never," Norris is griping, close to tears.

"Yeah, no, it's terrible, I know," I hear Charlie reply, less than convincingly.

Atwell unlocks the cell next to mine and invites Norris to take a closer look.

"Ah no, please, not a cell. I don't like 'em, I feel all closed in. Please Charlie, tell 'em," Norris starts to grizzle miserably.

Charlie puts this into legal speak for Norris and tells Atwell that his client suffers from claustrophobia and asks that he's not put in a cell.

"Don't worry, your client's slept over a couple of times before and we always leave a light on for him," Atwell reassures him.

"Oh no, that ain't Norris, is it? There goes the neighbourhood," I pitch in from my cell.

"Who's that? Bex? You shut your fucking gob!" Norris yells back.

"Oh my mistake, it's Oscar Wilde," I suddenly realise.

"Pipe down!" Atwell warns us.

"But he's trying to escape," I point out. "Quick smack him. We'll all back you up."

"I said pipe down!" Atwell hollers, then returns to the problem of Norris. "And you, go on, get in there."

Norris pouts pathetically but he's not going to escape fate today and he knows it, so he takes a few faltering steps inside his cell then turns to see Atwell closing the door behind him.

"Here, hold on, don't you want my belt and shoe laces?" Norris reminds Atwell.

Atwell thinks about this for no longer than half a second. "Nah, it's alright. You can hang on to them if you like," he says, slamming the door and twisting the keys in the lock.

"Honestly Charlie, I don't know how you can represent scumbags like Norris," Atwell chews.

"Innocent till proven guilty Sergeant, you know the law as well as I do," Charlie replies.

Atwell's not convinced though. "But Norris? I mean, he nicked and smashed up your daughter's motor."

"An offence he was never convicted of, so in the eyes of the law, he didn't," Charlie shrugs.

"Oh but you know…" Atwell starts, but Charlie can be the real deal when he wants to be and ain't having a word of it.

"What I know is neither here nor there, Sergeant. Everyone's entitled to legal representation."

"Ah yeah," Atwell cynically sneers, "just so long as poor old Joe Muggings tax payer here picks up the bill for it you mean?"

"Believe me, I don't like it any more than you do, I really don't," Charlie shakes his head as Atwell twists his keys in my door and reunites me with my friendly neighbourhood solicitor.

"Hey Charlie, how's it going?" I say, extending my hand to shake his.

"Yeah, not bad, fill that in will you?" he beams, thrusting a Legal Aid form into my outstretched mitt.

This narks Atwell no end, and I can't say I add much to his mood when I turn to him and ask, "Got a pen, Sergeant Muggings?"

*

Back in the front office, reinforcements arrive in slinky shape of Belinda. "Oh Mel, hi, I got a message from Ollie saying he'd been arrested and was down here. What's going on?"

"Didn't he tell you any more than that?"

"No, only to set the video for *Trevor and Simon*, but I couldn't find what time they were on, so I'm recording everything on BBC1 tonight just in case," she explains.

Mel shakes these thoughts from her head, sits Belinda down and steers the conversation around to their current predicament.

"Look, was Ollie with you last night?" she asks.

"Yeah, but he didn't get in till three."

"Snap, so this is something they did then. The question is what?" Mel mulls.

"You don't think it was something illegal, do you?" Belinda asks.

"Belinda, we're sitting in a police station. What do you think?" Mel points out.

"I don't know, I can't think. I'm all confused. What are we gonna do?"

"Well, that's the real question isn't it?" Mel says, raising an eyebrow. When Belinda doesn't get it, she elaborates. "Bex's alibi will be that he was with me last night. It always is. Just as Ollie's will be that he was with you. At that time of night what else can they say? The question is, do we cover for them?"

The obviousness of the solution almost overwhelms Belinda and she beams like a girl who's just been told by a premium rate astrology hot-line that she's a genius.

"Of course, yeah, we'll just say they were with us and then they'll have to let 'em go."

"You sure about that? You sure you want to lie to the police and risk a perjury conviction for those thieving idiots, just so they can then go out and do it all again tomorrow?" my kill-joy girlfriend presses.

Belinda thinks on it for a moment but can't see a downside.

"Yeah," she confirms, then notices Mel's sceptical expression. "Why, ain't you?"

"Of course I bloody am," Mel confirms.

"Why do you do it then?" Belinda asks.

"Because he's my thieving idiot, and I'll be buggered if I'm travelling up to Brixton for the next two years just to see his sorry arse," Mel smarts.

Belinda smiles at this, relieved to have got the answer right, but her relief's short-lived when a thought suddenly occurs to her.

"Hang on, I weren't alone last night. I had someone over when Ollie was out last night."

"I thought you weren't like that no more?" Mel raises an eyebrow.

"Here, no, I don't mean like that. I was with Roland."

"Roland?"

"Yeah, he called round last night to ask about Ollie's birthday. He's Ollie's best friend see and he's got some big, spectacular, amazing sur-prise all planned and wanted to make sure Ollie would be around to see it next week."

"What's the surprise?" Mel asks.

Belinda thinks on this.

"Here, you know what, I never asked."

"Well you'll have to call him and tell him what's happened. Don't worry, Roland'll back up your story. I'm sure."

"I would if I could but I can't. He shot off to set it up and I ain't heard from him since. What d'you suppose has happened to him?"

*

What indeed? Could he be decorating Ollie's flat with streamers and balloons, flying the All Saints in for a one-off special concert in his best mate's honour or sitting inside a cake in a big oven, wondering just how he's meant to do the icing when it's finished baking.

Of course he was doing none of these things because you and I both know that he was in the cell just across from me, carefully scraping a mother-load of peas into the toilet bowl. Atwell had made sure his dinner had been piled high with his green nemesis and had warned Roland he wanted to see them all gone when he returned to collect the plate otherwise it would be a salad next time around.

So that was what Roland was happily doing, when he chanced a look over his shoulder to make sure Sergeant Atwell wasn't watching him cheat his vitamin C when his beloved turkey steaks made a break for freedom and dived off the plate to join the rest of his dinner down the bog.

"Ooh no!" was the anguished cry that echoed around the cell block that afternoon.

*

I hand Charlie his clipboard and completed Legal Aid form back and tell him to keep the change, and only then does he ask me how I'm doing.

"Oh, on the clock now are you?" I say, following him and Atwell down the corridor and into a side room.

Inside the room there's Weasel, a couple of uniforms and four assorted face-aches standing behind cardboard numbers.

"Oh not this, please," I sag.

"All right Bex, you know the drill. Pick a number and shut your cake hole," Weasel tells me, directing me to go and stand with my new mates up against the far wall.

I pick up a card with a three on it and step in the middle of the line, forcing the others to shuffle off in either direction and swap cards until we're all sequential.

"Afternoon chaps. This where we come for the boy band auditions is it? We reforming Ugly Rumours again then or what?" I ask my new mates. One of them (Number Four) is staring back at me intently. "You alright mate?" I ask him. "Can I help you with something?"

"I know you, it's Bex isn't it? Remember me, I bought that DVD off you last year?"

"Alright, Jesus, keep it down!" I shush him, nodding my head in the direction of Weasel and Atwell. Number Four shrugs an apology and asks me how it's going. "Yeah, cushty mate. Real sweet." Fucking doughnut. "How's that DVD working out for you?"

"Yeah, brilliant. Actually I was going to ask you, are you getting any more in d'you know?"

I blink at Four a couple of times. "Are you absolutely sure this can't wait?" Once again, the soul of indiscretion just shrugs. Still, as uncomfortable as it is having someone in the room who has the goods on me and a runaway gob, I quickly realise I might be able to turn this to my advantage. Particular when I see the quality of Weasel's key witness and just how far she'd strayed beyond her Best Before date.

"Actually mate, you could do us a little favour if you like. When they wheel the old dear past, give her a little wink will you? Just to baffle her a bit," I suggest.

Four thinks on this. "Fifty quid?"

"Fifty quid? I said wink at her, not assassinate her," I stress.

"Alright, forty then?" he tries again.

"I'll give you twenty."

Without warning, Number Two on the other side of me, suddenly decides he wants to be part of this conversation.

"I'll do it for twenty," he offers.

"Oi, get your nose out. This ain't out for tender you know," Number Four warns him.

"Look somebody do it for crying out loud, because here she comes," I tell them both, and we all quickly resume our positions and wait to be inspected.

"Okay then my dear, don't be nervous. We're right here," Weasel reassures her.

The old biddy nods, then ever so cautiously steps up to the plate and takes a gander at Number One. Unconvinced she moves along and out of the corner of my eye I see Number Two's open and close in a flash to give her a cheeky wink. He does it so quick that Weasel doesn't clock it, but judging from the old girl's reaction, she does and looks at him with confusion for a moment before moving on to run a beady eye over me. I'm like a statue and giving her nothing. In fact a swarm of bees could've flown in through the window and set up home on my chin and I still wouldn't have batted an eyelid. Alice frowns with indecision and moves on to stupid big mouth next to me. Subtlety not being his specialist chosen subject, he goes and gives her the full Charlie Chester treatment, and for a moment I think he's going to take her by the arm and ask her how everything's going. Weasel glares at Four, then turns his furious eyes on me, but I still don't move. Meanwhile, Mrs Doubtfurnace is off giving Number Five the once over and chewing on the handle of her handbag.

"Right then my dear, is the man you saw present?" Weasel asks her, still staring daggers at me and Number Four.

"I believe so Captain," she replies.

"Okay then, just go up and identify him will you?"

The old girl hotfoots it back down the line, straight past numbers Five and Four and stops directly in front of me. For a moment I think she's made a mistake and has confused me with Number Four, but she's absolutely positive that I'm tonight's mystery guest.

"This is the man," she confidently declares, laying her hand on my shoulder.

"Oh you miserable old bag!" I bark, much to everyone's dismay. Weasel, Atwell, the uniforms, and even Numbers Two and Four tell me to have some respect. Not to be left out, the old lady informs me that it's not very nice talking to people like that.

"What d'you mean? According to you I'm a burglar. I'm not meant to be nice," I point out.

"That's no excuse. My Eddie killed two men in Korea and a nicer man than my Eddie you couldn't wish to meet," she lectures.

"Oh really, I bet those Koreans wish they'd met a nicer man than your Eddie," I reckon, but Atwell quickly wades in and ushers me in the direction of the door before I can tell her what I really think of her.

I tell you, it's nosey old birds like her that make me cheer on the con-men whenever Watchdog's on. Behind me, my mate Number Four's finally given into the ghost of Charlie Chester and strikes up a conversation with the silly old bird.

"Well, for what it's worth, your Eddie sounds like an hero to me," he winks proudly.

"Oh you're too kind," she replies. "I just wish the government felt that way. But according to them, it's animals like my grandson who give England fans a bad name."

Ollie didn't fare much better when it came to his turn - or should that be fair? See, Eddie's granny picked him out with no difficulty whatsoever, though that was hardly surprising considering the line-up he was stood in.

Like I said, Ollie's shade of skin is barely darker than hue, but Atwell had taken his earlier protestations to heart and had assembled a foursome of brethren so black that they wouldn't have looked out of place running for their lives on Skull Island away from King Kong.

"Is this even legal?" Ollie asks, when the old dear successfully spots the odd one out.

"Honestly, there's just no pleasing some people," Atwell sighs, unclear as to what he's done wrong now.

"And what d'you mean by 'some people'?" Ollie starts up again, so Atwell gives Bennett the keys and gets him to escort Ollie to his cell.

"Okay then Charlie, we'll start with Bex first," Weasel says.

"Right you are, just give me a second," Charlie requests, then hot foots it through the station to the front reception. "Oh good, Mel, you are here," Charlie smiles when he sees his clerk waiting with Belinda. "Just a quick question, Bex was with you last night, wasn't he?"

Mel's a little unsure how to answer this, so Charlie helps her out.

"Let me rephrase that. Will you be telling the police that Bex was with you last night?"

This is a question Mel feels more comfortable answering and she confirms that she will indeed be giving the police that line.

"And Ollie?" Charlie looks at Belinda.

"Yes," Belinda replies cautiously.

"Then that's what I must've meant all along then, isn't it?" Charlie smiles, then turns to head back to the interview room.

"Wait Charlie, just tell us what the charges are?" Mel pleads.

"Oh no charge, I've stuck it all on the Legal Aid bill so it won't cost them a penny," Charlie reassures her before disappearing.

"You know what, I'll be glad when he's paid off that bloody swimming pool," Mel frowns.

4. The plot thickens

Ten minutes later I find myself sitting in an interview room with Charlie opposite Weasel and Bennett. The introductions all taken care of and my rights read once again, we go straight into it and take up our respective positions on the board.

"I'm telling you, I was with Mel. Ask her if you don't believe me, she'll tell you," I say for the record.

"I'm sure she will," Weasel responds.

"Well why shouldn't she if it's true?" I put to him.

Weasel brushes that thought aside and plays his first card. "You were formally identified by a witness to the break-in."

"Sergeant, please promise me this case'll go to court, because I'm so looking forward to your witness taking the stand," Charlie smirks. "If she can, of course,"

"Don't underestimate her Charlie, just because she's elderly," Weasel advises.

"I won't if the jury don't," Charlie promises with a grin.

"Admit it, you've got nothing," I tell Weasel. "The CPS'll throw this case out faster than your ex threw your clothes out."

Weasel scowls at me with genuine malice in his eyes. Which is good. Get under the Old Bill's skin enough and you can sometimes tickle them into saying all sorts of things for the tape that they'll live to regret when the transcript is read out in front of a jury. It's nothing personal, again just part and parcel of the game. But Weasel's not biting just yet. He still has a few cards to play before he's ready to cash in his chips and he tells me in no uncertain terms that he knows I did it, then gives me the usual old guff about how it'll go easier on me if I come clean.

"I did it?" I rhetorically repeat, shaking my head and smacking my lips. "I did everything according to you. I don't know if you saw it but someone spray-painted 'Happy Birthday Big Guy' across the top of the multi-storey carpark last night. I expect I did that an' all, did I?"

Weasel gives himself a big kiss. "No, we have someone in custody for that already."

"Oh really, why bother when it's so much easier to fit me up for it?" I ask.

Weasel reaches behind himself and places a large clear empty evidence bag on the table in front of me.

"We found this in your van," he says.

I hold the clear plastic up to the light to double check that I'm not missing something.

"Yeah, this does kind of go back to what I was saying about you having nothing," I tell him.

"There's a plastic covering in there. Exactly the same sort of cover-

86

ing that was on each of the twenty leather jackets that were taken in the burglary," Weasel informs me.

"Well gee, I didn't realise your case was this strong; Miss Marple's mum and two empty bags," I laugh. "I confess."

"Should we conclude this now before you seal your promotion prospects for keeps, Sergeant?" Charlie suggests.

"Well, I do have one other ace up my sleeve, Charlie," Weasel tells us.

"I'm bracing myself," Charlie says.

"The jackets in question were part of a greater haul. A haul stolen in an earlier robbery in fact, a lorry hijacking, by a couple of notorious Turkish brothers…" Weasel tells us, placing mugshots of two evil-looking bruisers on the table in front of us. I recognise them in a heartbeat and I feel my bladder tighten at the shock. Weasel notices this and his grin broadens in response. "Didn't you know who the shop belonged to Bex? Well, last night's break-in led us right to 'em and we made quite a few arrests off the back of it. Half the family in fact and I must say, they weren't best pleased with you." Weasel suddenly remembers himself. "Or whoever, obviously."

Charlie shifts uncomfortably next to me, not a good sign. "Just what is it you're proposing, Sergeant?"

"Simple, he puts his hands up to the break-in and we'll fast track him through the system. Otherwise I will put him on the stand in the same courtroom as the Hassans. And I don't think he'd like that, would you Bex?" Weasel turns the tape off, his hand played out before us. "Interview terminated."

Me and Charlie don't know what to say, so Weasel suggests something.

"Now tell me I've got nothing."

*

Now, I don't know if you've ever heard of the Hassans. If you've led an upright, honest and God-fearing life, then chances are you won't have, but for the rest of us, they were the big fish that one day a few years back swam into our little pond and now kept the rest of us skulking amongst the rocks. I'd never had any dealings with them myself. In fact, I was reasonably confident they didn't even know who I was, and I was champing at the bit to keep it that way.

Abel and Omit Hassan made for extremely poor business partners.

There was also no touching them. Oh I know Weasel said they were all banged up but I wasn't about to stake much on them staying that way. They had a nasty habit of shaking off sticky charges and after some five trials across eight years had yet to share a courtroom with a guilty verdict. Basically, if they were germs (and some would argue that they were), they would be those hard as nails little one per cent motherfuckers who happily swam about in Domestos and gave other germs a bad name.

I didn't need to explain any of this to Charlie though. He was only too familiar with their work, despite having the discerning sense to always be on holiday whenever they needed a brief.

"We can't be mixed up in this mess Charlie, not even by implication. Not the Hassans. You've got to help us," I tell him.

Charlie thinks on this carefully and nods in agreement. "Look, leave it with me and I'll see how many rabbits I've got left in the hat. Remember, it's never over until the fat lady spills her guts."

"Are you allowed to mix up your euphemisms like that?" I ask.

"Yeah, I don't see why not," Charlie ponders. "It's all grist to the mill anyway. So look, just sit tight and I'll see what I can do about reuniting my favourite client with my favourite clerk."

"Alright," I agree, then decide to show Charlie my pluck by joking, "But don't tell Mel 'cos she's the jealous type, you know."

Charlie nods affably at this, but then goes and spoils it. "There you go, laughter in the face of adversity. Just the ticket for a man in dire straits."

Charlie leaves me to stew in my own misery and heads out to speak to Weasel. At the time, I didn't know what he was up to. It was only later on that I found out the sort of deal my solicitor was cutting with the enemy.

"Well?" asks Weasel when Charlie emerges from the cell block.

"He's finished and he knows it. But you're still going to have trouble pinning him down," Charlie replies.

"Don't worry, he'll come round," Weasel says, now flushed with confidence.

"Maybe," Charlie muses. "But you know what, it seems to me that I have two borderline cases this afternoon; Bex and Ollie, and young master Norris in cell three. How would you like to do a deal?"

Weasel's wary though. He knows how slippery Charlie can be so he treads carefully on this one. "What sort of a deal?"

"I'll give you Bex and Ollie, if you drop the charges against Norris. Just give me a victory. Just for my reputation," Charlie implores.

As enticing as this deal sounds, there's something Weasel doesn't get about Charlie's offer. "Hang on a minute, you want to get Norris off, even after he nicked and smashed up your daughter's motor?"

"The law says otherwise Sergeant," Charlie replies, nice and casual-like, almost as if they were discussing the weather forecast and not the blessed union of Jackie Taylor's Renault 5 and the A10's central reservation barrier. Charlie now fixes Weasel in the eye and spells it out for him. "Just as the law says Bex is essentially right too, without the jackets you don't have much. Give me a victory and I'll give you more."

"What can you do?" Weasel wants to know.

"Oh, you'd be surprised. It's just a question of having faith in people," he smiles.

Shortly afterwards, Charlie finds himself in Norris's cell touting for volunteers, though Norris is far too caught up worrying about his own wretchedness to hear Charlie at first.

"I never done it Charlie, honest I never," he's snivelling.

"Yeah, I got it first time around, so belt up will you?" Charlie tells him. "Now listen, they're willing to drop the charges if you'll just co-operate. All they want is a small favour."

This actually does make it through the self-pity and into Norris's brain and the moment he smells a chance to save his neck, he's on-board like a shot. "Anything," he agrees enthusiastically.

"Well, how can I put this? They were wondering, while you've been in this cell like, if you'd overheard Bex and Ollie talking about a job they pulled last night?"

"Oh yeah, I heard everything I did. Everything," Norris splutters, almost tripping over his own willingness to help.

"This might mean giving evidence against your friends, in court even," Charlie warns him, though this is pretty far down Norris's list of concerns.

"I'll do it, I don't mind. They got it coming anyway for planting that charity box in my car..." Norris starts up again, but Charlie tells him he can drop that one now.

"Just tell us what you heard?"

"Well, they were going on about this warehouse..." Norris says, so Charlie corrects him.

"Shop."

"Oh yeah, that was it, this shop, where they nicked these DVDs..."

"Jackets."

"Yeah them an' all."

"No, just jackets," Charlie insists.

"Yeah, no, that's right, I remember now, just jackets. I tell you, shouting about it they were, I swear on my mum's life, the miserable old fucking..." Norris trails off, so Charlie sets his pad down and decides Norris might benefit from a bit of the old Janet & John.

"I'll tell you what, why don't we write some of this down? Just to help jog your memory," Charlie suggests, going through his pockets for a pen. "Hang on, I had a biro in here somewhere, unless you've had it away," Charlie grumbles, but Norris isn't listening. He's suddenly far too busy reading what else is written on Charlie's pad. Namely, the location of twenty stolen leather jackets, that I've given Charlie, and the details outlining a possible property return plea-bargain deal.

*

Half an hour and one sworn statement later, Norris is striding confidently out of the station when he encounters Mel and Belinda in reception.

"Here for me are you?" he asks.

"That's right, worried sick we were," Mel conforms. "What were you doing in there?"

"Nothing. Just handing in some lost property, a cat or something," Norris replies.

"Did you see Ollie?" Belinda asks, all hopeful.

"Yeah, and Bex," Norris nods. "Look, I'll be straight with you right, but things ain't looking too hot for your dreamboats."

"And what would you know about it?" Mel dismisses.

"I knows it cos I grows it, gorgeous. Got the full S.P. didn't I and the Old Bill's stitching them both right up."

This confuses and panics Belinda all at once. "How?"

"Don't you worry about that, you hear. You just stay strong for them, Pocahontas," Norris winks.

"What's Charlie say?" Mel demands.

"He says you've got to stay here cos he wants to talk to you. Me though? I've gotta run, see a man about a dog," Norris nods knowingly.

"Huh, cats and dogs? You're a regular animal lover, aren't you Norris?" Mel sneers.

"I have my moments, Sugar Pants," Norris chuckles, rubbing his hands together with glee. "I have my moments."

*

Back in the cells, Ollie's calling out for me but I'm not there to hear it.

"Bex ain't here," Roland confirms.

"Where is he then?"

"I think he's off talking to Charlie again," Roland tells him. "Went about ten minutes ago." Ollie's yet to even see Charlie and completely in the dark as to events. To be fair, I've seen Charlie twice now and I still haven't got a clue as to what's going on either, so he ain't missing out on much.

"What's going on?" Ollie asks Roland.

"I don't know, but he should think himself lucky. My brief ain't even come yet."

"Who's your brief?"

"I ain't got one," Roland confirms.

Ollie thinks on this. "Well how the hell's he gonna come if he don't even exist? What's he gonna do, pop down the chimney with your defence strategy?"

"Nah, I don't mean like that, I just mean I ain't got no one regular like. Sergeant Atwell say he's gonna dig us one out the *Yellow Pages* if he gets a chance later on."

"Roland, how long have you been in here for crying out loud? You're

90

entitled to legal representation," Ollie replies in disbelief.

"I know, but I don't like to be no trouble," Roland shrugs.

"I've got news for you mate, you're already in trouble. You need a brief."

"I suppose," Roland miserably accepts, though he's got more pressing concerns on his mind at the moment. "Big Guy?"

"Yeah, what?"

"Can you still eat stuff if it's fallen in the bog?"

Ollie looks at the caked and dirty shitter in the corner of his cell. "Call me picky Rollo, but I generally prefer not to."

5. Repaying the faith

Across town, Norris pulls up outside Mel's late uncle's garage. Mel never uses this place and her uncle certainly doesn't any more. It also only costs about a packet of Hula Hoops a year to rent off the council so me and Ollie keep hold of it and occasionally stash stock here. Obviously, the rental agreement's still in uncle Vic's name, as council garages are all but impossible to come by these days, though this is doubly handy because it means if the Old Bill ever want to take a peek inside they'll have to take their warrant up to Tatley cemetery and serve it against a jam jar full of daisies.

Unfortunately, the pros of a place like this often serve as its cons as well. Our garage is out of the way, there are no nosey neighbours overlooking it to report our comings and goings, and the surrounding street lights in the alleyway leading up to it have been smashed (by us, as it happens, for all the above reasons), so it's also an ideal place to break into without drawing attention to yourself, as Norris is joyfully discovering while we're detained elsewhere.

He levers the padlock off the doors and drills the frame until he can get to the Chub, then quickly hacksaws that in under thirty seconds. Not a bad job, I have to admit.

Inside the garage, under a tarp at the back, he hits the jackpot as our garage pays out to the tune of twenty top notch unreportable stolen leather jackets. Norris breaks out into a grin of self-congratulation and he quickly transfers the lot on to the back seat of his Escort Estate.

"Mrs Norris, your son is a genius," he beams. "Unlike you, you squealing old bitch!"

*

Our gooses are just about as cooked as they're ever likely to be at this point. We're not only in the frame for the job and the Hassans' wrath, we've now lost our one and only bargaining chip - the jackets themselves. If we still had them, we might've been able to turn them over to the Serious Crime boys who were investigating the original lorry-jacking in exchange for lighter sentences, but this opportunity's now speeding off down the road with our erstwhile cell-mate.

At least, it is until Mel's phone receives a text message.

"What is it?" Belinda asks when Mel pulls out her phone to see what all the beeping's about.

"It's from Charlie."

"What's he say?"

"He says… 'trust me' and…" Mel starts reading, but tails off as she tries to read between Charlie's lines.

"Yeah, I used to have a boss who texted me stuff like that an' all, usually around midnight after he'd had a few drinks," Belinda sympathises.

"What else he say?

"I'm not entirely sure," Mel says, springing to her feet and giving the "ring for attention" bell some more abuse.

Once again, Weasel appears looking like he's just woken up from a wonderful dream, only to discover to that he's still a shabby DS in a shabby backwater cop shop.

"Mel look, just go home."

"I've got some information for you."

"Look, I'll take a statement off you later..." Weasel begins but Mel tells him he's got it all wrong.

"No, this isn't a statement, this is just information. An anonymous tip-off like."

"If you want to be anonymous, phone *Crimestoppers*. You can be as anonymous as you like with them, but please, just give it a rest because I'm busy," Weasel says, turning on his Hush Puppies and making to head back into the station.

Mel pulls out her phone and speaks into it before he reaches the door though.

"Hello, *Crimestoppers*? Yes, it's about twenty leather jackets," she teases. This catches Weasel's attention and he lets go of the door handle and returns to the desk.

"Okay then Mel, what's this information?"

"Hold on," Mel mouths. "I'm just on the phone."

*

Norris is buzzing when he strolls into Electric's shop with nineteen leather jackets under his arm and one on his back. It's not a pleasant sight. I've seen Norris when he's in a good mood before and it's enough to make you bring up your dinner. Some people just don't suit happiness and Norris is one of them. I can handle him when he's all morose and sucking on his bottom lip, but the moment things start to pick up for him I want to slap him about and remind him that one day he's going to die, just to stifle his joy because it set my teeth on edge so much.

"There you go old man, best quality leather jackets, times twenty. Well, nineteen," he shrugs, admiring his new jacket in the mirror behind Electric's counter. "Thought I'd give myself an early Christmas present, know what I mean?"

Electric feels the lapels and takes a peek at the labels.

"Yeah, these are nice, ain't they. Very nice, in fact. Where d'you get 'em from?

"Uh-uh, ask me no questions and I'll spare you the *Jackanory*," Norris winks.

"Norris, if this were a charity box, I wouldn't need to ask, but these jackets are just a bit too nice."

"Expensive too, dad," Norris points out.

"So Where d'you get 'em?"

"You ever heard of Rumpelstiltskin? Huh, look who I'm asking. Well I'm a bit like him, see. Got a load of little mateys holed up in the wall who knock 'em out for us," Norris explains.

Electric thinks about this. "That weren't Rumpelstiltskin, that was The Cobbler's Tale," he corrects him.

"Well I never believed it myself, mate," Norris chuckles, giving Electric a flash of his pearly yellows.

"Are these the jackets that got the Hassans busted?" Electric asks, momentarily catching Norris off-guard.

"Uh?" he double-takes, before quickly remembering his pitch. "Ah nah, no. These are cool these are. No problem," he assures Electric, though mention of the Hassans has brought an element of unease into Norris's mind.

"Then tell me about them," Electric insists.

"Look, let's just say they fell off the back of a lorry," Norris simplifies.

"Let's not hey. Because I reckon I know the lorry in question. And I also reckon I know what become of the driver. And I wouldn't touch these with a ten foot barge pole, not if I want to steer clear of one myself," Electric says.

Norris decides that's enough foreplay for one day and cuts to the chase. "Gis two grand for 'em."

"You ain't listening to me are you, Norris?"

"Alright, fifteen hundred," Norris reluctantly concedes, "but only cos I want to get shot of 'em quick like."

"Norris, if these are the jackets I think they are, they're twenty hospital invites," Electric tells him.

"Nah nah, honestly, it's not like that, it's just..." he tries again but, Norris suddenly feels like a man who's found something on a beach, dug it up, taken it home and looked it up on the internet, only to discover he's got an unexploded landmine sitting on his mantelpiece.

The Hassans.

The Hassans.

The Hassans!

Norris is rapidly swamped by an overwhelming feeling of doom.

"Yeah," Electric sees. "Now you know what I'm talking about, don't you? Bit of excitement, in' it? Get shot of 'em. And I don't mean ditch 'em. Put 'em back where you found 'em."

"Sod that!" Norris snorts, bundling up the jackets and searching his mind for a suitable dumpster to drop 'em in.

"Norris, you ever play pass the parcel?" Electric asks, as Norris scuttles to the door.

"No why, d'you fancy a quick game or something?" Norris replies.

"When the music stops, you don't just sling the parcel over your shoulder. Last person holding it's 'it'. And someone is always 'it'," Electric says, then demonstrates the point by asking Norris who else he's been showing his new jacket off to. A bolt of fear spears Norris's heart when he recalls the beer and chat he had with old big mouth Keith, the town bulletin board, when he stopped in The Badger for a cheeky half on his way over. This settles it and Norris immediately realises that he's got to get the jackets back the lock-up as quickly as possible so that me and Ollie can take the rap for them, or else he'll be the one left holding the landmine.

He turns and runs through the door, but Electric calls him back again. "Norris?"

"What?" Norris barks.

Electric smiles and winks.

"Love your new jacket."

A couple of expletives later, Norris is in his car and going through the gears like Stirling Moss on a promise when his rear view mirror starts flashing blue.

"What the fuck…" he turns, only to see a police cruiser flashing and indicating for him to pull in. "Oh no no no…" he panics, scarcely believing what's happening to him. "Not now. Not with this stuff in the car." But Norris is a rabbit caught between a police car's flashing headlights and he knows he has no alternative but to pull over and try to charm his neck out of the noose. So he indicates to stop, but does so as slowly as possible, buying himself a few precious seconds in order to stuff an enormous pile of leather jackets out of sight with his free hand.

Once parked, a knuckle raps on the driver's side window and a torch shines in to illuminate Norris's legs and arse. Norris climbs back into the driver's seat and smiles into the torch light.

"Wind it down," Weasel tells him.

"It's broken," Norris explains apologetically.

"Then open the door."

"That's broken too," Norris shrugs.

Weasel gives the door handle and yank, spilling Norris out of his seat and into the road.

"There, that seems to have fixed it. Right then, where are you off to in such a hurry, Lewis Hamilton?" Weasel asks. "Tax man after you or something?"

"Nowhere. Just home. Honest, I ain't done nothing," Norris assures him.

"Really? Well we got a tip-off that a vehicle matching this description was transporting stolen goods. You wouldn't know anything about this, would you?"

Norris thinks on this long and hard but it doesn't seem to ring a bell.

"Nah, honest," he hyperventilates.

It's about now that Weasel decides to direct his torch light over Norris's shoulder and take a closer look at that enormous mysterious bulge clogging the back seat of his car.

"Well I never! What's all this then?" Weasel asks, treating Norris to the full *Dixon of Dock Green* experience.

"Honestly Sergeant, they ain't mine! I swear on me mum's life," Norris protests.

"You know what, Norris, for once I believe you. I don't think they are yours," Weasel agrees.

Norris thinks about this. "No, that's not what I mean..." he says but it's too late, the landmine explodes, the trapdoor opens and the wheels spread the bunny across the road. Whatever euphemism you care to use, it pretty much amounted to the same thing.

"You're nicked," Weasel spells out.

*

Some thirty minutes later, Atwell comes and gets me and Ollie from our respective cells and reluctantly tells us to follow him. He's in such a sombre mood that I half-expect him to lead us into a room with a couple of ropes hanging from the ceiling, but instead he just leads us into the custody suite where Charlie is waiting to greet us with a grin.

"What's going on, Charlie?" I ask, as Atwell busies himself behind the desk returning our property.

"They've dropped the charges against you," Charlie says quietly. I look to Atwell, but he can't even look us in the eye.

"You what?" I ask.

Charlie elaborates a little. "It seems an arrest was made earlier on and property allegedly connecting you with the Hassan case was found in another individual's possession."

"Really? Who?" Ollie asks.

"I can't really say, but he knew all about the job and had even sworn out a bogus witness statement stating as much. I'm afraid the police had no choice but to switch the focus of their investigation." Charlie looks around to make sure Atwell's out of earshot then whispers; "Let's just say, he was someone I had a great deal of faith in."

"So, are we really in the clear then?" I ask, scarcely daring to believe.

"Yes, the fat lady has spilled her guts. Watch your step lads," Charlie says proudly.

"Charlie, I don't know how to thank you," I gush, so Charlie leans in to make a point.

"No need to thank me Adrian, you were innocent after all, remember?"

"What? Oh yeah," I suddenly remember.

"Well, cheerio then chaps. I'll see you again soon, no doubt," Charlie

96

confidently predicts.

"Here Charlie, before you go, can you look in on Roland in cell two? His brief still ain't come," Ollie says, aiming an accusing eye at Atwell.

Roland's voice comes echoing back from the cells. "But only if it's no trouble."

"Will do Ol, right after I see my latest customer," Charlie promises.

"You got someone else in then, Charlie?" I ask.

"Yep, no rest for the wicked I'm afraid," Charlie smiles, before disappearing. "God bless 'em.

"Right then, sign there and there, and the Constable here will show you out," Atwell says, laying our property and release forms on the counter in front of us.

I sign mine with a flourish and even half-think about leaving a tip. "Well, that was a really lovely stay, thank you very much Sergeant, though the room service was a little tardy," I tick our proprietor off. Atwell's not in the mood for any of my lip though, especially when my material's been lifted straight from his own.

"Oh disappear Bex," he grumbles, before turning his sights on Ollie. "And you, where's my newspaper?"

"Oh, I folded it into little boats and flushed 'em down the bog," Ollie tells him.

"What d'you do that for?" Atwell gawps.

"Well I'd finished reading it and was bored, weren't I." Ollie explains all matter-of-fact.

"Oh, you stupid, pointless, juvenile, little moron," Atwell seethes.

"There you go, that's better," Ollie congratulates him.

Atwell glares at Ollie in confusion. "Huh?"

"I'm just saying, we can have a chat without you turning it into a race issue every time."

*

In a police cell, not so far away from where I was five minutes earlier, Norris and Charlie are reunited after an extraordinarily short separation.

"Honest Charlie, I never done it, honest I never," Norris is explaining tearfully.

"Okay, settle down. First thing's first. Let's get these Legal Aid forms filled in, shall we?" Charlie says, attending to the important stuff first.

"But I already filled out one of those this afternoon," Norris tells Charlie, but Charlie puts him straight.

"No, that was for the old case. You've got a new set of charges against you now and a new set of charges requires a whole new claim. See how it works?" Charlie beams. "Right, name?"

Norris chews on his bottom lip miserably and reluctantly goes through the motions for a second time today. "Clive Norris."

Charlie repeats this parrot-like as he fills in the boxes. "Clive -

97

Norris. Occupation?"

Norris decides to clear the air between them first before they go any further, just so that there's no overhanging resentment between the two of them. "Look, Charlie, I never stole and smashed your daughter's motor up, honest I never," he says as sincerely as he can.

Charlie fills this in. "Not - stealing - and - smashing - up - my - daughter's - motor," then turns and fixes a sharp eye on Norris. "Date of birth?"

But Norris is suddenly too choked up to reply.

*

The girls are waiting for us in reception and rush into our arms as if we've been away for a couple of years. Which I guess was a distinct possibility.

"I thought they had you this time," Mel whispers into my ear.

"That's funny, I thought they had me this time an' all," I agree, prompting Mel to shove me away violently and start barking.

"So are you going to finally give this silly nonsense up or what?" she demands.

I figure now's not the time for serious dialogue, just comfort and consideration, so I give her a bit of the old flannel. "Mel luv, I promise you, that's me done. I'm giving it up once and for all. It ain't worth it," I reassure her for simplicity. Mel rewards me by resuming our hug.

"You promise?" she sniffles.

"Yeah, I promise," I tell her, in for a penny, in for a pound. "First thing in the morning I'll go out and look for a job."

This restores Mel's spirits no end. "I hope so Bex, I really do, for your sake, because your luck's going to run out one day."

She could be right about this. I'd certainly had more than my fair share of it just lately, but still there's no need to panic myself into making any hasty decisions, so I amend my promise slightly to give myself a better chance of actually keeping it. "Well, maybe not first thing. I'm not really much of a morning person to be honest. After lunch or something," I repromise, then notice Ollie hanging over the back of Belinda's shoulder making lunchtime pint signals at me.

"Oh come on, let's get out of here shall we?" Mel finally says, taking us by the hand and leading us out to the car park.

The cool night's air feels good in my lungs and I take an enormous belt of freedom before reaching into my pockets and flavouring it with a Malboro.

"I can't believe it. I simply can't believe it," Ollie keeps muttering to himself, an enormous look of relief and gratitude etched across his face.

"Old Charlie, yeah?" I guess, when I see his expression.

"What a miracle worker! I tell you, we were dead and buried in there and he still got us out. I don't know how he does it," Ollie gogs.

"No," I say, stopping to admire a gleaming top-of-the-range Jag with CH4RL1E front and back parked outside the station. "But I reckon I know why he does it."

So thank you Joe Muggings. Thank you for pulling us out of the firing line, for picking up the tab and for sorting it so that me and Ollie survive to play the game another day.

I really am most obliged.

Oh, and cheers for the pen, Sergeant Atwell. Turns out he rather naïvely forgot to ask for it back when I left the station.

THE TEAPOT JOB

1. A quiet pint at lunchtime

It's a quiet Wednesday lunchtime and me and Ollie have a final few quid in our pockets following a weekend on the tiles. The tiles in question belonged to a self storage depot on the trading estate and we'd filled our van to the brim with a dozen people's excess crap that they didn't have room for at home. Put like that, it sounds like we actually did them a favour. Anyway, Electric had taken the lot and coughed up almost five hundred quid for the privilege, so like Lions lollygagging on the Serengeti after a surfeit of zebras, me and Ollie have spent the last few days enjoying the shade of The Badger and the lovely feelings our pockets have been making while they've slowly shrunk back to empty.

"Can we swap back yet?" Ollie asks, giving up on my *Harry Potter* book after only two pages while I pore over his *Daily Mirror*.

"In a sec, I'm just reading this," I reply.

"But I'm bored," he mopes like a big kid.

"You've only been reading it for five minutes," I point out.

"Yeah, and I've been bored for four and a half of 'em."

"Well do more of whatever you were doing for that half a minute you weren't bored," I tell him.

Ollie thinks about this. "What, ask you if we can swap back yet and tell you I'm bored?"

There's no point talking to Ollie when he's like this so I try to ignore him and continue reading my feature. But Ollie's in no mood to leave me in peace and soon he's at it again, distracting himself by distracting me.

"What are you reading?"

"It's about the oldest woman in the world. She just died," I pause to tell him.

"What did she die of?" Ollie then asks, which does catch my attention. I look up from my paper and think about this for a moment.

"She was eaten by a crocodile," I tell Ollie. Ollie explodes with excitement and makes a grab for the paper.

"No! Where?"

"Get off," I tell him, whipping the paper from his grasping grubby paws. "Not really Ol. What d'you think the oldest woman in the world's going to die of? Old age, of course."

The disappointment momentarily calms Ollie, at least until he asks how old she was and I tell him she was forty-seven.

"Get out!" he gasps, trying to wrestle the paper away from me again.

"For crying out loud, Ol, put up a bit of a fight," I encourage him.

"Oh, right yeah. No actually I was going to say, I thought forty-seven sounded a bit young," he concedes.

"What, for the oldest woman in the world? Yeah, it does a bit, doesn't it, especially when your mum's fifty-two."

"Yeah well, like I say," he shrugs. "So how old was she?"

I skim down the article, find her age and tell him. "A hundred and nineteen."

Ollie stares at me sceptically.

"No Ol, she was, look. A hundred and nineteen is actually quite old, you know," I say, showing him the paper.

Ollie looks for himself, then studies the picture of her in her wheel-chair sleeping through her last birthday party in the queue outside Stringfellows.

"Imagine being the oldest woman in the world. You'd shit yourself, wouldn't you? You'd be like, 'oh God, help, help, I'm going to die any second. Help'," Ollie shudders, then spies two old fellas sitting across the pub from us. "I mean, even at their age you must get up every morning wondering if this is it. If today's gonna be the day."

"Not looking forward to retirement then?" I surmise.

Once again, Ollie shudders as if a load of matey's with particularly cold feet are running across his grave. "Terrifies me it does, the thought of getting old," he admits.

I think on this myself, look at the old fellas and disagree. "I don't know. Be alright. No job. No worries. Get to sit in the pub all day with your mates having a laugh," I ponder. "Can't wait myself."

At that moment, the door on the far side of the bar flies open and in steps another old fella we know only too well - Electric.

"Speaking of coffin dodgers, look who's here? What are you doing up and about in daylight, 'lec?"

Electric's scowling, but then again Electric's always scowling, so the first inkling I have that something's wrong is when his boot lands in my side and I tumble backwards off my stool.

"You thieving little scumbag!" he shouts as his left boot quickly follows up his right, then both go at it together. "Give it back. Give it back!"

Those old boys who Ollie was feeling sorry for a moment ago are suddenly up on their feet cheering Electric on, as if Electric's striking the first blows of the oldies revolution, while Keith shouts at us from the safety of the bar to behave ourselves.

"Jesus Christ! What the hell's got into you?" I yell, as I desperately scramble under tables and across the floor to get away from the deranged bastard's boots.

"I ain't joking, it all comes back to me, NOW!" Electric shouts, picking up a stool and lobbing it in my direction. The stool misses me, but takes out a table chocker with empty pint pots that Keith's been too lazy to collect, carpeting the pub floor with broken glass. This puts me off the idea of further scrambling, so I jump to my feet, spin the stool around and give Electric a taster of the legs.

"You bastard! You bastard!" he's snarling, but I'm able to ward him off long enough to bring something to everybody's attention.

"Hold on," I shout. "Just fucking hold on a minute, yeah? Before we go any further, just give me a moment here, will you?" Electric drops his dukes and agrees to a temporary truce. "Ta," I thank him, then look over at Ollie who hasn't moved so much as an eyebrow in the last thirty seconds. "Not disturbing you over there are we mate?"

Ollie looks about and gawps. "What?"

"Oh nothing," I tell him. "It's just good to know I can look to my mates in times of trouble, that's all."

"Bex, he's an old man, have a bit of respect. It doesn't take two of us to fight him now does it?" Ollie patronises.

"Incredible. And this bloke's meant to be on my side," I tell the pub, before turning back to Electric. Electric's still scowling at me, but judging by the way he's puffing and panting, it looks like he's blitzkrieged himself out, so I figure it's safe for me to drop the stool and ask him what his problem is.

"You know damn well what my problem is pondlife and if you don't give it all back I'm going to splash your plasma all round this fucking boozer," he shouts.

"Listen, if it's all the same to you, would you mind being a tad more specific so that me and Ol can join in with this conversation as it all sounds terribly exciting," I suggest.

"Point that smart mouth at me one more time boy and you'll see just how exciting things can get!" Electric warns me.

"He's definitely upset about something," Ollie reckons.

"Just tell me what I did," I demand, but Electric's still not playing the game and refusing to even entertain the thought that I might not know what he's talking about, so I quickly rack my brains for a way around this impasse. "Okay, let's think about this logically. Even if I do know what you're talking about, I ain't going to admit nothing, am I? So innocent or guilty, one way or another, eventually we're going to have to go through the charade of you telling us what I done just so we can move onto the next round of denials, so why don't we just fast forward to that bit and take it from there, hey?"

Electric thinks about this and agrees it's a fair point, then lays his cards on the up-turned table.

"You two turned me over last night, that's what."

"Did we? That was rotten of us," I reply, then a technical detail occurs to me. "Hang on, if you're saying we both turned you over, why d'you only come after me?"

Electric glares. "You don't smack Emu in the gob when Rod Hull keeps grabbing you by the nuts, do you?" he tell us. Ollie laughs at this, then creases his beak and says he doesn't get it. Electric doesn't bother explaining. "Now I want my stuff back. Everything you took."

"And what exactly did we take?" I ask.

"Not what you were hoping to, that's for sure," Electric replies.

"Really? I don't know why we bothered then?"

"Yeah well, you would've had all my stock away if I hadn't clobbered you in the act," Electric snarls, recounting how he found a late night shopper going through his stuff when he arrived back home the previous night.

"When did you do this?" Ollie makes a point of asking me.

"Oh don't you start. Though, that is a point, when did I do this?" I ask Electric.

"Last night, when I got back from the theatre. About half eight."

Ollie stifles a smirks. "What, you go to the theatre?"

"I do when I get a letter telling us that I've won Local Trader of the Month, a ticket to the star-studded extravaganza *Starlight Express* and a free slap-up with the cast afterwards. Only the extravaganza weren't quite as star-studded as the letter made out. Was it?" Electric fumes.

And he weren't wrong. Electric had got all tarted up in good faith, run a comb through his hair and damp cloth under his pits on the off-chance that one of the better-looking performers fancied seeing what the back room of an award-winning junk shop looked like. But thirty seconds into the show, he knew his ablutions had been for nothing when the stage filled up with toddlers and a teacher started bouncing her fingers over a piano in the corner.

He checked the ticket, then compared it to the programme, but there'd been no mention of the performers' age in either. Just what the hell were the Traders' Association playing at? Why on Earth had they thought he'd be interested in hobnobbing with a cast of kids after a bloody school play?

Electric was pondering these imponderables and grumbling to himself, when he noticed a dozen anxious young mums, whispering amongst themselves and scrutinising Electric's craggy leer. Electric might not have known what the Traders' Association had been thinking, but he had a pretty clear idea as to what they were. And it was at this point, when the audience murmuring got so bad that the kids could no longer hear the piano, that Electric really regretted bringing his camcorder.

"And somebody turned you over while you was out?" I say, connecting the dots for myself.

"Jesus, you fell for that one, did you?" Ollie scoffs.

"Yes I did. Only I had to come home early after... well trouble up at the old..." Electric flaps, trailing off at thoughts of said trouble. "Anyway I come home and caught you mid-rob!"

"Look, first off, it weren't us. We was in here winning the Tuesday night pub quiz as usual," I tell him, pointing him towards a blackboard with mine and Ollie's names sitting proudly atop a list of results. Everyone else uses team names but me and Ollie always call ourselves Bex & Ollie, so that everyone knows where we are most Tuesday nights for this very reason. Well we've got nothing to hide on our night off so why not?

Electric scans the list in disbelief. "What, you two brain donors?"

"Smarter than your average brain donors," Ollie winks.

"Secondly, why d'you even think it was us? All the scumbags you must know!" I surmise.

"I ain't singling you out. I'm seeing all my boys this morning."

"Oh yeah, and how are the boys?" Ollie asks.

"All well rested after a night in, would you believe?" Electric frowns. Ollie loses interest and heads off to the bar, but I press the point, being as I'm the injured party.

"And thirdly, what are you moaning about if nothing got robbed?"

"I didn't say nothing got robbed," Electric snaps. "A few bits did. And I want them all back. From you or from anyone. I don't care. I just want them back."

I smell a rat, though it could just be Electric's pits. "What is it you're not telling us?"

Up at the bar, Ollie's already forgotten about Electric's troubles and is busy working on a few of our own.

"Here, Keith, you got the old wotsname for next week?" he winks, less than subtly.

Keith plucks a plain envelope from behind the till containing next Tuesday's answers and swaps it for an empty crisp packet full of silver and notes, his share of our quiz winnings.

"There. And try getting a couple wrong next time, for crying out loud. I thought we were gonna get lynched last night," Keith glares.

"What's the difference? A win's a win, in' it?" Ollie shrugs.

"No one gets a hundred per cent you doughnut, especially not when they turn up twenty minutes late. Drop a couple of points for chrissakes!"

"Is it our fault we know the answers?" Ollie asks.

"Yeah, but you don't know the answers, do you? You're meant to memorise the sheet I give you, not just write your name on the top and hand it back in, you lazy fuck!"

"Aye aye, skullduggery ahoy," I say, when I join my quiz league partners. "Get this, old Electric's bag of stuff ain't quite as worthless as he'd like everyone to believe."

Ollie perks up at this. "No? Really? How much is it worth then?"

This is typical Ollie. "Don't you even want to know what's actually been took first?" I suggest. "You're like those vultures on The Antiques Roadshow who's eyes glaze over until someone mentions money."

Ollie rolls his eyes and wearily folds his arms. "Go on then, what got took?"

"A teapot. Though this ain't no ordinary teapot, this is a very special teapot indeed," I tantalise.

"Really, how much?" he asks.

"Oh, I give up," I sigh. "Two grand."

"Two grand for a teapot!" Ollie exclaims. "Bit steep in' it?"

I suddenly notice Keith earwigging our conversation as he pours us a couple of his famous cappuccino lagers, so I decide to deal him in properly to save my flat being repeatedly turned over by the blokes at the other end of Keith's Chinese whispers chain as they search for an electric teapot with two grand inside it.

"Here Keith, can you keep a secret?"

Keith doesn't even hesitate. "Yeah, no problem," he leans in.

"Never say no, do they?" I point out to Ollie, before filling in the blanks for Keith. "Well look, a mate of mine had an antique teapot nicked, only whoever nicked it don't know what it's worth, so keep your ears peeled and there could be a drink in it for you. And I don't mean a cup of tea."

"Will do Bex. Ear's open, gob shut," Keith enthuses, tapping the side of his nose. "You know me," he winks. Which I certainly do.

Keith moves off to pour someone else a pint of bubbles and the moment he's out of earshot, Ollie turns and asks me what I told him for. "Old big mouth Keith, are you sure?"

"Yeah, quicker than the internet, that bloke. Save us racing around town putting the word about ourselves, won't it?" I tell Ollie.

"Hang on, why do we care if Electric's lost his teapot?" Ollie asks, not unreasonably.

"Because Electric's throwing a paddy and threatening to shut up shop if he don't get his stuff back," I tell him.

"Where will we sell our gear then?" it suddenly occurs to Ollie.

"Oh gee you know what, I never thought of that."

"Yeah well you also never thought about what the bloke who nicked his teapot will do when he finds out what it's worth. Electric'll never see it again."

"No, but someone will when he tries to flog it, which is preferable to him thinking he's got a sack full of tuppenny tat that's only fit for bombing the ducks with. Also, he's putting up a Monkey for its return," I explain.

Ollie frowns, not understanding any of this. "Jesus, all this fuss over a teapot."

"Again, David Dickinson, it's a very special sort of teapot," I try again.

"So how are we going to find it?"

"Ye of little intelligence," I say, then notice Keith deep in conversation at the other end of the bar. "Come on, make that pint to go, we've got people to see," I tell Ollie, tucking my own pint inside my jacket.

Keith doesn't even look up as we pass. He's already far too busy going to town about this missing antique teapot that's worth millions, to some poor bloke who only came in for a read of the paper.

"Don't you go telling no one though. It's all very hush hush," he warns matey, but is cut short of embellishing the story any more when the telephone behind the bar jingles to life.

"Hello, The Badger?" I hear him say as we step through the door. If I'd stuck around, I would've heard him say a bit more. "No, she's not on till the evening, okay. But here listen, guess what Bex told us. What's that? You know, Bex - funny-looking bloke - burglar - drives that van with the dodgy MOT, though don't go telling no one I told you that right. Anyway, who's this?"

2. Legal assistance

We wander around to Charlie's office just up the high street. I drain the last of my pint and sling the glass into Charlie's bush just before I go in, smashing last week's glass while I'm at it. Ollie hangs onto his. He's a slower drinker than me, always has been, which is really annoying when you're in a round with him. And Ollie refuses to sign up to the pub etiquette charter which demands a person buys their round when the first person in said round has an empty glass, not the last, which is always him. The amount of times I've seen him nursing half a pint in the middle of a big group of angry blokes who are all spitting feathers at two minutes to last orders is beyond a joke. But then that's Ollie for you. He's got no shame.

"Ding-dong, Avon calling," I sing as I enter the offices.

Mel looks up at me from behind her glasses and asks what I'm doing here at this time of the day. "I thought you had that job interview this afternoon?"

"Did I?"

I think about this one, then look at Ollie, who simply shrugs and takes a tiny sip of his pint. I tell you, I'm gonna have to start writing some of the old bullshit I tell Mel down because I simply can't keep track of it all. Mel's still staring at me, waiting for an answer, so I quickly make something up. "Oh yeah, no that was this morning. Just come from it in fact."

"So, how'd it go?" she enquires.

"Cushty, went really well," I tell her to cheer her up, though I'm reluctant to go too overboard in case she starts to wonder why I didn't get the job then, so I qualify my bullshit with a bit more bullshit. "In fact, they want to get us back next Thursday for a second interview," which should hold her off for a week or so, by which time hopefully she'll have forgotton all about it.

Mel looks concerned. "But haven't you got your dentist's appointment that afternoon?"

"Er… no, that's been moved to the following Tuesday," I decide.

"So who's going to drive your dad to the airport that day?" Mel points out. I rack my brains, but come to the conclusion I haven't got time for this.

"Anyway, look never mind about that. I need a favour."

"Oh, lucky me," she grimaces, then notices Ollie drinking his pint. "Can I get you some peanuts?"

Ollie looks interested. "Have you got any?"

"Mel, how many fences has Charlie got on his books?" I ask.

"That's privileged information. I can't give that out, I'd be fired," Mel objects.

"I don't want you to give it out, just make a few calls."

Mel's face tightens into its default setting and she glares at me with suspicion. "What's this about?"

"Oh, it's complicated," I say, not wishing to burden her with the tiresome details. Far from thanking me for this - after all, I always hate being burdened with needless details, such as where things comes from, who they belong to and where the old people's home is going to find the money to replace them - Mel actually gets all smart with me.

"Oh, that's alright, I'm an intelligent girl. Admittedly, not as intelligent as you two if word on the pub quiz circuit is anything to go by, but I reckon I could just about keep up if you want to try me."

Ollie looks up from the legal book he's holding and I catch his eye.

"Honestly, this country hates winners, doesn't it?" I tell him, before returning to the problem of Mel. "Look, it's nothing really. It's just that er..." I quickly think, "the interview I just come from, old matey reckons he got turned over last night."

"Was it you?" Mel asks.

"No it wasn't actually!" I reply. Fuck me, she's got her suspicious head on today.

Ollie examines a packet sandwich he's found in her handbag behind her chair. "Are you gonna eat this?" he asks Mel.

"Yeah, with any luck, if I keep my wits about me," Mel replies, snatching it away from him. "Anyway, so what's matey getting turned over got to do with you?"

"Nothing, it's just that he said he had an antique teapot nicked, so I figured if I could get him it back for him, I'm a shoe-in for the job," I tell her, then congratulate myself on an excellent bit of joined-up bullshit, designed not only to camouflage my real agenda, but also spur on Mel's motivation to help. I always get a lovely warm feeling when I come up with a well-crafted lie like that, especially on the hoof, but Mel's not quite with the programme yet.

"Bex, you had an interview at a dry cleaners. This sort of thing isn't normally required of people hoping to work in dry cleaners."

"Gotta get ahead somehow, luv," I tell her. "It's a dog-eat-dog world out there and a man needs to have an angle."

"Have you ever considered just getting your head down and working?" Mel asks.

"Fuck me, one thing at a time please luv, let's just get his teapot back then we'll cross that whole minefield when we come to it. Anyway, put the word about will you? It's for a good cause."

Mel melts a little. "If I get five minutes, I'll see what I can do but I want your word that this isn't some scam."

"I give you my solemn word luv," I swear.

"Cross our hearts," Ollie adds, scattering pens and Post-It note pads from his sleeves as he does do. "They're mine."

As Ollie is scampering across the carpet bagging his stationery, I figure a little something extra is needed to sweeten the pot, so I tell Mel there's a slap-up feedbag in it for her tonight if she does the business.

"But I thought you had your football awards dinner tonight?" she points out.

I think on this, then decide that's been moved to next Monday. "Anyway, better scoot," I say and quickly skedaddle before she's able to complicate the moment with any more of my former excuses.

Outside on the stairs I look at Ollie counting his pens and tell him; "You know what, I swear I haven't got a clue what she's going on about sometimes."

Ollie tucks his pens away and agrees. "That's women for you," he says, like the old sage and onion stuffing he is.

"What's d'you mean?"

Ollie's not sure. He just said it as he thought it was his turn to say something and he didn't really have any better to offer.

"Nice. Well do give us a shout if you come up with anything else, won't you? No matter what time, day or night, if I'm not around you just bell us straight away, promise?"

Out on the street, we walk for a bit, me thinking, Ollie still drinking and kicking pebbles as we go.

Eventually, Ollie asks, "How old d'you reckon Electric is?"

"I don't know, sixty or seventy maybe."

"Just think about it. That's only half the age of that oldest bird in the world in the paper you know," Ollie ponders. "Imagine being twice as old as Electric? You wouldn't be happy about it, would you?"

"Well, if it's any comfort I don't think you'll ever have to worry about that. You'll be long dead before you get anywhere near either of their totals."

Ollie chokes on his lager. "Oh cheers, nice one you big fuckhead."

"True though. So I wouldn't worry about stuff you don't need to worry about. You wanna find something else to worry about if you really wanna worry about stuff," I suggest.

"Oh perhaps you can help us think of something. What d'you mean I ain't going to get near either of their totals? Sixty ain't old."

"It is for a mayfly who don't look after himself."

"What, you think I live unhealthily?"

"No Ol, I think I live unhealthily. I think you're waging war on your internal organs."

"And what's that supposed to mean?" Ollie demands.

"Ollie mate, look at how you live; you smoke, you drink, you don't exercise and you think cheese is a vegetable that counts towards your five-a-day. And then you don't bother with the other four."

"I eat fine," he objects.

"No Ol, not everything you eat should be golden. Try eating something green once in a while."

Ollie screws his face up as if Jamie Oliver's just pulled up outside his school. "Urgh, rabbit food!"

"Yeah, the thing about rabbits Ol, is that most of them can tackle a flight of stairs without honking up and talking out of one side of their face for an hour afterwards. You can't."

"And I suppose your body's a temple is it?" he counters.

"No, it just ain't no Happy Meal box like yours," I tell him, then stop dead in my tracks when I spot something across the road. "Oh, hold on!"

"What?"

"Ol mate, when something gets nicked around here, who's usually nicked it?"

"You?"

"Other than me," I amend.

"Who?"

I turn him around and point him in the direction of the war memorial across the road. Like many war memorials around the country, Tatley's is a simple stone obelisk inscribed with the names of those who fell in two world wars and one bloke who thought joining the RNLI sounded like a great career move, though a more appropriate memorial for this town might've been a stone bed with the names of all those who dodged the call inscribed underneath it. You would've certainly seen a few Beckinsales on that particular memorial, all the way back to Waterloo and beyond. We missed the lot, you know.

Anyway, just in front of the memorial is a fold out card table with a hand written banner hanging from the front of it saying "BRITISH LEGION POPPY APPEAL" and a bedraggled veteran in army surplus togs shaking a charity box at passing pedestrians.

Ollie's eyes widen when he recognises the veteran.

"Norris."

"Come on," I say, "let's go and have a word."

We circle around the back and put a boot into Norris's back, spilling him out of his camp chair and onto his face. Norris jumps to his feet and shapes to flee, then notices it's only us and stands easy.

"Oi, what is this, Tip Norris off his chair day?" Norris objects, brushing his German paratrooper jacket down.

"Yeah, comes round earlier every year doesn't it? I take it you've seen Electric then?"

"Yeah, him and what he's been stepping in. I tell you what short cuts has that bloke been taking, that's what I wanna know," Norris gripes.

Ollie picks up Norris's charity box and starts to peel back the handwritten Poppy Appeal sticker that's covering up an RSPCA logo until

Norris snatches it out of his hand. "Oi, get off that!"

"What is all this?" Ollie asks.

"Another day that seems to have come around early," I see. "I didn't know you were in the Legion, Norris."

"Yeah well, there's a lot you don't know about me," Norris asserts.

"I think I know where you're getting your poppies from. I wondered what you were doing going through the bins last November," I say, looking in his box and sorting through two dozen filthy and torn poppies, until I find one that doesn't look right at all. I pick it out and see that its stem is a green pipe cleaner and its flower's been cut from a packet of Park Road cigarettes. "Are you making some of these yourself?" I ask in disbelief.

"Oi, hands off, they're five quid each, they are?" Norris warns me.

This doesn't sit well with Ollie though. "Poppy's ain't got a price. They're voluntary, you know, however much you can afford."

"Oh don't you start, that's all I've had this morning. I tell you, this town's got a short memory," he shouts at a couple of old biddies loaded down with cat food and Werther's Originals.

"Anyway, talking of things you've had, where's Electric's gear?"

Norris blinks with innocence. "You tell me."

"Your place?" I take a pot shot.

Norris sneers. "Yeah, funny that, that's what Electric reckoned an' all, but I'll tell you like I told him, you can come round my place any time you like and have a look because I ain't got nothing to hide," he says, then qualifies that. "Well, nothing of his anyway."

"How about now?"

"Not now, I'm working."

"Give us your keys then and we'll take a look," I offer.

"On your bike, you think I'd give you keys to my place? Come round tonight," he says.

"Oh and you promise if you have got his stuff, you won't move it before then?" I check.

"Oh you're hysterical, you are. Now if you'll excuse me I'm busy doing my bit for my fallen brothers," Norris bristles.

"And where exactly did they fall?" Ollie asks, reading the inscription on one of Norris's shinier medals. "The Hampstead Heath 10k?"

Norris slaps Ollie's hand away. "Oi, fuck off that!"

"You been burgling joggers again then Norris?" I say, which is an old party piece of Norris's. What he does is watch the local parks, single out someone who likes to huff and puff around them of a weekend, then do a few laps of their flat the following Saturday while they're out circling the duck pond.

"Is there anything else you want because I'd hate to be keeping you from something?" Norris suggests.

"Just one thing. Did Electric tell you what he had nicked?" I ask.

"A bag of old tat he reckons."

"He didn't tell you about the teapot then?"

"What teapot?" Norris eyes narrow.

"The rare antique teapot that's worth two grand."

"Electric's got a teapot that's worth two grand?" Norris gawps.

"Well no, not any more he ain't," Ollie reminds him.

Norris shrugs this thought off. "Oh. No he didn't mention it then. Anyway, it don't matter as I didn't nick it," he shrugs, then smiles. "Though I'll tell you something if you like, I wish I had now."

Norris snaps his feet together and gives me his best Trumpton fire brigade salute.

"What a hero!" I frown.

3. Back to school

As part of our ongoing investigations, me and Ollie pop into the primary school that had put on the previous evening's production of *Starlight Express*. Behind the desk is a typical box-standard school reception battle-hatchet, whose face knits together in a scowl the moment we step through the door. There's a certain breed of mother hen who are supremely suited to working in primary schools. No qualifications required, all they need is a genuine love of children under ten and an outright, vicious fucking hatred for all the rest of us.

"Yes?" she glares.

"Oh yes, hello there," I say, giving her my bushiest bright-eyed smile. "Do you keep records of who buys tickets to your school plays?

"Could I ask what this is concerning?" she glowers.

"Of course, we're trying to trace the buyer of a particular ticket to last night's performance of *Starlight Express*," I explain.

"And who exactly are you?" she stares, giving me and Ol the old up and down.

Ollie smiles and nods. "I'm Ollie."

"No, what I meant is, are you with the police or something?" she spells out.

"Oh right, yeah, that's right. We're in the police," I confirm.

"Well could I see some identification then please?" she demands, rather pissing on that particular bonfire before I'd even got it properly lit.

"Oh. Er... no, we're not really, I just said that," I shrug.

"I see. I think I might ask you to leave now then," she forewarns us.

Ollie sees it's not quite going to plan, so he steps in and tries to reassure her. "It's alright, we're not dodgy or nothing. We ain't after the kids, honest."

This doesn't quite do the job and I can almost hear her bird brain start to frantically cluck as she faces down a couple of foxes who are trying to negotiate their way into the chicken coop.

"How very reassuring," I say, shaking my head at Ollie in disbelief and repeating his reassurance to underline just how ludicrous it sounded. "You see, you can relax because we're not after the kids."

It's at this moment that I notice a familiar face over mother hen's shoulder. Normally it's nice to see familiar faces, but not in this instance, not when it's on poster and captioned "CHILDREN BEWARE - TELL A TEACHER IF YOU SEE THIS MAN". Electric stares out at us from the poster and takes a moment off scaring the kids to remind us that we're still no closer to finding his teapot.

"Well, we'll be off then. Thanks for all your help," I tell the receptionist. "Just out of curiosity, do you keep those types of records anyway?"

The receptionist slams the hatch down on this particular line of inquiry. "No!"

"Brilliant." I turn to Ollie. "Come on then Gary, let's get out of here before she breaks the panic button under the desk." And with that we leave.

We head across the playground towards the school gates. It's weird to be able to do this without having some teacher running after us, as had been our daily ritual some fifteen years earlier.

Being back on our old stamping ground, Ollie succumbs to a bit of nostalgia too.

"You know what, it only seems like yesterday my first day in this playground," he says, stopping to look around. "Remember it?"

"I do. I remember it well," I confirm. "There you were, stranger in a strange land. Recently moved here from Reading. No mates. No one to talk to. Little boy lost you were. I remember seeing you and thinking to myself, I'm gonna fucking get him, I am."

"And you did," Ollie corroborates.

"Well you were on my bench."

"Life though, it just goes so quick, don't it? I don't feel any different now to how I felt back then. I still think the same as when I was thirteen."

"Get away."

"Don't you though?"

"No! I'm a big boy now."

"You know what I mean though? What if I'm still thinking like this when I'm eighty and still as frightened of dying then as I am now? That I haven't accepted it? What happens then?" Ollie frets, wringing his hands with worry.

"I'm going to stop reading bits of the paper out to you, I really am," I sigh, but this one's burrowed its way into Ollie's brain and it's chewing through all sorts of cables.

"It's doing my head in, Bex. It really fucking is," he starts hyperventilating.

"Ollie mate, you can't dodge it. no one can. We've all got it coming one day, no matter how much muesli we eat. All you can do is lead a rich and varied life. *Carpe Diem*. Seize the fucking day," I rally, before spotting another of our old school haunts just outside the gates. "Speaking of which, you fancy a pint?"

"Oh yeah, very varied," Ollie points out.

"Well what d'you want you maudlin git, jelly and a go on the bouncy castle? Come on."

We've barely ordered our beers when my pocket starts singing to herald the break in the case we've been waiting for.

"Hello, Bat Cave?" I say, whipping out my phone and answering.

"You owe me one very expensive dinner tonight," Mel tells me triumphantly.

"Really? How's that?"

"Local antiques dealer. One conviction. Five burnt fingers. Would very much like to avoid singeing them again," Mel spells out. "He has some information."

I quickly scribble down the little squealer's details, then pat Ollie on the shoulder and once again tell him to make those pints to go.

4. The wrong arm of the law

Half an hour later I'm standing in the stock room of an old dusty antiques shop while the owner twists his legs together in knots out front and tries not to wet himself all over a Persian rug.

I don't know what it is, but I love the smell of antiques shops. Same with old book shops. They have a reassuring smell about them. They're smells from another time, aren't they? A simpler time, when coal burned in every room, clocks chimed on the hour and children looked up to their elders, not slapped them about outside MacDonald's and posted films of them doing it on youtube.com. I can see why some people withdraw from modern life and surround themselves with knickknacks of yester-year, particularly nervy individuals like the owner of this particular bou-tique, a dapper old gent called Mr Cooper, who still ironed a shirt, wore a jacket and tied a bow tie, at a time when a good percentage of the pop-ulation had all but chucked in pulling their trousers up.

He whips back the curtain and quivers a lip at me.

"He's late. You don't think he suspects something, do you?"

"Not unless you've given him reason to suspect something, Mr Cooper," I reply. "What did you tell him?"

"Just that I'd had a change of heart about the item he mentioned, that's all."

"You didn't tell him you were assisting in the recovery of the item for the original owner?"

"No," he assures me.

"Or that you're buying it out of the recovery fee?"

"Of course not."

"Or that the police would be here?" I suggest.

"I assure you Sergeant, the last thing I want is for the criminal ele-ment of this town to know that I co-operate with the police," he scoffs.

I fix the little grass in my sights. "Quite right, Mr Cooper, you can't be too careful these days."

A passing car startles the poor little lamb and he turns towards the door anxiously. He watches it with trouser-tightening trepidation as I peruse his stock on the shelves just behind his head. An attractive silver cigarette case catches my eye and I pick it up to examine the hallmark. I wonder if I should tell Mr Cooper that I suspect it of being a clue or merely confiscate it while he's not looking but manage neither in the event when Mel steps forward and slaps it out of my hand.

"I can only apologise again, Mr Cooper and promise you that I had no idea the third party would turn out to be the police," she glares.

I turn on my best *Dixon of Dock Green* and give her the full toes-up routine. "Not to worry miss. It is miss isn't it, or is it ms?"

Mel thinks on this, then decides, "I'll keep you posted."

"Well miss, all we want to do is recover the item, palm off our sus-pect with the marked notes and see where the trail leads us. It's Mr Big we're really after," I reassure her and Mr Cooper.

Mel mutters something under her breath and shakes her head, but Mr Cooper's fully onboard with the whole scheme.

"Good luck Sergeant, because I don't mind telling you this town's gone to the dogs. It's full of scumbags, it is," he tells me. Mel chuckles in agreement.

"Is that right?" I glower, mentally crossing Mr Cooper off my Christmas card list.

"It certainly is. Germs the lot of them," he spits. "Did I tell you what happened to me?"

"In mind-numbing detail, sunshine," I sigh inwardly, bracing myself for yet another retelling of the most tragic story ever told - Mr Cooper and the hooky grandfather clock.

"A house clearance, that's what the gentleman said. A house clear-ance. I do half my business with house clearance firms and trust is everything," he vents. I didn't know who'd sold Mr Cooper the clock that had landed him in the dock but if I ever found out I'd shake that fella by the hand and buy him a very large drink indeed.

Across the road, Belinda's faring little better in the van as she finds herself on the wrong end of Ollie's impressively early mid-life crisis.

"… I mean, what if at eighty, I'm all alone, no family or friends, just a telly and a tin opener," he frets, while he and Belinda stake out the front of the shop. "I'd hate that I would, to be all alone and lonely and scared and no one to look after me."

Ollie's mind skips forward to the year 2062 and he pictures himself as old man living in a shack under the Tatley to Buenos Aires high-speed rail link, with nothing but robot cats for company and he shivers at the prospect.

But Belinda's already there for him. "You won't be lonely Ollie, because I'll look after you," she promises.

"Will you?" he perks up.

"Of course, silly. And I'll have fun with you when you're bored and give you a cuddle when you're scared," she smiles. "So you don't have to worry Olly polly."

"I'd like that," Ollie smiles, for the first time in a couple of hours.

"So would I," Belinda agrees. "So it won't be too bad, will it?" A thought then occurs to her. "And you know what as well?"

"What?"

"When you're eighty, I'll still only be seventy-seven!" Belinda gleams, then licks her finger and makes a sizzling sound as she presses it against her thigh, presumably implying that her tits'll be scalding-hot in fifty-five years time, because that's what she's more likely to find down there in the latter half of the century than anything thigh-like.

Ollie finally has something to look forward to either way and he gives Belinda a grateful hug, only to cut it short when a circling motor catches his attention.

"I don't believe it!" he gawks, snatching the company binoculars up off the dashboard and pointing them at the car.

"What is it?" Belinda asks, but Ollie's too busy thumbing his mobile and watching Mr Cooper's imminent visitor park across a KEEP CLEAR box.

Back in the shop, Mr Cooper's barely paused for breath and the conversation's taken no time at all to drift into slightly soapier waters.

"… I mean, it's getting to the point where we might as well just hand our country over to this lot because they're the one's who are coming over here and taking over," he tells me, giving me an assured nod.

My ringtone stops Mr Cooper in his jackboots and I look at the little screen to see it's Ollie who's calling me.

"Holster that anecdote Mr Cooper, it's my colleague, DC… er Bennett," I tell him, then answer in character. "Hello, DS Haynes?"

The line immediately goes dead.

"He's hung up," I tell Mel, then notice a perplexed Mr Cooper looking on. "Er, would you excuse us please Mr Cooper, police business," I wink.

"Oh right, of course, yes certainly Sergeant," he arse-kisses, stepping out of the stock room for a second. I dial Ollie's number and he answers cautiously.

"Hello?"

"What are you doing hanging up?"

"I think I just phoned the police by accident," he explains.

"No Ol, you phoned me. How else would I know you just hung up?"

"Oh yeah, that's a point," it dawns on him.

"Anything you wanted, at all?" I ask.

"You're never going to guess who's just pulled up," Ollie teases.

I think on this for approximately one second and sigh.

"Not Norris. Please tell me it's not Norris."

"It's like you're psychic or something," Ollie confirms.

"I told you we should've done his place over and seen who else he's been awarding Trader of the Month to."

"Yeah well, one man's 'told you so' is another man's 'didn't do', so stick that in your arse and smoke it."

"Is he coming in here?"

"Yeah, he's just got a bag out of his boot and is heading your way now so watch yourself," Ollie rings off, then grabs one of the heavy socket wrenches off the passenger seat and hands the other to Belinda. "Ready luv?"

"Ready?" she confirms.

Inside Mr Cooper's pokey little stock room, I hear the bell above his front door tinkle, followed by the dulcet tinkles of Norris's voice.

"Alright?"

Naturally, Mr Cooper shits his pants and overdoes it on the nonchalance front to the point where he might as well be wearing a police hat himself.

"Oh yes, yes. Fine, no problem at all. Everything's absolutely fine," he giggles.

Norris stops and sniffs the air. "What's up? You had people in here asking about me?"

"What? Oh no no, of course not."

"You sure?"

"Absolutely, I'd tell you if I had," Mr Cooper hyperventilates.

"You'd better. Because if you're lying to me, dad, I'll find out. I'm connected I am. I've got a lot of friends in this town," the world's biggest no-mates presses, cracking me up in the backroom.

"I promise you. I haven't spoken to anyone about this matter, honestly," Mr Cooper insists, finally finding his feet. "On this, I give you my word."

I take this as the perfect cue to enter and swish back the stockroom curtains to dramatic effect.

"'ello 'ello 'ello, what's all this then?" I enquire.

Norris jumps out of his shellsuit with fright and his legs wobble in the direction of the door, but he quickly regains his composure when he sees it's just me and Mel.

"Oh… Oh alright Bex," he nods at me. "Bex's bird," he nods at Mel. "How's it going?"

Mr Cooper, on the other hand, is outraged. "You said you wouldn't pick him up until he was well away from here, Sergeant. You lied to me," he fumes.

Norris's brow creases. "Sergeant?"

"Oh, he thinks I'm the police," I tell him. "Little tip for you Mr Cooper, a police badge doesn't usually have *Sheriff Woody* written on it, you big blindo."

"But you gave me your word!" Mr Cooper gnashes, turning purple with outrage.

"Yeah, and we all know what that's worth, don't we, chuckles?" I remind him.

Mel steps forward to smooth the waters and assures Mr Cooper that we're not here to cause trouble for him. "We're simply trying to recover some property, that's all."

"You buying Electric's teapot back for him then?" Norris deduces.

"And not just his teapot. He wants it all back," I tell him.

This comes as news to Mel. "Hang on a minute. Electric? You told me it belonged to matey from your interview. Remember?"

I rack my brains and realise my piss poor memory's just undone yet another one of my temporary truths. "Er... yeah, funny story. You'll laugh when you hear it."

"Only if it's told over a very very expensive meal tonight. My sense of humour's been known to suffer when I eat stuff out of a basket, if you know what I mean?" Mel scowls.

"Both barrels, sweetheart," I confirm, then return to the business in hand. "So, got the stuff then?"

"You got the money?" Norris retaliates.

I invite my beautiful assistant to step forward, but Mel's still clearly got the arsehole with me. "Oh I just love it when you snap your fingers at me. It makes me go all gooey inside," she huffs, parking our attaché case on the glass counter between Norris and Mr Cooper.

Norris smirks at my little domestic but the amusement soon falls from his face when he pops open the case.

"What the fuck is this?" he asks, picking out one of the bundles of newspaper that me and Ollie had spent the afternoon cutting up - which is actually a lot more fun than you'd think.

"Oh yeah, sorry, I didn't have anything bigger - like money," I apologise.

"What? You didn't even have the cash?" Mel spots, comparing this conversation to the one we'd had in the van on the way over to pick out the inconsistencies.

I realise an explanation's in order, so I tell her, "Well, if I give him the finder's fee, then I don't get to keep it for myself, do I? You see my dilemma?"

Norris figures he'll leave us to it, so he picks up the bag he came in with and heads for the door. "Well, this has been fun. Cheerio then," he waves.

"Hand it over or I'll tell Electric who took it," I warn him.

"Even if he believes you, which he probably won't, so what? I'll just find someone else to flog my stuff to in future. He ain't the only buyer in town, you know?"

"And deal with kiss and tell merchants like Mr Cooper here?" I point out.

"I ain't handing over a two grand teapot for nothing!" Norris barks, then hotfoots it out the door to freedom.

I look at Mr Cooper and smile. "He's a nice bloke, ain't he? Well, all the best Mr Cooper. Do give my regards to the local criminal element. I'm sure I must know a few of them," I reckon, then head on out the door after Norris.

"It's probably best not to mention any of this," Mel tells Mr Cooper apologetically as she leaves. "To anyone. Ever."

I catch up with Norris, who's pulled up sharply at the sight of Ollie and Belinda wielding their socket wrenches.

"Here guess what we did?" Ollie invites.

Norris looks at what Belinda's sitting on and sees it's a pile of worn and balding Michelins, while his car balances on bricks behind them.

"What the fuck..."

"We've got you by the nuts, Mr Norris," Belinda grins with delight, opening her hand to reveal sixteen greasy wheel nuts, before threatening to drop them down the nearest drain.

"See, there you go, you wouldn't be handing Electric's stuff over for nothing. You'd be getting four wheels for your car," I tell Norris, putting a comforting arm around him. "Pretty good deal I reckon."

Norris's shoulders sag against my weight. "I tell you, all this fuss over a teapot," he tuts.

Me, Ollie, Mel, Belinda and the traffic warden placing the parking ticket on Norris's windscreen all sympathise.

5. Electric's tea leaves

We arrange to meet the girls in an hour and head over to Electric's to claim our reward. We find him in the back room, ensconced in *The Times* obituaries page, checking birth dates and death dates to see who he's done better than.

"Greetings friend, we are wise men bearing gifts - which we didn't nick in the first place, incidentally," I remind him with a theatrical flourish. It feels good to have done something that's actually going to cheer someone up for a change, so I make no bones about savouring the moment.

Electric jumps out of his chair in a fit of anxiety and demands the bag.

"Give it here. Give it here!"

I hand it over and he burrows straight to the bottom. A look of relief washes over his face when his fingers touch what he's digging for, but it ain't got handle and spout, just a face full of numbers, a couple of hands and an old leather strap.

"Funny looking teapot," I say.

"Uh? Oh that, yeah, sorry. It was the watch I wanted back really," Electric shrugs, slipping the watch into his overcoat pocket and out of sight once more.

"With you so far," I confirm.

"I just didn't want anyone knowing it. People..." Electric ponders. "Well, let's just say, people get greedy when they know they've got something of yours you want back."

"And this?" I say, pulling a delicate china teapot out of the bag.

"That? Oh that, it's worthless. A tenner at best."

It's then that I notice two dozen such identical teapots on the shelf just above Electric.

"What d'you say it was worth two grand for then?" Ollie wants to know.

"To put a block on 'em selling me watch. You don't sell an old watch for peanuts when it comes from the same haul as an antique teapot that everyone's looking for, do you? You've been in the game long enough to know that," Electric says. "No, you sit on all your old crap until you've got rid of your prize first, then you flog that stuff afterwards."

At last, the penny drops. "Yeah, and bloke hocking a priceless white elephant all over town makes a hell of a lot of noise don't he?" I say.

Electric smiles smugly. "That he does."

"So how much is your watch worth then?" Ollie wants to know.

"Nothing really. At least not to you. But my dad give it to me in 1940 just before he went overseas. It's the only thing I've got to remember him by," Electric laments.

"Oh," Ollie says. "France was it? Where you dad went?"

"What? No, Canada. There was a bloody war going on in France."

"You know, I do hope none of this affects that monkey I heard so much about for your teapot's safe return," I interrupt.

Electric just smiles apologetically. "Maybe next time son."

"I don't believe this..."

"Hey, I'm the victim here," Electric insists.

"I tell you, all this fuss over a teapot," I say, then remember it wasn't actually the teapot, it was the watch. "Sod it, we ain't got time for this, the girls are waiting for us at Swanky McPricey's Oyster Bar in town and we're both potless. I tell you, it's going to be fun and games when the bill turns up," I say, turning to leave. "And I'll tell you another thing old man, we'll have some gear for you next week and we are so not haggling over it."

I stomp through the shop and back out into the sunlight. Electric's shop doesn't smell like Mr Cooper's shop. It doesn't have a reassuring aroma from yesteryear. It just smells like Electric. And seeing as I've known Electric for almost five years and have never seen him in a different shirt, I'll leave it to you to guess what that smells like.

Ollie emerges five seconds later clutching a memento.

"He gave me his teapot."

"What a result," I say, glad that it was all worth it then.

"You never know, Norris might give us a few quid for it if he still thinks it's valuable."

"Huh, as funny as that would be, I think I've had just about enough of this particular stream of karma for one day."

"And so what about Electric?"

"You win some, you lose some. Today we just lost some. Chalk it up to experience."

"So that's it is it, we're just going to let him get away with it?"

"Oh no, I wouldn't say that. I'm an extremely bad loser, you know."

I step back from Electric's window and show Ollie my handiwork. Against the glass I've stuck one of the posters we saw at the school earlier featuring the efit of Electric and warning; "CHILDREN BEWARE - TELL A TEACHER IF YOU SEE THIS MAN".

"Should get the locals chatting if nothing else."

"Nice," Ollie agrees.

We head off round the corner and up the hill, kicking pebbles and wondering just what we're going to tell the girls when we knock on the window of the restaurant they're sat in and point to the chippy across the road. I notice Ollie deep in thought and I have half an idea what about.

"Mildly surprised you didn't ask Electric if he spends his evenings sitting around in his hat and coat waiting for everything to go black," I say.

Ollie agrees. "I wonder if he does though."

"Nah, I expect he's far too busy laughing his socks off about us to find the time mate."

"He must be worried though. It must be on his mind. I mean, how could it not be when you get to his age?" Ollie says, then hands me the teapot and sprints off up the road."

"What are you doing now?"

Ollie points to an old lady who's just come out of the Post Office and tells me he just wants to ask her something. "For fuck's sake," I grumble as I watch him stop the old dear and press her for reassurances that everything's going to be alright when he's her age.

"Well? How was she, alright?" I ask him, when he eventually returns.

"I don't know, I think she's a bit batty," Ollie says, scratching his head. "Look, she gave me her purse."

"Why she do that? What d'you say to her?"

"Nothing, honest. I just asked her if she was scared, that's all. I said I would be if I was her, I'd be terrified in her shoes, and before I could say anything else, she gave me her purse and told me to take it."

An uneasy feeling comes over me as Ollie begins searching the purse for answers.

"Yeah, I think you may've just mugged her, mate," I point out.

Ollie looks at me as if I haven't been paying attention and tells me again. "No! I was just asking her if she was scared, that's all. I was just..." an internal plonk cuts short his explanation and the colour drains from Ollie's face. "Oh shit, I think I have, haven't I?"

"Come on, Let's go give it back to her, shall we? Before I start wondering how much is inside it."

We turn the corner to catch up with Ollie's unintended victim but pull up sharply when we see she's got company. Some burly beat copper with truncheon and pepper spray is trying to make sense of her hysterical ramblings when he spots us clutching her purse.

"Oi you, come here!" he yells, but we're already on our toes and legging it as fast as we can away from the sounds of an angry set of police issue boots, seven pound fifty in loose change exploding from the old lady's purse and a worthless white elephant of a teapot meeting its maker across the pavement behind us.

THE FOOTBALLER JOB

1. Scratch and sniffle

Once upon a time, there was a handsome young prince, who signed for Arsenal for just over eight million quid from St Etienne. At first, the local townsfolk were wary of this new prince because no one had ever heard of him before, and despite rumours he'd set his last kingdom alight with a twenty-five goals a season for the last three seasons, that counted for little with Arsenal's townsfolk because who the fuck were they over there anyway? If you see what I mean.

So it was with miserable resignation that the Gunner's faithful trotted out to welcome their new star the following Saturday afternoon against Blackburn Rovers. And although the town's criers heralded the arrival of a major new talent, the townsfolk knew, to a man, that this prince was just going to turn out to be the latest in a long line of jokers.

In fact, the prince turned out not to be a prince at all - but a wizard. We were seventy minutes into a stunningly dour nil-nil when the prince caught everyone by surprise by actually scoring. It was a weird sort of goal, one which ricocheted around the box like a pinball, but it was the prince who finally stuck a toe on it and bundled it over the line to put us in front. It was almost too good to be true.

But then things went from good to unbelievable when five minutes later he launched a free-kick into the penalty area, only to see it rebound off the goalie and into the net. We were two-nil up and cruising. It was now that the prince dipped into his box of tricks and astonished the faithful with an awe inspiring display of wizardry and finesse, the likes of which we'd not seen in red and white for a good long while, sending us home three-nil winners.

It had been a fairy tale debut for Prince Claude Delacroix.

For the next two seasons I, along with the rest of the Arsenal faithful, flocked to Highbury to pay homage to our prince, and with every passing match his status rose a little until eventually we were no longer worshipping a prince, we were worshipping a God.

But then, you know what they say; you should never meet your Gods, as you'll only ever be disappointed. And such was the case with Claude Delacroix. And how his star would tumble as a consequence.

"Hey you, get away from there," Claude shouts when he leaves the newsagents and sees some kid on a bike peering into the window of his precious Lamborghini - his handle bar perilously close to Claude's brilliant yellow paintwork.

"I'm only looking at it mate," the kid retorts without backing away, so Claude grabs his bike and forcibly dumps him back four feet. "Oi!" the kid objects, but Claude's not a man who likes his stuff messed with, especially not when it cost more than this kid would earn in a lifetime of shovelling chips.

"Go on, get, allez allez!" Claude shoos, warning the kid away with the back of his hand. "Don't touch what you can't afford. This car cost one hundred thousand pounds, you know. Is very expensive."

The lecture adjourned, Claude turns to climb into his chariot when he spots a tiny scratch on the door, roughly where the kid's brake lever was a second ago. It's microscopic, almost invisible, but it's definitely there. A scratch.

A scratch on his brand new Lamborghini!

That little bastard!!!

"Hey you, you do this to my car?" Claude asks, near apoplectic with disbelief.

The kid squints at where Claude's pointing, but just shrugs with confusion. "I never touched it, mate."

"You touched my car?" is all Claude hears.

"No, I said I never..." the kid objects, but it's too late. Not for the first time, Claude's famous temperament is making him see red.

"You touch my car," he declares with wide-eyed fury, "then I touch your bike!" And with that, he spills the kid onto the pavement and starts stamping on his front wheel.

"You like that? Huh? You like that?" Claude asks, but the kid most definitely does not and begs Claude to stop. But Claude's deaf to all pleas of mercy and holds the kid at bay until he's finished the reshaping job he's started.

"Please, don't, you're breaking it, please," sobs the kid, but Claude's in his stride by this point and there's no suddenly stopping him...

... particularly when he spots the canal opposite the shop.

He lifts the bike and marches purposely towards it, the kid hanging onto his coat every step of the way.

"No please, what are you doing? Please give it back. Please mate, don't," he cries, but before he knows it, his bike is over the railings and dangling over open water.

"Look and learn," Claude smirks, then lets it go.

"Nooo!" the kid shouts, as he watches his bike turn over and over in the air before crashing into the oily waters.

"Whoa, that made a good splash, no?" Claude grins. He turns to the little vandal and gives him an affectionate pat around the chops and a wag of the finger. "Hey, you mess with my stuff, I mess with yours. Au revoir kid."

The black surface of the canal churns and bubbles as the kid's bike sinks to the murky bottom, taking his guts with it. Behind him, Claude jumps into his precious Lamborghini and tears up the road with a triumphant roar.

The kid doesn't turn to look.

Not even when Claude gives him a toot.

2. Golden opportunities

Some days later, Saturday night to be precise, I'm standing at the bar of Glitzy's nightclub with my beloved Mel. Mel's looking off across the club and frowning as she watches Belinda shake her money-maker in the prestigious VIP Gold Lounge.

"You think Belinda's looking to get it tonight?" Mel finally asks.

"I don't know, that's Ol's department. I'm just the bloke in charge of making sure you get it tonight," I reassure her.

Mel thinks on this. "If by it you mean the cab fare home and the mop and bucket after you've honked up all over the stairs again then I have every faith in you."

"Yeah well, the work's it's own reward, in' it?" I smile, before handing Mel her drink. "There you go, for madam."

"Funny looking glass of Chardonnay," Mel says, reluctantly accepting the pint of Guinness I'm handing her.

"Leave it out, how am I meant to reach the Chardonnay from here?" I reply, keeping an eye on the bar staff at the other end of the bar as I go ahead and pour myself one as well.

"I don't know," Mel ponders. "How do other people reach it?"

"Believe me luv, if I had money, I'd spend it on you."

It's then that Mel spots the pattern in the creamy white head of her pint. "I see you still managed to do the shamrock though."

Not bad considering it was only my third attempt. My mate Keith down The Badger has been pouring pints most of his adult life and no one can make head nor tail of the weird shapes he scribbles in their stout.

"Anyway, getting back to Belinda," Mel says. "I'm not sure Ollie is in charge of his particular department."

"Hmm?" I hmm, then realise what Mel's getting at when I see one of her eyebrows making a dash for her hairline. "Ah no, Belinda's not like that no more."

"You sound like Ollie," Mel points out.

"Well, it's the party line in' it?"

"What, Belinda's home phone number?"

"Now now, retract those claws and be nice," I chide.

"Do you think you should pop outside and have a word with Ollie?" Mel suggests, as Belinda screeches with delight and disappears from view inside a burst of dry ice.

I think seriously on this one for a moment before concluding that this probably wouldn't improve the situation.

"No, I don't think so. He doesn't like being disturbed while he's working. He takes his job very seriously you know."

Mel turns her attention away from the Gold Lounge and looks around the rest of the club, which is almost empty by comparison.

"You don't say."

When it comes to nightclub security, Ollie operates a strictly zero tolerance approach to admission. As effective as this is at heading off trouble, it does somewhat jar against the basic principles of business, but Ollie doesn't concern himself with the nitty-gritty. He has a simple philosophy and it goes something like this; "If the manager had wanted his club full of beer boys, scrubbers and riff-raff, he wouldn't have employed me to keep them out now, would he?"

And so, armed with this single truth, Ollie has spent the last week standing at the head of an enormous line of people outside Glitzy's boosting the profits of every other pub, club and wine bar in the immediate surrounding area.

"No," he says, barely even looking up from his clipboard to afford the next punter a glance. The guy and his mate move off without saying a word and are welcomed with open arms and a free promotional cocktail in The Funky Hippo across the street.

"No," Ollie repeats, turning away a whole gang of lads with smoking pockets courtesy of all the end-of-week cash they're carrying. They too drift off and successfully empty them into El Gringo's cash register just up the High Street.

"Not a chance," Ollie snorts at his next hopeful, shaking his head derisively. This gets the hopeful's goat up good and proper and he's in no mood to shuffle off without a decent explanation.

"Why, what's wrong with me?" he demands, holding himself open to the light to show that he's tucked in his shirt, polished his shoes and ironed his trousers.

"Well, if you don't know by now mate, I can't help you," Ollie tells the trouble-maker, committing his face to memory for future reference.

"You're nothing but a jumped-up little power junkie, you are? You're no better than the Nazis," the hopeful shouts over his shoulder as he heads off into Saturday night.

Ollie calls after him. "That's right mate. And you're barred for life." Ollie turns just in time to catch the next punter looking at him in a funny way. A capital offence if ever there was one. "You too mush. Go on, hop it," he tells him.

It's at this point that Glitzy's' manager, Mr Andrews, decides to pop upstairs to see why his club's full of air on a Saturday night when the number one weekend pursuit in this two-horse town is getting paralytic and fingered on dance floors.

The moment he pokes his head out of the door though, Ollie spots him and wonders how he let someone that ancient get by him.

"Oi Granddad, out of there..." he starts to say, before recognising the worried brow of his employer. "Oh, sorry Mr Andrews, didn't see it was you," he apologises.

"What the hell's going on out here?" demands Mr Andrews. "Can you please let some people in before I go bankrupt?"

"Sorry Mr Andrews, I was just trying to keep the place a little selective, if you know what I mean," he winks.

"There's no one in there for Chrissakes!"

"Well, give the place a bit of chic and you'll have no end of punters trying to get in before you know it," winks Ollie.

"I've got no end of punters trying to get in now, you moron!" fumes Mr Andrews. "What d'you think the all-night happy-hour and free sausage & chips are all about? Just something to put on the posters?"

"Well, if you're not bothered what sort of place you run..." Ollie starts but Mr Andrews cuts him off with a frustrated wave of the fist.

"An open place bonehead! An open place. Now start letting people in and leave putting me out of business to my rivals for one evening, will you?"

Ollie watches Mr Andrews storm back inside, his words ringing in his ears, and turns back to face the queue of freshly optimistic clubbers.

"Come on then," he reluctantly sighs, stepping aside to admit the masses.

A torrent of flesh and hair gel begins pouring past Ollie, but the place has still got some standards, so the oily bozo with the unnervingly attractive date gets a reality check when Ollie grabs him by the collar and points him back towards the street.

"Yeah, not you mate, off you go," he advises.

*

Inside the club, Mel's making an effort to have a 'serious' conversation with me.

"Actually, I've something of a confession to make. I brought you here for a reason tonight," she says.

"You're pregnant?" I splutter into my pint.

"No."

"You're dumping me?"

"No!"

"You're in love with another man?"

"What?"

"Another girl?"

"Stop guessing, Bex."

"Oh go on then, what is it?" I give in.

"I want you to do me a favour."

"Oh luv, honestly, I'm waiting for a management position to come up..." I try to tell her, but this is a different 'serious' conversation.

"No Adrian, this is about Wayne."

"What, your little spanner nephew who had his bike thrown in the river?" I chuckle gleefully. Misfortune's always funnier when it befalls

135

someone else.

"Cousin. He's my spanner cousin," Mel corrects me. "Anyway, you know I told you it was one of Charlie's clients who did it?"

"Yeah."

"Well, he's here tonight. The client I mean."

"So?" I say, not liking the sound of this one little bit.

"Can you have a word with him for me?"

"I thought he paid for the bike?"

"He did, but this isn't just about money, you know," Mel says, evidently forgetting who she's talking to.

"Oh please, don't give me some old twaddle about this being about self-respect. He's thirteen years old for God's sake. He probably still thinks lighting his own farts and stuffing mud down his pants is a great way to meet girls."

"This is about self-respect, Adrian," Mel insists. "That overgrown ape took Wayne's away and only an apology can restore it."

"Yeah, that's right, then afterwards, perhaps we can all sit in a circle, hold hands and talk about the pets we've lost," I sigh. "Or backed over."

But Mel's got her teeth into this one and she's not for shaking.

"Please," she pouts.

As reluctant as I am to get embroiled in this whole bucket of bats, I'm equally not sure I could face the consequences of politely declining, not when she's in this sort of mood, so I unhook my St Christopher and slip it into my pocket, then ask Mel how big this bloke it then.

"No Adrian, I just want you to talk to him," Mel insists.

"That's all I was going to do, but talking to R2D2's stunt double's a lot easier than talking to someone who bangs their head going through the Channel Tunnel, if you know what I mean," I point out, psyching myself up for my impending 'talk'.

Mel frowns at me, then lands a bombshell on me. "It's Claude Delacroix."

"What? Arsenal's Claude Delacroix?" I can scarcely believe. "He's in here?" I turn and look in the direction of the Gold Lounge and see the man, nay the Prince, large as ninepence and up to his cuffs in flesh. "Hang on, that's who Belinda's with," I suddenly spot.

"Will you talk to him?" Mel asks.

"Yeah, of course, no problem," I enthuse.

"No, about Wayne, I mean? I can't because of my job."

"What? Oh yeah, leave it with me," I promise her, then it occurs to me that Mel's been holding out on me for the last couple of years. "Here, you never told me Charlie represented Claude. Why not? You know how nutty I am about 'the Arse'."

"Why? Because Delacroix's the most arrogant hateful scumbag I've ever met - and remember I've met all your mates; including that bloke who blew his wife's life savings paying for prostitutes to cry in front of him."

I have a think. "That weren't my mate. That was my uncle."

"Yeah well, the point stands. And Delacroix's even worse. So the prospect of begging him for free tickets and locks of his hair every other week didn't really appeal to me, to be honest."

"Oh, thank you very much. Very kind of you. You can lean across the bar and get your own fucking drinks from now on."

"Seriously, it wouldn't have done any good anyway. He's a total arsehole. He can't even bring himself to look anyone else in the eye, not unless they're another footballer, his agent, his bank manager or some bimbo who's begging him for sex. He thinks the rest of us are scum, the mud on his boots at the end of a match."

"Yeah well, I can see his point. I mean, even I look down on half this lot," I agree with Claude.

"You'll see what I mean," Mel nods knowingly.

"Just out of curiosity then, if this bloke's such a cock smoker, what chance have I got of getting an apology out of him?" I point out, rising to leave.

"Not much," Mel admits. "But no one'll even ask him, not even Charlie, because he's the great Claude Delacroix and we can't risk upsetting a hero of our times now, can we?"

"Well he is a God," I point out.

"Kicking a ball into a net doesn't make you a God," Mel disagrees.

"It does if you do it twenty-five times a season, including twice against 'the scum'," I explain.

"Who are 'the scum'?" Mel asks.

I think about this seriously for a sec. "Well, pretty much anyone who isn't Arsenal really."

I saunter over the Gold Lounge and find Roland manning the entrance. Roland's not really one of life's natural bouncers, but he leapt at the chance to work here when he found out he'd be in constant radio contact with Ollie.

"Alright Rollo, how's it going?" I ask.

"Pretty sweet, now that you come to mention it," Roland replies, currently chuffed to bits with life.

"Top work. Keep it up," I congratulate him, then continue sauntering on my way.

"Here hold up, where are you going?" Roland says, barring my progress.

"In there," I tell him.

"No Bex, that's the Gold Lounge. You have to be a Gold Club Member to go in there," Roland quibbles.

"I am a Gold Club Member though," I explain.

Roland looks relieved. "Oh, are you. Right okay," he says and is about to step aside when he thinks better of it. "Er, can I see your Gold card then?"

"Well I haven't got it on me, have I? It's in my wallet at home."

"Oh, sorry then Bex, then I can't let you in. I could get in trouble if I did," Roland shrugs.

"Rollo, don't be a plum."

"I have to I'm afraid, it's me job."

I realise there's no point in trying to reason with an immovable object, so I make a deal.

"Look, I'll tell you what, I'll give you twenty quid if you let me in for just five minutes. I've just gotta do something."

Roland chews on his lip and looks around the club for Mr Andrews, but fortunately the coast's clear. "Okay, but only five minutes, alright?"

"Cheers Rollo," I say and try to make my way past him again but the big doughnut's still standing in my way.

"Here, where's the twenty?"

"Rollo, didn't I just tell you I'd left my wallet at home?"

Roland folds his arms and shakes his head. "I'm sorry Bex, but I can't let you in."

This is more than a trifle annoying, so I fire off a few home truths before departing. "You've changed, you have. You used to be cool."

I'm already halfway across the club when I hear Roland calling back after me apologetically; "I'm still cool!"

"That was quick," Mel says when I get back to the table.

"I haven't seen him yet. Fucking Ginger Haystacks wouldn't let me in," I fume, then realise a way around this particular impasse. "Here, back in a sec. Just nipping outside."

Ollie's all but chucked in the towel as far as tonight's clientele's concerned, though there is still one face that immediately gets him snatching up the braided rope and barring the doors again.

"No no, sorry no."

Norris blinks at him in confusion. "What?"

"You can't come in. Off you go," Ollie spells out.

"Don't be an arse," Norris replies, trying to squeeze between Ollie and the wall to get at the club, but Ollie plugs the gap.

"You're not coming in."

"Ollie, let me in."

"Sorry Norris, if it was up to me..."

"It is up to you," Norris points out.

"You're right. Get lost."

I find Ollie and Norris still locking horns when I poke my head around the door and ask how things are going.

"Oh fine," Ollie replies. "Just saving the ladies' handbags inside."

Norris has never been so insulted in all his life, which I find hard to believe.

"Oi, I resent that. I ain't here to steal no handbags. I just want a drink," Norris insists.

"What's wrong with the places down the road then?" Ollie asks.

"Well I'm barred from all 'em, in' I?" Norris explains.

"What for?" asks Ollie rhetorically.

Norris sucks on his lip for a moment. "Never mind about that, you gonna let us in or what?"

"No."

Norris searches his soul and decides there's nothing else for it but to resort to sincerity. "Look, I promise I ain't here to steal no handbags, honestly. I swear on me mum's life. May she be struck down and die a thousand terrible deaths if I lie."

"You ain't coming in," Ollie repeats for the umpteenth time.

"Alright, how about I give you a cut of anything I make?" Norris proposes.

"Shouldn't you be getting home to see how your old mum is, Norris?" I suggest.

Norris curls up a lip in defiance. "Ah, sod you then. Didn't want to come into your stupid club anyway," he mopes, flicking us a finger and trudging off towards the High Street.

"Well then, that worked out nicely for everyone, didn't it?" Ollie calls after him, before looking at me. "Anyway, what do you want? I'm working."

"I need a favour. Claude Delacroix's in the Gold Lounge and I need..."

"Who?"

"Claude Delacroix. He plays for Arsenal. What is this total blank you have about football, Ol?"

"Well, it's a bit gay isn't it. Lot of men chasing each other around a field, kissing, cuddling and having baths together with their mates," Ollie says, nodding at me knowingly.

"Yeah, coming from a bloke who sits around in pink trousers watching cowboys getting off with each other," I point out.

"For the last time, my jeans are red and they faded. And it was you who told me to get *Brokeback Mountain* out if I liked a good Western," Ollie reminds me, which is true and something that brought me a lot of pleasure. "Oh, I'm glad you think it's funny because my dad's banned me from picking films for DVD Wednesday thanks to you."

"Anyway, never mind about that," I tell him "Get on your Bat Radio and tell Meatloaf Weasley in there to let us into the Gold Lounge, will ya?"

"Bex, the Gold Lounge is for Gold Club Members."

"Oh don't you start. What is it with you these days? You've changed. You used to be cool."

Me and Ollie have known each other for fifteen years, so we know each other about as well as two people can know each other. Certainly well enough to spot when the other's tactics change mid-gambit.

"You got that one out a bit early didn't you?" Ollie spots.

"Well I'm pressed for time here, in' I? So are you going to help us out or not?"

"Not. If you want to pay the Gold membership fee and..." he starts, but he's having a laugh in' he?

"Oh give over, I only want to go in there for five minutes. I'm not paying £500 just for that, am I?"

"Well I can't help you then," my best mate shrugs.

"Ollie, I'm doing this for you," I tell him.

Ollie looks dubious. "Me?"

"Of course. Look, Belinda's in there dancing her arse off and sooner or later Claude's going to whisk her off to the bog for forty-five minutes each way," I spook him.

"He what?" Ollie duly jumps.

"No no, calm down. She's fine for the mo, but you know what she's like after four bottles of champagne," I wink, only to have to hold him back when he tries charging into the club. "Ollie, don't be a spanner. If you go in there and kick off, Belinda'll get the right hump, won't she? Just let me go in and have a quiet word with her, okay?" I say, then indicate over his shoulder. "Besides, your handbags aren't safe yet."

Ollie looks and sees Norris lurking in the shadows by the rear of the club waiting for his chance.

"Go on, call Roland," I suggest. "He'll listen to you, he likes you."

"Oh really? I hadn't noticed," Ollie reckons, then speaks into his radio. "Roland? It's Ol."

Roland comes back loud and clear. "Hey Big Guy. How's it going?"

"I only spoke to him five minutes ago," Ollie points out before continuing his communiqué. "Yeah pretty good, Rollo."

"Here Ol, d'you want to come over to mine tomorrow night? I got out that *Brokeback Mountain* film you like," Roland enthuses.

Ollie glares at me as he replies. "No, I'm cool Rollo. Here look, let Bex into the lounge, will ya?"

But Roland's surprisingly uncooperative. "I can't do that, Ol."

"Just for five minutes. Special dispensation. It'll be fine," Ollie tells him, but Roland's not biting so I punch him in the arm and tell him to up the ante. Ollie frowns. "I'll consider it a personal favour Rollo."

"Okay. Anything for you, Big Guy," Roland agrees, then inserts a pre-condition. "And you'll come over tomorrow then, yeah?"

Ollie wrestles with himself and grits his teeth before answering.

"Yeah, alright. But we ain't watching anything even vaguely arty, you hear me?" Ollie tells him in no uncertain terms, before pocketing his radio. "Go on then, go and rescue Belinda. And then tomorrow night, you swing by Rollo's and you rescue me. You hear?"

"Absolutely," I agree, though I make a mental note not to be too early. See how he likes some of that for £500 for five minutes. Fucking arsehole.

I find Claude in the corner of the Gold Lounge tucking into some wannabe WAG who's all but sucking him off with her eyes.

It's weird meeting famous people. Weird and slightly confusing. Because there they are, as familiar as an old friend, with all that history behind them from a relationship stretching back years as far as you're concerned, but wearing a look of complete and utter incomprehension because they don't know you from Adam. And usually don't want to. It must be slightly disconcerting from their point of view too I guess, having a never-ending procession of total strangers asking you how it's going and phoning you up in the middle of the night as soon as your telephone numbers get posted on the internet. But then that's just the price of fame I guess. If these celebrities didn't want to be bugged and bothered by every cunt in the universe then surely they would've got jobs in WHSmiths in order not to get noticed by all us strangers and nutjobs.

I park myself next to Claude and launch straight into my hastily ordered schpiel before he gives me the slip amongst his WAG's thighs.

"Alright Claude, not interrupting am I? Here look, first off, I just have to say I'm a massive Gunners fan. Haven't missed a game in years - well, I missed six months once but that was just cos the judge was in bad mood. Anyway, I just wanted to say that you've been the dog's sausages for the last two seasons, so I know you won't mind if I ask you a small favour."

Claude eventually pulls his face out of his lady friend's tits and turns it a fraction of a degree my way.

"How did you get in here?" he asks.

"Oh, I'm a mate of the bouncer," I tell Claude, hoping that'll cut some mustard with him.

"What do you want?" he murmurs, already sinking back into her cleavage.

"Well look, my girlfriend's nephew is the kid who's bike you chucked into the river and..." I tell him and this does get his attention.

"That is with my lawyer," he snaps.

"Oh yeah, I know, no problem. And between you and me I don't blame you mate, I would've done exactly the same if the little fucker had scratched my motor too."

"Then what do you want?" he repeats.

"Well look, he's just a little kid. Ain't got no mates, still wets the bed more than likely. All he wants is an apology really."

"I paid for the bike," Claude says.

"Oh yeah, I know and that was great and everything, very generous, it's just that my bird was hoping..."

But Claude is more interested in what his bird's hoping for than mine and immediately goes on the attack. "If he wants trouble, I will instruct my lawyer to tear up the cheque."

"No, he don't want no trouble or nothing. He just wants..."

"Wants what? Me to get down on my knees and beg for forgiveness? Ha!" he laughs theatrically, snapping his fingers and summoning Roland.

"Sorry Bex, but you're gonna have to go," Roland apologises.

"No problem Rollo. Anyway, nice to meet you Claude. Give her one for me." The WAG winks to assure me that this is a cast-iron nailed-on cert and I leave the Gold Lounge through a sea of war-paint caked faces all watching like hawks for the first opportunity to steal Claude from under her.

Mel's waiting for me outside the Gold Lounge entrance with an expectant look in her eyes.

"Well. How d'you get on? What did he say?"

I hate to see Mel disappointed so I decide to salvage the evening by giving her a bit of flannel.

"Yeah, no problem. He's going to do Wayne a full written apology."

Mel seems surprised by this. "Really? How the hell did you get him to agree to that?"

"I dunno. I guess I'm just fantastic," I tell her.

Roland watches us drift off into the depths of the club, then something else catches his attention off to one side. A long, unravelled coat hanger is twisting through a little fan vent in a nearby side window. Roland watches it circle the window frame and eventually find the catch. A quick yank of the wire pops the catch and the window open and Norris clambers through a moment later, finding his feet just in front of Roland.

"Alright?" Norris says, when he sees Roland blinking at him.

"Alright," Roland replies.

"Can I go in there?" Norris asks, pointing at the golden doorway just behind Roland.

"No, this is the Gold Lounge," Roland shrugs.

"Alright, see ya," Norris says, moving off into the rest of the club.

"Yeah, see ya," Roland calls after him.

3. Enemy at the gates

"Can you really forge Delacroix's signature?" Ollie asks, as I carefully copy Delacroix's scrawl off a football sticker and onto the note I've just written.

"Yeah, enough to fool some thirteen-year-old spanner with water in his handle bars, I reckon. I mean, I ain't flogging it to Sotheby's or nothing," I tell him, finishing the job just as the school bell rings across the road.

Ollie drums the steering wheel he's holding a couple of times then asks if I'd do him one as well then.

"God, you're not still on about losing your job, are you?"

"Oh I'm sorry, am I boring you?" Ollie apologises.

"Trust me, it's just a temporary set back," I tell him.

"Oh yeah, and what makes you so sure?"

"Just how many blokes do you think there are in this town who want to stay sober on a Saturday night? Don't worry, you'll be back in there before you know it," I promise, but Ollie's still smarting.

"I'm a mate of the bouncer's," he mimics, shaking his head and muttering to himself under his breath.

A knock on the side window kills the moment and me and Ollie turn to see some nosey young biddy miming at me to wind it down, so I give the handle a bit of exercise and ask her what's up.

"Erm, excuse me, but are you waiting for your children or something?" she pries.

"No, we're waiting for yours," Ollie replies, before I have a chance to open my gob.

Unsurprisingly, our young biddy's features stretch to the four corners of her face and she rushes off in near hysterics to alert the rest of the herd that there are a couple of lions lurking in the long grass.

I turn to Ollie, who's looking particularly pleased with himself.

"What d'you say that for, you big fuckwit?"

"I'm only having a laugh with her. Honestly, some people have got no sense of humour," Ollie dismisses.

"I'll try and remember that when the neighbours roll up with pitchforks and burning torches," I tell him, looking to see where the young biddy's got to before spotting Wayne in the crowd. "Here, here he is."

I jump out of the van and wave across the road at him. "Oi Wayne!"

Wayne spots us and comes over. "Alright Bex?" he says, then looks at Ollie. "Einstein?"

"How's your bike?" Ollie retaliates.

I don't know what it is with these two. Wayne likes Ollie alright, but he likes needling him as well. Probably because he's an easy touch and Wayne's practicing for later life. You know what young cubs are like.

"Now now you two," I separate. "Here look, Mel told us what happened, so we went and saw Claude and he's absolutely gutted about it and everything. Really upset he is."

Wayne looks devastated. "Oh no, poor bloke." Piss-taking little fuck.

"Yeah well anyway, he asked me to give you this by way of an apology," I say, digging the note out of my pocket and handing it to Wayne.

"*Dear Wayne*," Wayne reads, "*sorry about chucking your bike in the canal. All the best...*" he screws up in face and looks at me. "I can't read what the rest of it says."

"It says Claude Delacroix. It's his signature," I tell him.

"No it doesn't," he looks again.

"It does."

"It doesn't."

"It does," I insist, pulling the football sticker out of my pocket and comparing my effort to Claude's official signature. "See. It's the same."

Wayne compares the two. "Oh yeah, very convincing."

It's at this point that I realise I've been rumbled.

"Oh well look, that's not the only reason we're here. How d'you like a new bike?" I offer.

"You're going to buy us new a bike?"

"That's right. We've got our credit card right here," Ollie winks, opening his jacket to show Wayne a set of bolt cutters. "I never leave home without it."

"Yeah, then we split the cheque three ways, what d'you reckon?" I nod.

Little Lord Fauntleroy's not keen though. "I don't want you nicking me someone else's bike," he snaps. "All I want is a replacement for mine and an apology from the twat who threw it in the river."

"It's not like we're not trying, Wayne," I point out, then decide this isn't going at all according to plan. "Oh look, d'you want a lift home then? We've got some puppies in the van."

"Gonna try and flog me one are you?" Wayne retorts, so I put him in a head lock and mess up his hair because he likes it when I do this. Or doesn't. Can't remember which.

Anyway, just as we're all climbing into the van, Ollie's mate, the nosey young biddy, comes tearing over with the royal arsehole screaming at us to stop and trying to block the van with her body.

"Stop! Stop! Quick, somebody call the police! Help! Help!" she's yelling, so I tell her to keep her hair on and calm down.

"It's alright, we know him. He's my girlfriend's nephew," I tell her.

"Cousin," Wayne corrects me.

"What? Oh yeah, keep forgetting. Anyway, he's cool, we know him," I reassure her.

Wayne peers out of the van and for one silly moment I think he's

144

going to corroborate what I've just said, but instead he just smiles at her and says; "They're going to put me on the internet."

I've been operating on the wrong side of the law for a few years you know, so I've seen a lot of speeding police cars in my time, but I don't think I've ever seen so many descend on one area so quickly in all my life. And it's a good job they did too, because I don't think there would've been much left of me and Ollie if the boys hadn't got there when they did. So much yelling. So much van rocking. So many snarling murderous faces trying to get into the van. If the world's ever taken over by zombies, like in that film, *Dawn of the Dead*, I'll be one step ahead of the rest of you lot because I've already seen what it's like, though I can't say it's something I'm particularly looking forward to.

"I tell you, between the two of you, it's a wonder there's a square inch of me left that hasn't got a tag on it," I fume, as the Old Bill tries to disperse the last clutch of hardcore vigilantes.

"It was only a joke," Wayne shrugs. "Honestly, some people have got no sense of humour."

"Here, that's what I said," Ollie agrees.

Weasel approaches and tells PC Bennett to take our cuffs off and let us go.

"Well, that's the worst of it calmed down, but I'd give the school run a miss for a few weeks if I was you, Bex," he grins.

"Cheers Tom, don't worry, we will. This little comedian can pour himself some Ready Brek the next time it's slashing it sideways with cats and dogs," I glower.

"Chip off the old gobby block are you son?" Weasel asks Wayne, committing his face to memory for future reference.

"I'm nothing to do with him. He's just banging my cousin," Wayne replies, earning himself a few mental notes in the margin.

"See what I mean. Kids today, they've got no respect," I despair, but Weasel's not giving up.

"How old are you, Wayne?"

Wayne chuckles. "Why, you want to bombard me with emails pretending to be the same age or something?"

"Adorable, in' he?" I say when I see the look on Weasel's face.

"Yeah, little git. Go on, sling your hook, all three of you."

This doesn't go down well with the crowd though, particularly the young hysterical biddy who didn't 'get' Ollie and Wayne.

"You're not letting them go, are you? You have to arrest them. You have to take them to the police station!" she rants, indulging in a spot of the nation's favourite pastime, ie. telling the Old Bill their job.

"Don't worry luv, your kids are at no risk from these two," Weasel tries to appease her. "Your purse and your handbag however? Now they're a different matter."

But our young biddy's determined to have the arsehole over something today and she turns on Weasel in a heartbeat.

"Don't you call me luv, you condescending prick!" she snaps, rounding on Weasel like Emmeline Pankhurst up on blocks. Weasel looks at me as if to ask what he's done.

"You want to run her in, Tom, she seems like a trouble maker."

"Here," Ollie says, joining in with the objections. "I don't nick handbags. I protect them."

4. A bit later in the pub

"Nice note. I could've done this myself," Mel says, inspecting my handiwork, as we sink a few in The Badger.

"Well why didn't you then?"

"Because we don't want a badly forged apology from you. We want proper apology from Delacroix."

"Yeah," Wayne joins in, looking up from the pool table just long enough to give his cousin a vote of support, before potting two reds and knocking my easy yellow safe. Cunt.

"Well get used to it, because forty-grand-a-week means never having to say you're sorry," I tell them.

"Blimey, imagine being on forty-grand-a-week?" Belinda muses from behind her curly straw.

"I can't even imagine being on a forty-quid-a-week, not now, thanks to my best mate over there," Ollie gripes miserably, determined to chew this particular bone in two.

"Look, fair's fair Ol, you did tell Rollo to let a non-member into the Gold Lounge. You really can't have any complaints," I say, giving him a taster of the needle he's been giving me these last two days.

"Yeah, got me sacked an' all Ol," Roland empathises.

"No Rollo, you were sacked because you were found asleep on top of everyone's coats," Ollie points out.

"Well I have trouble staying up past midnight, don't I?" Roland whines.

"Yeah, the fact remains that we still haven't got an apology out of Delacroix," Mel interrupts.

"Oh let it go. Jesus, just because he threw your bike in the river and got you two sacked. Who cares? Not me. Get off the bloke's back for, crying out loud," I tell everyone, annoyed that this constant bellyaching is messing up my game. And as if to demonstrate, I miss a simple snooker, clip one of Wayne's reds and go in off the black. "Bollocks."

Finally, someone agrees with me.

"Yeah, I thought he was nice. He even invited us all over to have Sunday lunch with him and the team next weekend," Belinda says.

"Did he?" Ollie says, like this is news to him.

"Yeah, we're all gonna have a roast together," she smiles, then stops when she sees Ollie choking to death on his pint. "What?"

"Anyone got any glove puppets?" I smirk.

"I think you're the one in need of a glove puppet demonstration, Bex," Mel continues to bang on.

"What do you mean?"

"Oh for God's sake, open your eyes. Do you know how I knew where Delacroix was on Saturday night? Because he propositioned me last time he was in the office. Ditch your boyfriend darling and meet me Saturday night," Mel hams in her best '*Allo '*Allo* accent. "I'll show you what a real man can do, you little slut."

Belinda's impressed. "Here that's dead good that is, you sound just like him," she reckons.

"Yeah, I see. That must've been awful for you," I venture.

Mel scowls. "You're not even that bothered about it, are you?"

"Well it's not like he had much luck," I reason. I mean, who can blame a bloke for trying?

"God, you've really got it bad, haven't you?" Mel glares, so I decide it's time for a practical demonstration, glove puppets or otherwise.

"Look, I want to show you lot something," I say, snatching Wayne's last red ball off the table just as he's about to knock it in.

"Oi, put that back," he objects.

"Keep your hair on, I'm just using it to demonstrate a point," I tell him. "Right, are you lot watching? Okay then, now this red ball is Delacroix," I say, nice and slowly for the benefit of more boneheaded amongst them. Roland already has several questions, but I ignore his raised hand and carry on. "And them down there, the yellow balls," I say, pointing at the six yellows I've still got in the table, "they're the opposition. Now, all those yellows are more scared of this single red than he is of them. And it's this same arrogance that makes him such a God on the park, that occasionally causes him to rub people up the wrong way off it. But what d'you wanna do?" I tell them, resetting the red.

"Oi, put it back where it was," Wayne moans.

"That was where it was, weren't it?"

"What, snookered behind the black? No it wasn't actually."

"Oh," I say, looking at the balls before knocking them with my cue. "Well I guess we'll have to void this game then."

"Afternoon chaps," an unwelcomingly familiar voice wishes us as it sidles close. "Talking about Delacroix are you?"

"What's it to you, Norris?" I ask.

"Oh nothing, I could just hear you crying about him from over yonder, that's all," Norris smirks.

"I ain't crying about him, it's this lot," I correct him.

"Well whatever. You ain't going to have to worry about him now that he's sodded off to straw donkey land whatever the problem was," Norris consoles me.

"You what?"

"Look, up there, on the telly as we speak," he says, pointing up at the Sky Sports broadcast on in the corner.

Sure enough, there's Claude sat at a big table with his agent, publicist and the manager of Barcelona, grinning like a Lottery winner.

"What the fuck?"

I jab the buttons to get the sound up and Claude's laying it on thick for the benefit of the gentlemen of the press.

"It is a great honour to come to a big club like Barcelona and get the chance to challenge for major trophies. When I was a little boy, I was always a fan of Spanish football and Barcelona in particular," he tells a sea of flashing bulbs.

"That piece of shit!" I exclaim.

"Norris, what's happened to your eye?" Mel asks, scrutinising the delicious bruise on Norris's face.

"That were them weren't it, old thick and thicker," Norris complains, pointing an accusing finger across at Ollie and Roland.

"Just doing our bit for handbags everywhere, weren't we Rollo?" Ollie freely admits.

"That's right. We were like them two cowboys from that film," Roland proudly agrees.

"Yeah," Ollie nods, then thinks about this for a second. "No, hang on, he's talking about *Butch and Sundance*, not them two from that other film."

"So which one of you's Butch?" Wayne chuckles.

"I've a good mind to sue the pair of you," Norris scowls. "Assault and battery that is."

Mel offers the benefit of her legal expertise. "You should you know. Nothing tugs the heartstrings quite like a purse snatcher with a shiner. You could be on for millions with the right jury I reckon."

"This is unbelievable. What a Judas! We should do him for this. We should do the bastard," I'm finally able to splutter after finding my voice again. Claude is now in his Barcelona top and smooching all over the badge, just as he'd smooched all over ours for two seasons. I feel hurt, betrayed and inconsolable. It was one thing to try and kiss my bird, but quite another to kiss a different club's badge. That two-timing bitch!

Mel picks up on this point. "What, we should do the bastard for daring to leave Arsenal?"

"Oh you know, and for trying it on with you, obviously, getting Ol sacked and offering to play pass the parcel with Belinda," I remind them, appeasing the crowd. "But perhaps most importantly of all, Wayne here deserves a proper apology."

"That's alright, I knew you'd cheat if I started beating you anyway," Wayne shrugs.

"Not from me, from Delacroix. Look, it don't matter what our reasons are, all that matters is that this guy needs taking down a peg or forty-thousand so are you lot in or what?"

"Bex, we've been in from the start. You're the one sprinting after the bus with his General's hat on," Mel says.

"Well it's a good job I'm here now then isn't it, because you've done a right shonky job of it so far," I point out.

"Remind me why I go out with you again?" my girlfriend asks.

"Because I'm the man with the plan."

"You got an idea then?" Ollie spots.

"Well just a flicker of one," I mull, "but with a little fanning it should set my cotton buds on fire the next time I clean me ears out."

"Clean your what out with what?" Ollie furrows.

"Mel luv, can you find out what legal areas Charlie actually handles for Delacroix?" I ask, beginning mobilisation.

"On the QT, presumably."

"If you can. And Wayne, perhaps you should try appealing to Claude's better side just one last time?" I suggest.

"I don't think he's got one, has he?" Wayne replies.

"It would appear not, but we can only try."

Ollie is reinvigorated by our sudden togetherness and feels moved to words. "Man, this is well good this is. It's like we're all pulling in the same direction for once. With a common cause and goal."

"All for one, hey Big Guy?" Roland suggests, wrapping his arms around his beloved best friend.

"You're not wrong Rollo," Ollie agrees.

Unfortunately, when you've got mates like I have, these moments of togetherness are inevitably short-lived.

Belinda's the one who goes and ruins it.

"Here, where's my handbag gone?"

5. A moving farewell

"Well of course it is your decision, but Charlie really thinks it'd be in your best interests if you issued a simple apology," Mel tells Claude.

Five miles away, Claude stands in ten acres of greenbelt land, in front of a seven bedroom manor, by his Koi carp pond and immaculately sculpted topiary hedgerow, but he's too angry to notice any of it. All he can see is the scuff on the door of his Lamborghini, which he'd since mentally enlarged to match his rage, and the cocky grinning face of some gobby little shitehawk who expects him to grovel for forgiveness. For what? For throwing a bike in the river which he'd since paid for?

Who paid to have the scratch removed from Claude's paintwork? Not the kid, that was for sure, but Claude himself. Admittedly, it had only required a little working with T-Cut, but that was besides the point.

The point was that he'd done it. So Claude had done his bike. But being a bigger man that the kid, he'd paid to have the bike replaced (on Charlie's advice). Now the little fucker wanted an apology too!

It was an outrage too far. Well if he wanted a war he could have a war. The thirteen-year-old kid who could get the better of Claude Delacroix was yet to be born.

"Listen, damn it, if this boy wants trouble, tell Charlie to drag his ass through every court in the land until his family home is a one-man tent in a muddy field. Then we kick down the tent," Claude tells Mel, outlining his overall legal strategy.

"Mr Delacroix, this might impinge on your transfer to Spain if the boy goes to the papers. Think of the publicity..." Mel continues to try, but Claude could give two ha'penny fucks about that.

"In England, not in Spain. In Spain, they won't care. They'll even be on my side when they hear the truth. Let him say whatever he likes," Claude says, heading for his patio doors.

"It's really not too late. I even have him with me at the moment if you want to speak to him," Mel says, looking across the desk at Wayne.

"He is with you now?" Claude stops, conscious of the fact that his house is full of eavesdropping removal men and preferring not to be overheard, particularly in light of what he's got to say to the kid. "Okay, put him on, but I will only say it in French, yes?" he sighs.

"Here, he wants to speak to you," Mel says, handing the phone to Wayne.

"Hello?"

"Hey kid," Claude mulls, "pardon my French but, kiss my fucking ass you little cocksucker!"

Claude presses the red button and chuckles to himself. That was almost worth it.

Back in the office, Wayne shakes his head at Mel.

"You were right, he was never going to apologise, was he?"

"No, which is probably just as well really," Mel says, stopping the tape recorder and removing the sucker cup mic from the phone. "Still, useful to get him on tape in case we ever need it."

Charlie pops his shiny head out of his office to have a quick word with his Legal Secretary. "Er Mel..." he starts, then spots Wayne. "Oh hello young man. Get your cheque alright, did you?"

"Yes thank you Charlie."

"Jolly good, now don't go spending it all on sweets, you hear," Charlie winks.

"What four hundred quid?" Wayne asks.

"Yeah, it's possible. Reckon I could probably do it," Charlie ponders, breaking Wayne's compensation down into weights, measurements and pick 'n mix in his mind.

"Er, was there something you wanted Charlie?" Mel asks.

"Oh yeah, I was just seeing if you were still on the phone to Claude. Just need a quick word with him like."

"I can call him back, it's not a problem."

"No, it's alright, I'll do it," Charlie waves, heading back into his office.

"Er, well you do have someone waiting, regarding Claude actually," Mel says, all circumspect then nods a knowing nod. "Another one."

"Huh?" Charlie pokes his head around to corner into the waiting room and sees a young lady in short skirt, high heels and tears.

"It was that footballer man. He molested me," Belinda hams, barely able to draw a breath.

"Did he?" Charlie raises an eyebrow. "Well you'd better come in for a little chat then hey."

Charlie looks over at Mel and says quietly. "Mel luv, bring the cheque book in will you please?"

Belinda shuffles past him, her pants protruding from the bottom of her mini and her blouse more tits than actual material. Charlie makes a quick mental recalculation.

"On second thoughts, make that the petty cash box. Oh and yeah, give Claude a quick bell will you and tell him the removal firm's going to be late. Somebody broke into the depot late last night and glued up all their lorries' locks."

"Sure, I'll let him know," Mel promises.

*

Claude sits at his private bar watching the backs of the removal men he's hired. Like all British workers, they are lazy and stupid. Claude knows this, so he stays at hand to make sure they don't skive off and stop for a tea break every five minutes. He wants to get out of this miserable grey shit-hole of a country as fast as possible, and he wants to find his valuables in one piece when he arrives in Spain.

One of the removal men begins dragging a large wooden crate towards a dolly, which makes Claude leap out of his seat and give him a warning.

"Hey, be careful with that box, it is very valuable see."

"Really?" the removal man gawps, turning to face Claude.

"Hey, do not look at me," Claude warns him, averting his own eyes lest theirs accidentally meet. Claude doesn't like eye contact. Eye contact makes him uncomfortable, especially from people inferior to him. He'd had it his whole life, a waiter or shop assistant would say "please" and "thank you" with their lips, but "fuck you" with their eyes, and Claude would look a fool when he complained, so these days people didn't look him in the eye. His people took care of that. Charlie should've given these fools the same instructions, but they'd obviously taken no notice or were just trying to be clever, but they'd see. When he was all moved and finished with them, Claude would teach them to cheek him.

"Sorry," the removal man mutters, turning away.

"Now, this crate is worth more to me than everything else," Claude instructs. "Even my five-thousand pound TV. It is very precious, you understand? Handle with care."

The removal man tugs his forelock and chalks a mark on the side of the crate as Claude returns to the bar. "Well, I guess we'd better take this one first then."

The removal man turns to his colleague who's ten feet away and beckons him over. "Here, Dave, you want to give me a hand with this?"

His colleague doesn't react.

"Oi, Dave," the removal man repeats, then takes a cloth out of his pocket and throws it at his colleague's head. His colleague turns round and looks at him blankly.

"What?" says Ollie, unsure as to why I'm calling him Dave.

"Come here and lift this with me."

We lift the heavy crate and carefully carry it through the hallway and towards the front door. On the way, we pass two other familiar faces also done up like removal men.

"Here Bex, are we even gonna get this lot in the lorry?" Roland asks, wrapping a jewel-encrusted carriage clock in bubble wrap and dropping it into a crate.

"No, and Mel just rang to say we've probably only got another half an hour left, so just grab the best stuff and let's get out of here," I tell him.

"How do we know which stuff's the best stuff?" Roland asks.

"Easy, just pick something up and look like you're going to drop it and Claude'll come charging over and tell you how much it's worth."

Norris gives me and Ollie a black look as we pass him by the door, though he'd struggle to give us any other kind of look now that his second eye had been given a shiner of its own in the course of reuniting Belinda with her handbag.

"Yeah, so work hard now and there might even be some bamboo shoots in it for you," Ollie mocks with great delight.

"Oh fucking ha ha Ol, you're so hilarious. Well let's see who's laughing when my lawyer gets involved shall we?" Norris promises.

"I thought your lawyer said he'd break both your legs if he ever saw you again?" Roland reminds him.

"Oh belt up, will ya Rollo."

We manhandle the crate into the back of the lorry we've borrowed for the occasion and I'm tempted to take a peek inside at exactly what Claude regards as his most precious possession, but we've simply got too much work to do and too little time to do it in.

"Jesus, I'm knackered," moans Ollie, mopping his brow. What an unfit bastard. We've only been here twenty minutes.

"Yeah, hard work in' it? Just imagine if we were doing this for real for just a wage? How depressing would that be?" I put to him.

"Not sure I'd bother, to be honest."

"What, help Claude move? Wouldn't you?"

"Oi, you two," Claude hollers from an upstairs window. "No slacking. Get back to work, allez allez!"

"He's a slave driver, in' he," Ollie puffs. "Can't he see, we're nicking as fast as we can?"

*

An hour later we're rolling open the back of the lorry outside Electric's backdoor and showing him our spoils.

Electric's mightily impressed. "Jesus, how much stuff d'you get?"

"A lot. Delacroix really worked us," I tell him. "Can you move it all?"

"Oh I can move it, that's not the problem. I just don't think I'll get much for it, that's all," Electric tells us, somewhat predictably.

"Leave it out Terror Hawks," Norris objects, "that telly's worth five grand alone."

"Oh aye, well that'll shift like hot cakes out of my shop then won't it because I'm exactly the sort of bloke you'd buy a five grand telly off, in' I?" Electric scoffs, then notices Norris's complete set of black eyes. "How's Sooty keeping? He alright, is he?"

"Look, we'll just take half of whatever you make," I tell the old man, reasoning that we probably wouldn't get much more than that anyway, no matter what sort of a deal we struck with this old crook, so we might as well just press on.

"Oh will you now?" Electric postures, still in negotiations mode.

"Electric mate, we're on the clock, so let's save the haggling for later

154

as we need to dump the lorry, alright?" I spell out.

"Alright," he agrees. "Get it in the shop then. And make sure you wipe your feet. One of you trod dog mess all through my place last time you were here."

"Hey, that were me," Roland gleefully admits.

*

We dump the lorry an hour later in some woods just off the motorway and within another two, it's plastered with Old Bill. Weasel's there too, with our old mate PC Bennett and the man-of-the-moment himself, Prince Claude Delacroix. Weasel's having a difficult time figuring out what's wrong with Claude and can't quite get a handle on him. Normally the victims of crime are in his face from the off but Claude won't even look at him. Weasel wonders if he's had a hand in the job himself, or more likely let rip in the police car on the way over and is trying to disown it. Either way, Claude's getting under Weasel's skin to the point where Weasel's ready to file this one CASE UNSOLVED the moment he gets back to the office. But there are procedures to go through before he can get to that point, so Weasel sets about ticking them off one-by-one.

"So, if you can just identify this as the lorry that took your property away, then that would be a big help Mr Delacroix."

Claude barely looks at the lorry and shrugs. "I don't know. Yeah sure, why not? It's a lorry, non?"

Weasel rolls his eyes at Bennett, but presses on. "And the men that came with it?"

"I told you, they were men. You know. Five, six, seven. I don't know," Claude pouts.

"But you did get a good look at them, didn't you?"

"Hey, this is not my job to find these men," Claude snaps. "This is your job, so do your job, yeah?"

"But this is the lorry, is it?" Weasel tries one last time.

"Hey, I said so. Didn't I just say so?" Claude paddies, so Weasel decides to take that as a positive ID and look inside.

"Terry, do the honours will you?"

Bennett folds open the tail board and runs the back shutter up. The lorry is all but empty. Only a single wooden crate with a distinctive chalk mark on the side remains. Claude spots it and is immediately overwhelmed with an enormous sense of relief that his most prized possessions are safe.

"And can you identify this then?" Weasel asks, but Claude is already charging into the lorry to get at the crate.

"My shirts. Yes, my shirts!"

"Er, hold on sir. One second, please. Terry?"

Bennett blocks Claude's path and is almost pushed over for his troubles, but Claude remembers at the last moment that he's dealing with the police, not his gardener, so he backs off until Weasel can join him.

"So, do I take it you positively identify this crate as yours then sir?" Weasel asks.

"Yes, of course this is mine," Claude tells the two idiots.

"And can you describe its contents?" Weasel presses.

"They are my shirts," he tells them again.

"Shirts?" asks Weasel.

"My football shirts. I swap them at the end of the games with other players, non? Gerrard, Lampard, Rooney, Zola." Claude's shoulders sag heavily at being confronted by such flat-footed stupidity and he lets out a groan to demonstrate his impatience. "Ohh, they are football shirts, in frames for my wall, d'accord?"

"Football shirts," Weasel clarifies.

"Yes yes yes, they are irreplaceable," Claude spells out.

Weasel gives Bennett the nod, so he cracks open the case and reaches inside. Claude watches expectantly, but the colour drains from his face when Bennett pulls out not an original framed Premier League shirt, but a rusty and muddy kid's bike - with a busted front wheel.

"Hmm, looks likes someone's managed to replace them," Weasel deduces, then remembers himself. "Sir."

Only now does Claude look Weasel in the eye.

6. Shirt tales

Electric is in his back room cataloguing his new stock when the bell tinkles out front to indicate he has a customer. He pops his head through the beaded curtains all eagerness and smiles, only to see Weasel examining the bottom of one of his teapots.

"Er, morning Sergeant. What can I do for you?"

"Well, you could stop buying stolen goods if you wanted to. I guess you could do that for me," Weasel replies, setting the teapot down and joining Electric at the counter.

"Stolen goods? Me?" Electric blinks in confusion. "There must be some mistake. I'm completely legitimate, respectable and above board I'll have you know. I wouldn't even look at anything that was stolen. I give you my word Sergeant. Especially not since my last conviction."

Weasel fixes Electric in his sights. "Why must we go through this pantomime every time? Look, I know you're still operating and you know I know it, so let's just cut through the lies for once and for all shall we and behave like grown-ups. It demeans us both."

Electric relaxes his guard a little and agrees. "You're right, Sergeant. You're right."

"So, has anyone been in offering you any stuff over the last couple of days?" Weasel asks.

"No," Electric replies without drawing breath.

"Well don't think about it or nothing, whatever you do."

"But they haven't, honest," Electric insists.

"I could go and get a warrant if you want to play it that way," Weasel warns him.

Electric relaxes even more. "Meaning you haven't got one now?"

"Well no, but I could go and get one," Weasel insists, but Electric's not for bluffing. He's long enough in the tooth to know that if Weasel had strong enough suspicions, he'd have a warrant with him, not just the threat of one. Which settled it, Weasel was just fishing, but Electric knows better than to flap his fin in the water too vociferously, so he plays this one nice and carefully.

"Sergeant, what exactly are you after? Just so's I know what to steer clear of like," he winks, making it clear that information isn't entirely out of the question. After all, one of a fence's prerogatives is stitching up and selling out his rivals.

"The proceeds from that footballer's robbery. I'm sure you saw it in the papers."

Electric just about recalls it. "Oh yeah. Tragic that was. Very sad. Why's it always the good ones?" he laments.

"The tragedy is the stupidity of the men involved," Weasel informs him.

"How d'you mean?"

"Among the haul was a number of framed shirts. All original, signed and unique. Stuff like this is unbelievably traceable. The moment they surface... and they will... we'll have 'em." Weasel takes one last look around the shop then heads for the door. "I'll see you later."

"Oh, well best of luck," Electric wishes him. "Let us know how you get on with that."

Electric breathes a sigh of relief and returns to his back room to continue cataloguing his stock. On a nearby five-thousand-pound TV, one of Claude's DVDs is playing. Electric regards the screen for a moment. It's Claude, three years ago, at his Arsenal press conference.

"It is a great honour for me to play for a great club like Arsenal. When I was a little boy in France, I was always a fan of English football and Arsenal in particular," he tells an earlier sea of flashing bulbs.

Electric turns the telly off.

"Pranny."

*

Of course, Weasel was absolutely right, there was no way we could sell Claude's shirts, as they were far too traceable. I knew that the moment I jemmied open his precious crate and saw what was inside.

Ollie asked if we should leave 'em then, and let Claude have 'em back if they were no good to us, but there was an alternative school of thought.

Claude's frames hit the nearest builder's skip while their contents accompanied the rest of us over the local recreation ground for a kick-about. The last time they'd been worn, they'd stretched across the shoulder of footballing Gods who could afford greenbelt manors, koi carp and five-thousand-pound tellies. Now they're being worn by us, half a dozen council estate thoroughbreds who can barely afford a ticket to see these shirts in action.

But you know what, football shirts are just football shirts at the end of the day. And between hanging on a wall in Barcelona or haring around a field after a ball again, I think I know which they'd chose if they were able to have their say.

Result.

THE OFFICE JOB

1. A foot in the door

You know, I never really worry about job interviews. Well, what's to worry about when I don't actually want any of the jobs I get sent for in the first place and only go along in order to keep getting my fortnightly dole cheques? No, under the right circumstances, job interviews don't unduly trouble me. I stick on my old suit, turn up when I'm meant to, smile politely when I think it's appropriate to do so and chat for twenty minutes with well-dressed strangers who are interested in the things I have to say for myself. Then I loosen my tie, go to the pub and buy myself a congratulatory drink. Yep, I think it's fairly safe to say that job interviews can be a mildly diverting little day trip if there's absolutely nothing whatsoever riding on them.

Today's job interview is different though. Today's job interview has a great deal riding on it.

Accordingly, I make a special effort.

Mel pops into the bedroom with a cup of tea and vocalises her approval.

"You know, you look really handsome in a suit," she sexually harasses me.

"Yeah, don't polish up too badly, do I?" I agree, finishing off my tie in the mirror.

"How much did you say it cost again?" she asks, feeling my jacket's lapel.

"I didn't. I'm a right man of mystery, me."

"Well it was high time you got a new suit. That old one hanging up in the wardrobe wouldn't even fit me any more."

"And how would you know? Been trying it on when I'm not around, have you? Well fair's fair. Me and Ollie try on your things when you're out," I admit.

"Yeah, I can well believe it."

"Anyway, you should never knock a man who's suit don't fit him. In some respects it's a mark of success," I tell her.

"How d'you figure that?"

"Because it shows he hasn't been up before the beak in a while," I tell her which is a fact. Some of the happiest crooks in the world have got burgundy waffle suits hanging up in their wardrobes with big moth holes under their armpits.

I rock back a few steps and admire my handiwork in the mirror.

Mel looks at my enormous Windsor knot and the six inches of tongue hanging from it and leaps across the room in a single bound to interfere. I tell you, few things in this life irritate Mel more than the way I do my ties.

"Oh for God's sake Bex, you're going to a job interview, you're not bunking off Geography. Come here, let me do it," she insists, half-strangling me in order to redo my tie.

"No, get off, leave it. This is how I like 'em," I object, trying to hold her at bay.

Left uninterrupted, this could well have ended in a punch-up but a blast on the doorbell distracts Mel and I'm able to put some distance between her meddling mitts and my triple-Windsor.

"Who's that?" Mel asks.

"Bit tricky to tell without opening the door I'd say," I do indeed say.

"Are you expecting anyone?" she asks.

"Like who?"

"That would be the point of expecting someone. You generally know who you're expecting."

"I don't know then. Must be your fancy man," I hedge.

"No, he's not coming over until three," Mel tells me.

"Maybe he's come early?"

"Yeah, that'd be just my luck," Mel replies, going for the door, "having a boyfriend and a fancy man who both did that."

I mull this over a moment then wonder why either of us bother with the sarcastic old cow.

Mel finds a dapper-looking Ollie shining his new shoes on the backs of his legs when she opens the door.

"Oh look, it's Captain Mensa," she sighs, less than surprised.

"Reporting for duty, ma'am," Ollie theatrically salutes.

"Here, what are you doing in a suit too? And the same suit as Bex, come to that?" Mel then notices.

"Oh this, yeah, part of a job lot, weren't they?" Ollie explains.

"Yeah, 'Job' being the operative word, I reckon," Mel ventures, as Ollie invites himself inside.

He finds me in the kitchen. "You're early," I tell him, checking my watch.

"Yeah, my toaster's broken. Thought I'd come round and use yours," Ollie says, pulling a couple of slices of Mighty White from his jacket pockets.

"Hang on, I'm lost here. I thought you were going for an interview this afternoon?" Mel flaps, three pages behind me and Ollie.

"I am. We both are," I say.

"The same interview?"

"It's the Job Centre who're sending us up for it," Ollie explains.

"Perhaps they're sending every idiot in town for it."

"Yeah, but a job's a job in' it - a foot on the ladder," I reason.

"And what exactly is this ladder of yours leaning up against?" Mel wants to know.

"Oh luv, you old cynic you."

162

Ollie goes one step further. "That's hurtful, just plain hurtful, that is."

"Look Mel, you keep saying you want me to get a real job, well this is me trying. Is it my fault they're sending us both up for the same position?"

"In the same suit?" Mel continues to chew.

"No, that was my fault," I concede. "Or at least, M&S's for having a sale on."

"So you didn't nick 'em then?" Mel presses.

"Practically. It was a hell of a sale," I pucker.

"Yeah, might as well have just left the till open," Ollie confirms.

"Still, look the business don't we?" I brim, pleased as Punch with my new duds.

"You look like a couple of Scientologists," Mel reckons.

"Thanks," beams Ollie. Ollie doesn't get many compliments.

Ollie's toast decides to join in the conversation at this point, jumping out of the toaster to get a clearer look at our suits.

"There you go, lift off. What d'you want on your toast?" I ask, opening the fridge.

"Couple of eggs and a bit of bacon, perhaps?" the cheeky bastard chances.

*

Half an hour later we're pulling into a little residential side street just off the town centre. There's a multi-storey car park just around the corner but the prices they charge border on criminal, so me and Ol prefer to make our own arrangements.

We pull up and check the sign on the lamppost. PERMIT HOLDERS ONLY. VEHICLES PARKED ILLEGALLY ARE LIABLE TO BE CLAMPED OR REMOVED.

Perfect.

We jump out, open the back doors and set to work fitting a wheel clamp to our back wheel. I tell you, this thing's fantastic. We've had it just over a year and it must've saved us hundreds in parking tickets and fines in that time. It's like the ultimate free parking permit. I can't understand why everyone doesn't get one, but don't ask me where you do because me and Ol simply found ours - on our van as it happens. Some silly bastard had the poor judgment to fit it to our back wheel, now he's one clamp lighter and me and Ol get to park where we want.

"So why ain't Mel at work today? Lazy in't she?" Ollie asks as we fit the clamp.

"She's just using up her holiday. Had three days left so she had to use 'em or lose 'em before Easter," I tell him.

"How many days she get then?"

"Twenty I think."

"Jesus, imagine only getting twenty days off a year? How would you

163

find the time to do anything," Ollie shudders at the very thought.

"Like what?" I ask.

"Like... I don't know... telly. How would you be able to keep up with all the telly? That's a full-time job in itself."

"Yeah, and that sitting around on your arse ain't going to take care of itself either, is it?" I agree.

"It's mental though, isn't it? Working. It don't make any sense," Ollie frowns as I finish locking the clamp off and he spreads a 'Vehicle Clamping Securities' sticker across our windscreen warning STOP: DO NOT ATTEMPT TO MOVE IT.

"Yeah well, think about those old mateys who built the pyramids. They never got twenty days off a year. They never even got weekends off. They just worked until they dropped," I tell him, in an attempt to freak him out.

"Nah, you wouldn't do it, would you. You'd just jack in and go on the dole," Ollie dismisses.

"Oh yeah, I can see that," I chuckle, as I lift the windscreen wiper and slip our Penalty Charge Notice underneath. "'Excuse me Ramesses the Third, but my Giro never come. So what's the deal, is it late or what?'"

Ollie's brain refuses to marry into this concept and he stares at me blankly as I grab our briefcases out of the cab and hand him his. "Why would it be late?"

*

Just around the corner from our theoretical discussion, a man is standing in an opticians trying on a pair of frames. Nothing too unusual there you might think, except that this particular man doesn't actually need to wear glasses. There are any number of things wrong with this particular gentleman, but his eyesight is one of the few things he can be envied for.

The man grimaces at his reflection for a moment, before peeking around the mirror at the pinstriped businessman across the busy shop from him.

Like everyone else in the shop, the businessman is trying on frames, but unlike the man who's watching him closely, the businessman is unable to fully appreciate his mirrored appearance through the clear plastic lenses the display frames have been fitted with. The businessman leans in and squints a little harder, then picks his own glasses up off the side again and tries wearing both at the same time to get some sort of perspective as to what these new frames might look like on his face.

The businessman decides against them, then picks out another promising-looking set. These ones have steel rims, like the ones Mulder occasionally wore in The X-Files, and they always looked good on him, the businessman remembers. He sets his old glasses on the side again, leans a little closer into the mirror and squints once more. Again, the clear

164

plastic lenses and unnecessarily chunky anti-theft tag make it all but impossible to tell if they suit him or make him look like a big fucking joke. The businessman wonders how it is that scientists can show him what mankind will evolve into in two million years time, but they can't show him what he'll look like wearing a new pair of glasses without him having to fork out the three hundred quid to get the bastards made up.

He puts the designer frames back in the rack where he found them and reaches for his old set again, but confusingly, his fingers only touch shelf. He squints down and runs his fingers along the shelf, then feels around the floor by his feet, but his glasses are nowhere to be felt.

As he's widening the search, a man with perfect eyesight casually picks up the businessman's unattended briefcase and quietly exits the shop, setting an old pair of glasses in a rack by the door as he leaves.

Ten seconds later, that same man with perfect eyesight is piling into me and Ollie just up the road as he hot foots it away from the shop.

"What the…"

"Norris! Who are you legging it from?" Ollie asks, as we catch him by the collar to stop him from getting away.

"No one," he denies. "Can't a bloke run for a bus in this town without being accused of nicking someone's briefcase?"

I look at the briefcase he's carrying under his arm and the anxious guilty expression flittering across his face and reason he hasn't just come from an executive board meeting.

"I don't remember mentioning anything about your briefcase," Ollie says.

"That's funny, 'cos I don't remember mentioning anything about yours either, but I could if I wanted to," Norris warns us, nodding down at our cases.

"He's got us there, mate," I concede.

Norris suddenly notices our threads.

"Anyway, what's with the party frocks? You two up in front of the beak today or something?" he asks.

"For your information, we've got a job interview," Ollie proudly tells him.

"What you going to a job interview for?" Norris asks, all confused.

This stumps Ollie. "What do people normally go to job interviews for?" he retorts.

Norris thinks about this one. "I don't know. So they don't get their dole stopped?" he hazards.

"True," I tell him. "Usually. But in this instance we're making the leap and joining the ranks of the professionals."

Norris looks even more confused now. "Why?"

"Why? Because we don't want to spend the rest of our lives scratching a living out of nicking of course. I mean, do you?" I put to him.

"Dunno," Norris replies, sticking out his lip and sliding a chewing gum around inside his mouth. "Haven't thought that far ahead to be honest. I'll probably be dead in a couple of years time anyway so what's the point in planning?"

Norris suddenly pulls us together to make a wall and ducks behind it. "Shit, quick hide us," he urges.

A hundred yards up the road, a pinstriped businessman and a couple of irate opticians have fallen out of Mr Spectacles and are frantically scouring the High Street.

"Oi, he's over here!" we shout, stepping aside to give them a glimpse of the hare.

All three yell at us to stop the thief and start storming in our direction, but it's not our chase, so we wish Norris all the best and leave him to play with his new mates.

"Oh thanks a lot," he yells back at us as he sprints away. "Do the same for you some time."

The businessman and the opticians fly past us at a lick, but I don't fancy their chances. Norris with a bag under his arm and a head-start is a foregone conclusion. Cancel your cards, buy some new pens and move on with your life. That's my advice mate.

We watch them all tear up the High Street and disappear off over the horizon.

"That's one of the most beautiful sights in the world that is," I tell Ollie. "Norris going away. No sunset comes close."

2. Horace and Doris

"So... Doctor Harrington," Horace smacks his lips, as he reads Ollie's CV.

"That's me name, don't wear it out," Ollie clicks in response.

"Er yes, well quite," agrees Horace a little uncertain. "Anyway, so what exactly is your doctorate in?"

Ollie ponders the question in order to give Horace the fullest and frankest explanation possible, then when he realises he hasn't got a clue what he's going on about he simply looks across the desk blankly and asks, "you what?"

"Your doctorate. What's it in?" Horace repeats, almost willing Dr Harrington to do well so that he can rubber stamp his application.

"Er... dunno. I didn't even know they give you an 'at," Ollie finally admits.

Now it's Horace's turn to look blank. "What?"

Ollie reciprocates. "What?"

Horace turns to his colleague, Doris, who decides to have a go.

"I'm sorry, but I think we're somewhat at crossed purposes," she concludes.

Ollie looks at her and blinks. "What?"

"You do have a doctorate, don't you?" Horace presses.

"No. Like I say, I didn't know they gave you one so mine's probably still in the doctor's hat shop or something, but I just never bothered with it, if you know what I mean?" Ollie explains.

Horace and Doris take a closer look at Ollie's CV and draw the obvious conclusion. "Er, yes, something tells me you're not actually a real doctor, are you?" Horace goes out on a limb.

"Well no, not technically, no."

"Then in what sense are you a doctor?" Doris wants to know.

"Well, I just always tick that box when I fill in forms," Ollie elaborates. "Bit more interesting really, in' it? I mean, everyone's a mister, aren't they?"

Horace shuffles his papers and bristles. "Quite. Well, Mr Harrington..."

"Please, call me Doctor," Ollie offers.

"Er, yes, okay. Well thank you Doctor Harrington for coming in."

"No problem," Ollie reassures them, then notices his time's up. "Here, hang on a minute. I haven't asked about my holiday days yet. Do sick days count as holiday days an' all or are they separate? And if so how many of them do I get?"

Neither Horace or Doris seem to know.

I fare a bit better when it's my turn to face the firing squad. In fact, old Horace is so bowled over by my CV that it takes all his self-control to keep his arse in his chair and the shirt on his back. Quite right too, when it took me all of half an hour writing it the previous evening.

"Well Mr Beckinsale, I must say your CV's very impressive," he smacks, as he runs his eyes up and down my list of qualifications.

"Good quality paper too, five quid a box that stuff is," I nod.

"Er, oh, right. Yes, very good," he agrees, fingering the weight accordingly. "Anyway, with qualifications of this calibre, we were wondering if perhaps you might be a little over-qualified for a job in telemarketing. What do you feel about that?"

"Oh no, crack on, I don't mind," I reply. "Better than a kick up the jacksy with a rusty bike, that's what I reckon anyway."

From the look on Horace's face, I guess he's not really one for euphemisms.

Doris steps in once again to butter Horace's roll for him. "Yes, I think what my colleague's getting at is whether you see this job as merely a temporary stop-gap until something else comes along or whether you really do see a career for yourself in telemarketing."

"Ah no, telemarketing all the way," I affirm. "This is the job for me and you're going to have one hell of a job turfing me out at sixty-five but we'll cross that kettle of bananas when we come to it. Just give me this chance, please." I even clasp my hands together to show them how much this means to me, which goes down a storm across the desk, so they swap little nods, slap on their congratulatory smiles and prepare to welcome me to the family.

"Well, I must say, it's good to see such enthusiasm in a young man. I can't understand why you haven't found suitable employment before now," Horace gushes. "So, if we can…"

"Oh, there is just one thing," I figure now's as good a time as any to tell them. "I won't work with blacks."

A pin drops.

Ollie's waiting for me outside the interview room when I leave.

"How d'you get on?" he asks.

"Not bad," I tell him as we walk down the corridor. "Though there was one nasty moment there when I thought they were actually gonna offer me the job so I had to call on the big guns to get myself out of schtuck."

"What, not the old 'I won't work with Ollie's mates' line?" Ollie chuckles with delight. As it happens, it was Ollie who'd originally come up with it over a few beers while we'd spend a pleasant evening in the pub compiling the top ten phrases a person would do well to steer clear of if ever invited to appear on Parkinson. My own best effort had been, "Paedophiles? If you ask me, they're as much the victims as the children they repeatedly abuse."

"Yeah," I confirm as we turn the corner and head for the lift.

"What did they say?"

"Well Doris weren't too impressed, I'll tell you that much, though I reckon I'm still in with a shout judging from the funny handshake Horace gave me on the way out."

This saddens Ollie and he shakes his head. "Terrible in' it. It's rife in big business it is, racism, you know."

"Yeah, good job we work in an equal opportunities industry then ain't it?" I reassure him, stopping just short of the lift outside the Gents. "Anyway, what was I going to say. Oh yeah, that was it; do you fancy a Jimmy at all?"

"Yeah, I think I do as it happens," Ollie confirms.

"Then you're gonna love this place," I wink, pushing open the bog door and heading inside.

*

Norris's pinstriped businessman doesn't heed my advice and fruitlessly chases Norris all over town before Norris finally loses him in the shopping centre. Whatever it is he keeps in his case, he really wants it back. Norris takes heart from the businessman's persistence and clings onto his prize with an unyielding grip until he has the breathing room to examine its contents.

Finally, in an alleyway just behind the supermarket, Norris is all on his own.

He squats down behind a dumpster, lays the case on his lap and pulls out his picks. Thirty seconds of digging around inside the locks and the catches spring open.

The first thing he finds of use is a sandwich wrapped in clingfilm. Norris tears into the cellophane and stuffs the whole lot into his mouth in one go, he's that hungry from his long chase. But no sooner has it connected with his taste buds than it's leaping from his gob and hitting the side of the dumpster.

"Fucking Jesus!" he spits, wiping his tongue and opening the bread up to see lettuce and tomatoes alongside the ham. "For crying out-loud!" he spits, emptying the rabbit food out onto the tarmac, putting the bread back together and stuffing what's left back into his face.

The rest of the case is surprisingly light. There's a couple of coloured pens, some wordy files and this month's edition of Caravan Enthusiast, but precious little else. Certainly nothing that would've got Norris haring all around town like an idiot after it, he mopes.

He throws the files out and rips into the pockets and eventually finds a little box marked TOP SECRET. Norris's eyes instantly widen and he finally understands why the businessman chased him for so long.

His hands are trembling as he opens the box and inside he finds a small, sleek, black plastic device. He examines it carefully, turning it this way and that as he tries to work out what it is and how much he should demand for it from the businessman's competitors.

He sees something deep inside the slot of the device and cautiously pokes his finger inside. When he withdraws it, the tip of his finger is bright red. It's then that it dawns on Norris what he's dealing with and with one quick slap of the device, he prints the word TOP SECRET on the lid of its own box.

"Fuck's sake!" he barks, throwing the lot against the fence in disgust. "Running all over town..." he grumbles, half-tempted to go back and give his businessman a right-hander for wasting his time.

*

Back on the homestead, Mel's fancy man still hasn't shown up, which is just as well because she's got way too much ironing to do for any of that nonsense anyway.

She's halfway through ironing the duvet cover when... I know, pointless ain't it, but Mel irons everything. Socks, pants, jeans. Everything. I've even seen her iron a tea towel before now. Makes absolutely no sense to me, but Mel's a bit special-needs when it comes to ironing. I expect it's some sort of cry for help but it keeps her busy and out of the living room when Football Focus is on so I'm reluctant to pry. Anyway, like I was saying, she's halfway through ironing the duvet cover when someone gives our doorbell a ring downstairs.

She rushes down to open it, foolishly fantasising that it's me with my arms full of flowers and champagne, celebrating a new job and unable to reach my keys. Instead, she finds Weasel kicking our milk bottles about.

"Oh Jesus, what now?"

"Lovely to see you an' all Mel. Is Bex home?"

"No he's not, and before you go sending out an all points bulletin, whatever it is you think he's done, this time you're wrong," she tells him.

"Oh am I? Oh well thanks," Weasel replies, digging out his notebook and scribbling inside it. "'Bex - didn't - do - it. I'm - wrong - again!!' Wow thanks Mel, I wish all my suspect's girlfriends were this helpful, I'd get my work done a lot quicker if they were."

"No problem," Mel replies, trying to close the door shut but finding Weasel's foot.

"Where is he?" Weasel repeats.

"Oh for God's sake just leave him alone will you. Especially today alright, just give him a break," Mel pleads.

"Why especially today?"

"Look, he's turning over a new leaf. I know you've heard it all before but this time it's true. He's really making a go of it and you could mess it all up if you go storming in after him in your size twelves."

"Mel, I just want to talk to him, that's all," Weasel reassures her.

"Yeah, in connection with some break-in I bet."

"Well of course. We're not mates you know."

"Please, Sergeant, just give him the benefit of the doubt this one time. Please," Mel implores, but Weasel has a police badge where his heart should be.

"Mel, I'll happily give Bex the benefit of the doubt, as many times as he likes, but when someone goes shopping at M&S at three o'clock in the morning and leaves with twenty-five Italian suits, I do need to rule people like Bex out of my enquiries before I can go back to giving them the benefit of the doubt. So, for the last time, where is he? What's he doing today?"

The colour drains from Mel's face as she pictures me in my handsome new suit, and once again she realises she's been made a mug of. Weasel notices the change in her demeanour and presses some more while she's still rattled.

"Where is he Mel?" Weasel demands.

Mel sighs and shakes her head sadly. "The pub," she eventually concedes.

"Oh yeah, he's a real changed man, isn't he? Are you sure it's even him?" Weasel agrees, before turning business-like again. "I don't suppose you can tell me which pub he's in?"

"I can't remember," Mel shrugs.

"Of course you can't," Weasel scowls.

*

Norris returns to the scene of his crime and looks about. He keeps well away from Mr Spectacles but hunts the surrounding area for signs of me and Ollie, convinced we're up to some no-good of our own.

In a residential side street just off the town centre, he finds our van and examines our parking ticket and clamp.

"Yeah right," he sneers, then pulls out his picks and once more goes to work.

Five minutes later and our van is sitting unguarded in a permit holders only parking space while Norris keeps watch from the pub across the road.

He chuckles to himself and readies his camera phone to catch the entertainment.

3. An Empty Office

The main open-plan office is in darkness, but a couple of lights still flicker in two side offices. The first goes out and Doris emerges with her coat over her arm, locks the door behind her and heads for the lift.

As she passes the second office, that light also goes out and Horace steps out already wearing his coat.

"You off are you?" Horace spots.

"Yes, another day done," Doris smiles. "Good night."

"Fancy a quick drink at all?" Horace suggests.

The smile falls from Doris's face. "Look, I've told you a dozen times already, this is harassment. I'm not interested. And if you keep pestering me, I will report you to Colin."

Horace is completely taken aback by this reaction. "Oh gosh no, I didn't mean like that, I just meant, you know, like friends."

Doris jabs the button for the lift and spells it out to Horace. "Stop it, okay? I'm telling you now and for the last time, to stop it!"

The lift arrives and they both step in, neither looking at each other and both burning with embarrassment. Horace figures it's up to him to say something to smooth the waters, so he lets the doors close then turns to Doris.

"I love you," he sobs, a small erection unfolding in his trousers.

*

A few feet away, me and Ollie are still in the toilet, though you wouldn't know it to look around the place as we're up in the ceiling. We lift a panel out and check to make sure the coast's clear when we hear the lift descend.

"Fuck me, I thought they'd never go. What time is it?" I stretch.

Ollie looks at his watch. "Six."

"Don't tell me we've been up here for two hours. My back's killing me," I groan.

"What are you lying on?"

"I don't know. Some sort of electrical conduit. I bet it's giving me cancer an' all," I complain, which would be just my luck. I tell you, nothing ever goes for me.

"Nah, you'll be alright," Ollie reassures me. "It's asbestos you want to worry about. That's the real killer."

"What, you think there might be asbestos up here?" I fret, suddenly picturing my lungs as two sacks of coal.

Ollie shrugs. "Could be."

"Well what d'you follow me up here for then?" I ask.

"Because you told me to."

"Oh right, so would you jump off a cliff if I told you to?"

Ollie considers this. "Yeah, I guess," he concludes with a shrug.

We climb down out of the ceiling, stopping only to pick our wallets out of the open toilet when they both fall in, and pop our briefcases by the Gents door. I find a little angled dentist's mirror in one of my case's compartments, then open the door an inch or so and poke it through the crack.

"What can you see?" Ollie asks my ear'ole as I check the walls for cameras and detectors.

"Shhhh, you stupid big mouth," I warn him, but Ollie's like one of those little kids who has to be involved in everything and tries in vain to crane his head around mine in order to get a glimpse of the tiny inch-wide mirror. "Get off!"

"Just show us, will ya?"

"Just a sec…" I try to push him off, but Ollie pushes back and before I know it he's piling head-first into the door and slamming it shut on my mirror.

"Whooah!" he goes over.

"Oh, you big donkey!"

Ollie rights himself and watches as I try to extract my mirror from the door jamb. "Sorry mate, not my fault," the clumsy great fuck insists as the whole thing snaps off in my hand.

"Oh, nice one. Look at that, you've bust my looking-around-corners mirror. What are we supposed to do now?"

Ollie thinks about this. "I don't know, just sort of…" he mimes peering round a corner and nodding to confirm the coast's clear, "… that, you know."

"Oh brilliant. Very *Mission Impossible*. That should get round the motion detectors alright, shouldn't it?" I fume.

"Well what d'you want you old misery? I've only got so many sorrys in me before I lose interest you know, so let's just get this thing done shall we?" he says, snatching up his briefcase and yanking open the door to storm out into the corridor in a fit of pique.

"Nooo…" I screech after him, and Ollie quickly rejoins me again.

"Sorry, I forgot," he grimaces apologetically, then presses his back to the door and peers out into the hall. No security equipment in sight, he looks back, gives me the nod and moves out again.

"Why don't we get caught more often?" is all I can ask myself.

*

In a side street just around the corner, a council tow truck driver is licking his lips at the sight of our illegally parked van and reversing into position.

Norris is laughing so hard in the pub opposite that he can barely keep his camera phone steady to record the event for posterity.

*

Meanwhile back at the office, my worst fears are realised.

"I was right, motion detectors. One in each corner," I say, shining my torch beam through the glass doors to the main telesales office and sweeping the walls.

"Ow no, not motion detectors," Ollie tuts.

"What d'you expect; key in the lock and a hand with the gear? If you want something in life, you've got to work for it Ol," I remind him. "Right now, come on. And remember, move slowly. No more than six inches a second, yeah?" A thought suddenly occurs to me. "Huh, look who I'm telling?"

Ollie creases his brow for a second then scowls. "Oi, I got that," he objects, but I'm already through the door and moving at a snail's pace towards the nearest motion detector.

There are ways and means around most security equipment and a clue to a motion detector's Achilles heel can be found in its name. Motion detectors detect motion, so if you move slowly enough you won't set them off. Six inches a second is most motion detectors failsafe speed, which they have to have so that curtains and pot plants don't keep summoning the police every time a gentle breeze gusts through an air vents. Residential motion detectors have a second weakness in that they don't detect all the way to the floor, so that cats, dogs and mice can wander about freely without waking up the neighbourhood too, but few offices keep pets, so moving slowly's how we get around these.

"Shush, just ke' quiet right. Don't even 'ove your lips," I remind Ollie, ventriloquist style.

"I know, I hav' done this 'efore you know," he responds.

I lift my left foot and take four or five seconds moving it forwards before slowly shifting my weight and moving the right.

"Easy does it. Just go slow," I tell myself, only to hear Ollie offering himself the same words of encouragement across the office.

"Nice... and slow. Nice... and slow.

I cover the distance to my motion detector in a little under five minutes and drag a chair under it to get at the bastard.

"Are you there yet?" I whisper, barely daring to breath this close to the detector.

"Yeah. But you know what?" he replies.

"What?"

"I've forgotten me fucking tools."

"Huh?" I huh. Very very slowly, I turn my head and see both our briefcases back just outside the door. I feel my pockets as I watch Ollie start back towards them and realise all my tools are there too.

"Oh gollocks!" I sigh.

*

Fresh from her brush with Weasel, Mel's searching for me. Honestly, I don't know what would happen to the town if I moved away, everyone's

174

that dependent on me for their daily dose of drama.

After checking all my usual haunts, she calls in on Belinda at the golf club's nineteenth hole to see if she knows anything.

"Hey Belinda, sorry to drop in on you at work," Mel apologises.

"That's okay. You wanna drink?" Belinda replies, indicating to the pumps and optics scattered around the bar.

"No, it's okay, I'm fine thanks."

"That's just as well because you have to be a member anyway," Belinda says. "And a man."

"Belinda, where's Ollie?"

"He's at his interview," Belinda says.

"For three hours? What did they do, spring a written test on him?"

"Oh, I don't know then. Have you tried his house or the pub then?"

"No Belinda, this members-only golf club was the first place I thought of looking," Mel quips, but quips are spent ammo on Belinda.

"Well he ain't here. Hold on, I'll try his mobile," Belinda says, dialling Ollie's number.

Four miles away, in a dark and silent office, Ollie's mobile suddenly bursts into song in his open briefcase just across the office from us.

"Didn't you turn your 'ogile off?" I hiss, my hand hovering over my still-active motion detector.

"I gorgot!" Ollie yelps, as his painfully loud ring tone echoes around the office and out into the corridors.

"You're going to wake up sequrlity you fucking idiot. Shu' it uck," I urge him, so Ollie starts back towards his mobile at a breakneck speed of six-inches-a-second.

"I'n conguing. I'n conguing," he calls to it, but he doesn't get to within eight feet before it rings off. "Oh."

"Just do your detector first. You're right there beside it," I plead with him, but me and Ollie suddenly have other things to worry about.

"Bex, security!" Ollie shrieks, spotting a flashing torch beam rounding the corridor and coming our way.

"Oh shit!" I wobble, standing on a chair in the middle of an office, five feet from the nearest cover and unable to move more than six inches a second.

Ollie dives in slow motion towards the nearest desk while I sink off my chair and sprint as slowly as I can for a bank of filing cabinets.

"Hurry," Ollie urges me, when he sees I'm hardly moving.

"I can't you fucking doughnut."

The torch beam arrives at the main office doors and shines through the window. I'm still a good two feet from cover as it begins its sweep around the office, so I summon every last ounce of resolve I have left to make one last headlong dawdle for safety and make it a split-second before the beam hits me. I might've moved slower than most Antarctic lichen move when there's not much food about but I'm dripping with sweat and gasping for breath all the same.

"Anything on the motion detectors Arnold?" I hear the guard outside the door ask his radio.

"Negative," his radio crackles in response.

"Probably just someone left their phone at work. Turn them off and I'll have a look around," the guard then says.

I pick up a heavy-looking file and prepare to repel boarders, but for-tuitously Arnold comes to his mate's hat's rescue at the last moment by informing him that; "… the kebabs have just arrived."

"Oh have they? I'll be right down then," the guard replies, declaring the office clear and excitedly rushing away to investigate his dinner.

*

Back at the golf club, Belinda's fairly philosophical by her failure to reach Ollie. "Well, I expect he'll turn up sooner or later," she figures.

"Belinda, they're wearing stolen suits. If Weasel finds them before I do, he'll nick 'em before I get a chance to kill Bex," Mel insists.

"Why don't you try the place they had their interview today then?" Belinda asks.

"Well duh… I would if I knew where it was," Mel points out.

"I know where it is," Belinda admits.

This catches Mel completely cold. "Do you?"

"Of course, Ollie tells me everything," Belinda says, then notices Mel's demeanour. "Doesn't Bex tell you everything then?"

"Only when all else fails," Mel scoffs.

"Ohhh!" Belinda bristles, her spirit a-tingling with one-upmanship, or whatever the female equivalent is called. Clump-trumping Ollie reck-ons.

*

There are twenty-five computers in the telesales office, each with a flat-screen, hard-drive, keyboard, headset and handset. There are even a cou-ple of state-of-the-art ink-jet printers and an overhead projector. Everything a company might need to kit out a successful telesales office in fact. Which, now that I come to think of it, is probably what Electric's buyer plans to do with it all. Which make sense if you think about it.

Once the motion detectors are disabled, removing the gear is a rela-tively quick and painless process and twenty minutes after our security guard mate sinks his face into that first delicious bite of seasoned lamb, I'm lowering the last of our hard-drives out of the window to Ollie, who's in the alleyway below.

Ollie unties it, gives the rope a yank and looks up at me.

"Okay, that's the last one," I tell him via our walkie-talkies. Well, security guards aren't the only ones who get to play with toys you know. "I'll have a last look around up here while you get the van, okay?"

"Affirmative good buddy. Oscar bravo, over and out," my walkie-talkie crackles.

"Ollie?" I add.

"What?"

"You're an idiot."

"Roger," he confirms.

Ollie legs it off to go get the van, while I abseil down to the alley-way. We order all our climbing gear through a website from a place in Germany and the ropes we get are about the most common a climber can buy, so they're pretty untraceable, which is just as well seeing as we still haven't figured out a way of untying them and taking them with us once we've abseiled out of a place. I'm sure there's a way but for the life of me I can't think of it.

Ollie comes sprinting back in a big old panic.

"The van's gone!" he flusters.

"What?"

"The van, it's gone."

"It can't be."

"Can't it?" Ollie says. "Tell that to the empty bit of kerb out there then."

"But we put the DO NOT MOVE sticker on it."

"It's this bloody council in' it? If it ain't welded down, they'll have it away. I've a good mind to complain, you know," Ollie fumes.

"To who? The Great Train Robbers? They're about the only ones who'd be on our side," I point out.

"What are we gonna do?"

"What indeed?" a voice behind us asks. We spin round and see Norris leaning against one of the dumpsters, picking his fingers and admiring our computers. "Get the job, did you?" he cackles.

"Norris, you arsehole. Did you nick our van?"

"Nah, the council took it away," he naturally denies.

"And why would they do that when there was a sign on it forbidding its removal?" I ask, already knowing the answer.

"I don't know, but perhaps we should talk about it over a pint once we get these computers out of here," Norris suggests.

"We?" Ollie snaps. "When did we start to include you?"

"When you had your van towed away I reckon," Norris asserts.

"Why you scheming little..." I start but Norris puts a hand up to stop me.

"Ah no, let's not go saying anything we can't take back shall we? I'm only offering to do you a favour, that's all," he says. "Take it or leave it."

"What sort of a favour?" Ollie wants to know.

"Well I'll keep an eye on these computers while you two rustle us up some wheels," he smiles triumphantly, like he's offering to donate us a kidney each.

"Hang on a minute, you mean to tell us you haven't even got transport?" I gawp, this fucker's cheek knowing no bounds.

"No, but I have got a mobile, so I can give you a bell if I get wind of someone phoning the old Bill," he winks. "I mean, if someone were to do that while you were lumbered with all this stock and no wheels, where would you be then?"

"Hunting you to the ends of the Earth with a cricket bat and a bicycle chain," I confidently predict.

Norris has us over a barrel and he knows it. We can't very well tell him to sling his hook because he'd phone the law on us in a heartbeat just out of spite, so we have no choice but to take him on or blow off an entire night's work. It's really that simple.

I stretch out a reluctant hand and offer it to Norris.

"Okay Norris, you've got a deal," I sigh.

Norris beams like it's his multi-billionaire twin brother's birthday. "You know it makes sense," he says, pumping me by the arm.

Actually, scrub that, we do have a choice. And a fairly obvious one at that.

"I certainly do," I glare, hanging on to his fingers when he tries to get them back. But I ain't letting go.

All at once, a look of horrible realisation flashes across Norris's face and he desperately fights to extract his hand from the trouble it's cooked itself, but it's way too late for that. Ollie is now hanging onto his other arm and Norris is tumbling towards the cold hard deck, as the first lengths of rope are coiled around his torso.

4. A date with disaster

Electric's never looked so smart in all his life. Well, everyone looks smart in a new whistle, don't they? Particularly a nice Italian knock-off from M&S, the same as mine and Ollie's, and he's marking the occasion with an interview of his own.

Of sorts.

The peroxide MILF in the seat opposite flutters her eyelids and cleavage in his direction, but Electric only has eyes for the latter.

"Well my dear, I must say..." he starts to schmooze, only to be interrupted by the ringing of his mobile in his inside pocket. "Sorry about this, didn't even know I had it on," he apologises, pulling out his phone to turn it off, then grimacing in frustration when he sees my name on-screen. "I'm sorry my luv, but I've got to take this," he says, pressing the green key to answer. "Hello Bex, look I can't talk at the moment."

"I'm sorry mate, but this is an emergency. Those er... things you need to fill your order. You know?" I hint. "Well we've got 'em, but we've lost our wheels."

"What d'you mean you've lost your wheels?" Electric asks.

"I mean we're standing in a couple of buckets of custard," I crack. "What the fuck d'you think I mean? I mean, we've lost our wheels. We're stuck."

"Well what d'you want me to do about it?" the cavalry asks, smiling across at his date and promising to be off the phone in two ticks.

"Come and get us. Bring your van," I tell him.

"I can't, I'm with someone," he hisses.

"Well bring 'em along then, they can help us load up," I try again.

"Not that sort of someone," he explains, but I ain't giving up that easily. We've finally struck it rich and brought down a wildebeest only to discover that the rest of the termite colony are too fucking preoccupied to give us a hand carrying it home.

"Electric mate, help us for crying-out-loud, we've got a good score here, we're all going to earn out of it," I plead in frustration, but Electric's not for budging.

"Bex, I simply can't get away."

"Well look, if we come to you, can we just borrow your van then?" I compromise.

"Alright. But I need it back by ten," he agrees. "I'm in Spenny's, up by the Green."

Visions of Spenny's and Electric don't quite go together, one being a fancy social club that's also home to the local Rotary mafia, while the other's a grizzled old misery guts who wears his clothes to bed to save himself the hassle of having to put them on again in the morning. I wonder if he's scoping another job, so I ask, "What you doing there?"

"I'm on a bloody date, what d'you think I'm doing. Now sod the fuck off," he barks, hanging up on me and leaving me with one or three unanswered questions.

"Sorry about that luv, urgent business, couldn't be helped," Electric smarms, lifting his eyes just long enough to check that his date's still smiling, before dropping them again. "Right now, where were we?"

Before he can pick up where he left off though, another ringing interrupts him, this time the ringing of a bell from the direction of the stage. On it, a mumsy organiser in a flowery cardy clasps her hands together with delight and calls everyone's attention.

"Okay then, that's three minutes, all change," she warbles, barely able to contain her delight.

Electric watches in despair as his date parts with a little wave and moves along to the next table. The gentleman sat there beams with glee and starts chatting up his new companion as if they're old friends while Electric mopes over his loss.

Electric's not given long to mope though as an almighty thump opposite heralds the arrival of his 'new date' and he turns to find himself confronted with a sack of King Edwards wearing a Spenny's Speed-Daters badge on her lapel.

"Oh, bollocks," he chews.

"What?" she asks.

"Oh nothing. I was just waiting for her to come round for the last half hour and now I've missed out on her," Electric explains, presumably fishing for sympathy and understanding from his new date.

"Oh no, what a bummer," she says, almost shaking Electric out of his socks with the iciness of her glare. "And now you're stuck with me for the next three minutes. Isn't life crap?"

Electric miserably agrees, especially when he glances over and sees the guy's hands and his former date's knockers all over each other like Spring rabbits.

"See, they feel real, don't they?" his ex is saying. "Five grand a tit they cost. Go on, feel them some more."

The sack of King Edwards notices this too and shoots Electric a keep-away scowl.

"Don't even think about it," she warns him.

*

Ollie goes off to get Electric's van while I watch over Norris. We've tied him up with our spare rope and gone through his pockets and sure enough he wasn't lying, he doesn't have his car with him. Unbelievable.

We ponder our respective positions for a while and chat as we wait for Ollie to get back, Norris telling me about his TOP SECRET stamp while I tell him about our interviews and things are cordial enough between us. Well, there's no point being any other way once you've got

180

business done and dusted, is there? I even offer him a chewing gum.

"What flavour?"

"Peppermint," I tell him.

Norris screws his face up like I've questioned his sexuality. "Nah, you're alright," he scowls.

"So, how did the interview go?" another voice asks as it storms towards me from the far end of the alleyway.

I look up and see Mel with a face like thunder approaching fast.

"Oh shit!" I gabble.

"You can say that again," she fumes.

"Mel, I swear, it's not what you think," is the first thing that pops into my head.

"Oh really?" she squawks, eyeing the pile of computers that have been stacked up underneath the open window with the rope hanging from it. "Go on then, do please tell what it is, because I can't wait to see how you're going to explain this lot away."

I have a quick rummage around the old excuse maker and decide upon a course.

"Well look, first off, let me just say that the interview went really well. I think they really liked me," I nod enthusiastically.

*

Ollie piles up at Spenny's and manages to blag his way inside without paying the thirty-quid cover charge by telling the organisers that his mum sent him down here to tell his dad that dinner was ready.

He finds Electric at the back of the busy hall, treading water with his latest date, but rapidly running out of puff.

"Electric. Electric mate, it's me, Ol," Ollie calls from across the hall.

Electric uses up a smile he's been saving for later to apologise for the intrusion. "Excuse me my dear, would you give me a second?"

His date looks up from her watch. "I'll give you a hundred and eighty of them if you like, but that's it," she broods.

Electric regards her for a second longer but Ollie's suddenly upon him.

"Alright 'lec, how's it going?" Ollie says, then turns and nods at Electric's date. "Ma'am."

"Yeah, enough of that," Electric rushes him. "Here, here's me keys, now sod off and make sure you get it back to me by ten, cos I'm gonna be needing it."

"Cheers," Ollie accepts, pocketing Electric's keys and stopping for a fag while his hands are in the vicinity. "Here, you ain't got a light have you? Only I left my matches at work."

"There's a pop-out one in the van, now just sling your bloody hook will you, I've only got a minute left of her," Electric points out with mounting urgency.

"Oh really, going somewhere are you?" Ollie asks Electric's date.

"Ollie, for crying out loud!" Electric snaps at him.

"Blimey, I'm only being polite," Ollie tells Electric, before giving his date a little wink. "He's a miserable old git, ain't he? I dunno what you see in him luv."

Electric's date gives Ollie a considerably larger wink back and runs her eyes up and down his lithe young figure, causing Ollie to break out in ants all over.

"Er yeah, well… er… thanks for the van," Ollie says, retreating a step or two. "I'll bring it back later yeah."

And with that he turns and heads out the way he came in. A thought suddenly occurs to Electric so he calls after him.

"Here Ol, one last thing, there's an old mattress in the back. Shift it to one side if you've got a lot of stuff but don't go slinging it, alright?"

Ollie gives Electric the thumbs up and disappears. Electric turns back to his date but her face has descended several storeys from where he last left it.

"Urghh! You came speed dating in a van with an old mattress in the back?" she recoils.

Electric's suddenly aware that the room has fallen silent and he looks out to see four dozen disbelieving eyes all staring in his direction.

"No no, it's not like that…" he tries to explain, but the crowd's already in mid-murmur when the bells rings again.

His date leaps to her feet and almost sprints across to the next table to get away from him. Ten seconds later, all the women have found new seats, but one chair remains empty.

And if you guess which one, you could win yourself a couple of minutes in the back of a van on an old dirty mattress.

*

"…so really, I was just seeing if I could do it," I'm free-wheeling in Mel's disbelieving ear'ole. "I didn't actually want to do it, just see if I could. Because it's only when we master our demons that we're able to free up our potential."

Mel asks an obvious question I've overlooked.

"So you're going to put it all back then are you?"

"Well no," I shrug. "Not now that we've got it out. I mean, it's a long old schlep up that rope."

"Silly to, really," Norris agrees.

"Keep out of this you," Mel warns him.

"Yeah, keep out of this," I concur, spotting an opportunity to plant my flag next to Mel's.

"What are you barking at me for? I'm on your side, mate," Norris insists.

"Now listen 'ere, Norris…" I warn him, but Mel's having none of it.

"Oi, do you mind? One row at a time please and I was first in the queue," she points out.

"Technically sweetheart, I think I was actually," Norris corrects her.

"Oh for crying-out-loud, haven't you got a gag for him?" Mel beseeches.

"Er yeah, I have actually," I say, then turn to Norris. "Knock knock?" Well, it was on a plate wasn't it. Norris cracks up, but Mel's several time zones from smiling.

"You're never going to change are you?" she suddenly realises.

"Oh Mel, don't be like that," I try, but she's having none of it.

"No it's okay, I'm fine. Really I am, because this is my own fault. I knew what you were when I started going out with you, so I've got no one to blame but myself. I just thought you would've moved on by now."

"Mel, I am trying."

"Yeah, I can see that," she snarls, pointing at the computers. "You're really making an effort, aren't you?"

"Look, this ain't something I can buy patches for. I've got to eat... pay the rent..."

"Buy scratchcards..." Norris contributes.

"Seriously Norris, belt up," I warn.

"If you put half the effort into working that you did into thieving you could have your own business by now," Mel tells me.

"I have got my own business," I argue, pointing out that I'm just about as self-employed as any man can get.

"No Bex, you've got their business," Mel indicates to the office. "There's a difference you know."

A hoot at the far end of the alleyway calls time on this particular conversation as Ollie returns with Electric's van and starts backing it up.

"Mel luv, I really don't want to fight about this and this isn't the time anyway, so please, can we just talk about this later?" I plead, then realise a little sweetener's probably in order. "Over dinner perhaps? On me?"

"On who?" Mel double-checks.

"Alright, on them," I admit, nodding towards the office. "But either way ceasefire, yeah?"

"It's always another time with you, isn't it Adrian?" Mel says sadly.

"Mel please..." I try to appease, but before I can, Norris jumps to his feet and legs it off up the alleyway.

"Oi, get back here!" I shout, haring after him before he can get us all rumbled.

I don't know how it happened, all I do know is what Ollie told me after the event. But when Norris sprints up and past Ollie as he's reversing, he clips the van's wing mirror, startling Ollie and causing him to drop his fag into his lap. Instinctively, Ollie tries to push away from the red hot fag tip, only to floor the accelerator in the process and hurl the van back at thirty miles an hour.

Mel screeches and just about manages to fling herself clear of the careering van, but the twenty-five computers we've carefully stacked up have only a fraction of a second to encode themselves a quick prayer before Ollie cooks their chips good and proper.

The almighty crash stops me and Norris in our tracks and we look back to see Electric's Transit coming to a stop on top of our night's work.

Ollie leaps out brushing the front of his jeans.

"See that? Almost burnt me fucking nads off. And who says smoking's good for you?" he asks, before noticing the mass of broken circuit boards he's just parked on top of. "What the...?"

Mel steps out from behind a dumpster. "You all done for the evening then? Only there's a lovely little Indian round the corner and I think I'll take you up on that offer of dinner after all."

Norris likes the sound of this too. "Can I come?" he asks optimistically.

*

Several beers and an onion bhaji later, I'm finding solace in a plate of chicken madras and chips while Mel's claiming the moral high ground with lentils and Saag Aloo.

"Look, I don't want to nag, but seriously, how many years of shinning up drainpipes do you think you have left in you?" Mel asks.

I give this considerably more thought than I might've done had we got away with the computers tonight. "Not many, I'll give you that," I reluctantly admit.

"Then don't you think it's time you got a plan and stuck to it?" Mel presses, instantly going back on her word about not nagging. Seeing my shoulders sag, she decides to flavour this sentiment with a few words of encouragement. "I'm not joking when I say this, but you could be anything you want to be if you put your mind to it."

"Think so?"

"I know so," she enthuses. "But don't get too far ahead of yourself because you could just as easily end-up a broken-down alky ex-con who splashes his life up the wall, if that's the way you'd prefer to go."

"So basically what you're saying is, the world's my oyster?"

"Hmm, interesting spin. Perhaps you should try out for a job in PR," Mel advises.

"I could do that," I confidently predict. "I'd be great."

"Then do it, otherwise you won't be the only ex around here if you go down," she warns me, spoiling the mood somewhat.

I've heard this threat plenty of times before, but I still can't decide if it's a bluff or real. A few years ago I would've staked my flat (alright, Mel's flat) on it being a bluff, but these days I ain't so sure. I guess we're both older now and time does funny things to people - women in partic-

184

ular. When they're in their early twenties, they love nothing better than flying along on the back of Johnny Rebel's motorbike, chugging beer from the can and flashing their tits at passing buses. It's exciting, it's dangerous and it's exactly what their parents spent their teenage years pleading with them not to do. But time and a few ticks of the biological clock later and it's no longer sexy to still be doing this at thirty-four when everyone else's tits have kids hanging from them. Oh no, it's suddenly a bit sad and Johnny Rebel goes from being a leader to a loser without even noticing it. But Mel wasn't thirty-four. Not yet she wasn't. Not for a few years at least. But like the woman who finds herself holding onto the rope of a runaway hot air balloon, the realisation's quickly dawning on Mel that the longer she hangs on to it, the harder it'll be to eventually let go.

"Are you going to eat both your samosas?" I ask, but Mel's distracted by something passing the window. I turn to see what she's gawping at, only to see Weasel gawping back at us.

"Hey look, talking of losers, it's Weasel. Shall we throw some chips at him?" I chuckle, but Mel's suddenly in a flap.

"Oh God quick, I forgot, your suit!" she splutters in a panic.

"What?" I ask, as I watch Weasel turn and head towards the restaurant entrance.

"He knows you nicked it from M&S. He's been looking for you all day," she tells me, jolting me into action.

"I never, honestly," I promise her, whipping my jacket off the back of my chair and frantically stuffing it out of sight underneath the table.

"Bex, you're actually lying to me while you're hiding your jacket," Mel points out.

"What? Oh yeah," I realise, then admit, "I've got a problem, I know."

Weasel marches in and stops at our table, looking super-pleased with himself for a change. "Evening Bex? Mel?"

"Evening Sergeant. Here, pull up a poppadum," I offer.

"No thanks, not while I'm on duty, if you don't mind," he formally replies, and I swear he rises a mil or two off his toes.

"Not a social call then?" I deduce.

"No, purely business I'm afraid. I'm sure Mel's told you all about it already."

Mel throws her napkin onto the table and snatches up her handbag in a fit of disgust. "Actually you know what, Sergeant, think I'll just go and powder my nose. I'm not sure I can stand to hear any more of his pathetic lies," she growls, turning on a heel and marching off in search of the Benghazi.

Weasel watches her go then pulls a face at me. "Been upsetting her have we?"

"Oh don't you start. Honestly, women: can't live with 'em, can't bury 'em under patios," I bristle. "Anyway, what's up now?"

But Weasel doesn't answer. He's suddenly way too preoccupied admiring my shirt and tie and milking the moment for all it's worth.

"You're looking very dapper this evening Bex. New duds, by any chance?" he smiles.

"What, this old thing? Nah, I've had it ages," I shrug.

"Really? Let's see the jacket that goes with it then, shall we?" he suggests, practically licking his lips.

"Didn't come out with a jacket," I say, at the risk of disappointing him.

"Is that a fact?" he chuckles, checking the back of my chair then glancing underneath the table.

His face immediately drops and his triumphant demeanour turns to disbelief. "Stand up!" he orders.

"What?" I try, buying myself another second or two.

"I said stand up now!" he barks, almost shaking me out of my chair.

Reluctantly, I push it back and rise to my feet to reveal my shirt tails, stripy boxer shorts and a rather fetching set of knobbly knees, but as far as stolen Italian suits go, there are none to be found.

Weasel scours the carpet under the table, then it hits him like a brick.

"Oh shit!" he gasps, and dashes towards the bog after Mel. Unfortunately, all he finds is an emergency exit swinging open in the wind.

I knock over four tables and a dozen dinners scrambling out of the front door and spot Mel a hundred yards up the road and fleeing for all she's worth, my trousers and jacket flapping from her bag.

"Run!" I scream after her as Weasel rounds the corner and hares after us like an Exocet on overtime.

You know what, some days are like this, aren't they?

At least, they often are for me.

THE KEY JOB

1. A new start

Two years later, some sour-faced servant of Her Majesty twists a big bunch of keys in a lock and opens a door for me one final time.

"Go on then, sling your hook, Beckinsale," Mr Benjamin says, nodding me in the direction of the great outdoors - or at least, the great outdoors's car park.

I pat my pockets and shrug.

"I'm sorry my good man, but I don't appear to have any small change on me at the moment."

The peak of Mr Benjamin's cap turns to face me, though there's still no sign of his eyes. "Yeah, well I'm sure you'll do something about that before too long, won't you?" he sneers.

"Oh charming," I grumble. "What happened to the benefit of the doubt? A fresh start?"

"What happened to my Thermos?" he barks, before shoving me out into freedom and slamming the door behind me.

I'm just pondering whether or not to knock on the door and paint him a picture when a van hoots at me from across the road. I turn and see Electric flashing his lights and teeth at me in no particular order and my shoulders sag at the sight.

"How do Bex, how's it going?" he grins, when I eventually wander over.

"Well the day started out pretty good, then someone hooted at me and here we are," I tell him.

"We've come to give you a lift," Electric says, indicating over at Ollie in the passenger seat.

"Well I didn't think someone had finally come to visit me, did I?" I reply and I weren't kidding. In the last two years, Tatley Bottle Museum had had more visitors than me - and that was even after they'd accidentally locked that cat in over the Bank Holiday Weekend. Oh yes, I'd been dropped like a hot brick and no mistake.

Of course, they'd all been there in court to see me and Ol win our first serious stretch. My mum, my dad, my sister and her fella, Mel naturally, her entire extended family, everyone I'd ever been accused of ripping off, Weasel, the lot. Oh yes, they'd bussed them in from far and wide just for the occasion. There couldn't have been a high horse anywhere in county with anyone still on its back that morning as they were all sitting in court number three hoping and praying to see their least favourite scumbag burst into tears as vitriolic justice was meted out in the name of Queen Elizabeth II. Well, there was no way I was going to give them the satisfaction, so when the judge gave me four years and banged his hammer, I gave the cheering public gallery a defiant thumbs up and headed off to the cells as if I was heading into space. It was a different

189

story with Ollie though. Just as we were being led away, he asks the judge if he knows what time it is.

"Why, you got to be somewhere or something?" the judge replies.

"No, it's just I haven't got my watch on me," Ollie explains, but that's the extent of their conversation.

"You ain't going to need to know the time for a good few years," the prison warder in the dock with us chuckles as he's showing us down.

"What's up with you? You just find a hole in your pocket or something?" I ask him.

"No, I just love my job I do. Brings me a great deal of satisfaction," he savours, "putting filth like you in their cages."

"That's not very nice," Ollie says.

"Yeah, what you getting so personal for?" I ask.

"Shut your mouth you filthy maggot. You speak when you're spoken to. You're in my world now," he jabs me angrily.

I cast Ollie a look and he reads it instantly.

"Hang on, did you just call me a nigger?" Ollie asks.

"What?" the prison guard yelps.

"I'd like to see your supervisor if I may," Ollie then says.

Little flies. That's all we could muster. Little flies in his ointment. Nothing that would hurt him for real of course but enough to keep him staring at his bedroom ceiling worrying about his career for a few nights, that was all.

Me and Ollie were separated shortly after that, but a couple of outstandingly well-behaved years later, I open Electric's passenger-side door and am reintroduced to his warm smile.

"Hello mate, bet it feels like your birthday don't it?" he says.

"Put on a paper hat and serve me cauliflower and cheese three times a day and you'd have our 'hilarious' prison cook off to a tee, you would," I point out, but Ollie's confused and starts asking who I mean. "Oh never mind," I respond in frustration, suddenly remembering Ollie's twenty-questions party piece.

"So where d'you want dropping?" Electric asks, starting the van and pulling away.

"Mel's," I tell him. "Better face that music sooner or later I guess."

See, me and Mel might've been able to outrun Weasel that night, had it just been him after us, but he quickly got on the blower and flooded the area with his mates, so that we were picked up after only twenty minutes more on the lam. A warrant was later issued off the back of our arrests and Ollie came home to find his flat had been transformed into a police station and the next morning all three of us were charged in connection with the M&S raid; me and Ollie for burglary, and Mel, much to her dismay, for attempting to pervert the course of justice. Charlie however, petitioned that his secretary had not realised she was carrying stolen property in her handbag - after all, it had been me who'd stuffed the items in there, not her - and called in all his outstanding favours until eventually Mel's charges were dropped.

Bizarrely enough, rather than being happy about this, Mel was even more livid than usual and blamed me for everything, which was a little immature if you ask me. Still, that was two years ago, this was now. How long could a girl hold a grudge?

Ollie, never one to read between the lines, turns and asks me how Mel's doing. "I haven't seen her for a couple of years," he explains unnecessarily.

"Snap," I trump him.

Yep, one last glimpse of her scowling at me in the dock and a letter while I was in Erlestoke to let me know that all my Arsenal videos now had *Friends* recorded over them and that had been the last I'd seen or heard from her. This didn't exactly bode well for the touching reunion I'd been hoping for on my release, which was worrying because I'd really been hoping to touch something with tits today (and possibly get it to knock me up a bit of lunch afterwards), but there was nothing I could do about the past. Mel's stall was set out. All I could do was pop round during opening hours and hope she wasn't currently serving anyone else.

I'm just dwelling on these thoughts when something else suddenly occurs to me. I look at my watch, then I look at Ollie and notice he doesn't have the same prison demeanour as me, which is decidedly odd seeing as he should have got out this morning too. "What time did you get out?"

"About the same time, nine o'clock," he replies.

"Ollie, you can't have. It's nine o'clock now. And you were down in Sussex, so when did you get out?"

"Last week," he tells me, much to my consternation.

"Last week? But we got exactly the same sentence. How d'you get out a week before me?"

"I dunno. Just got me head down and kept me nose clean," he shrugs. "Didn't you?"

"Joking ain't ya. The last thing I wanted to do in that place was get my head down. You never knew what was waiting for it down there," I shudder.

Electric chuckles. "Nothing that'll keep your nose clean, that's for sure, hey lads," he savours, like a man who'd seen both ends of some of that plenty of times before.

"Urgh, don't," I object, trying to convince my breakfast not to jump ship.

Electric duly changes the subject, though I'm no less dismayed at where it pitches up. "Anyway, you're out now, and about time too because I've got stacks of jobs lined-up for you two," he promises.

"Are you sure you didn't want to shout that across the road at us when you hooted?" I ask him.

"You what?" he blinks in confusion.

"Electric mate, I've just got out, and you're already booking my bunk for next season."

"Ah well, obviously I know you've got a few things to do first," he concedes with a wink. "Have a beer? Visit a lady?"

"Have a shit with the door closed?" Ollie joins in with the game.

"Yeah, that's the one I'm really looking forward to, to be honest," I agree.

"So no problem," Electric smiles. "Take a day or two if you like, but don't go getting too comfy 'cos I've only just kept me head above water these last two years waiting for you two to get out."

"And your hair and most of your clothes by the looks of things," I point out, making Electric sniff his coat. "Let's get one thing clear shall we? I ain't going back inside, not now, not ever again, I'm straight from now on."

Electric's absolutely stunned and disgusted in equal measures. "What sort of defeatist talk is that? Your first serious stretch and you're packing it in? Blimey, look at me. I've been in and out my whole life and I'm still in the game."

"Yeah, but that's because you're a loser mate, and that's what losers do," I agree.

Electric is staggered by my effrontery and demands to knows what I'm talking about. "I'm doing alright," he insists, giving me a flash of the fake Rolex he's wearing and the Ratner's St Christopher around his neck.

I also point out the bed made up in the back.

"You've been living in your van again, haven't you?"

"Well, it's cheaper than having a house, isn't it?" he explains.

*

On our way back to town, we pass a beaten-up old Ford Escort Estate on the hard shoulder, accessorised with obligatory go-faster stripes, balding tyres and ticket-writing traffic cop.

"…driving without due care and attention, overtaking on the inside, driving in a bus lane, failing to stop at a stop sign," Bennett rattles off as Norris rubs his face and sighs. "… failing to stop at a pedestrian crossing, reversing the wrong way up a one-way street, using your horn to hoot at a party of school girls…"

Norris vehemently objects. "Oh come on, didn't you see that little blonde one? You can't blame us for that, she knew the score if you know what I mean."

Bennett pushes up the peak of his cap and appeals to his charge. "Norris please, one set of offences at a time? I've only got three pages left in my notepad. Right now, where was I…" he tries to recall.

"Hold on look, there's no need for all this, is there?" Norris interrupts, forcing a smile. "Here why don't you take a butcher's at my licence? I think you'll find everything's in order," he says, checking the coast's clear before handing Bennett his documents.

Bennett looks down at what Norris has slipped him and sighs. "Norris, are you trying to bribe a police officer - with a fiver?"

"What?" Norris stares. "Well it's all I've got ain't it? Me dole ain't due till Thursday for fuck's sake. Can I owe you the rest?"

*

Electric stops just up the road from mine and Mel's flat. I'm about to leap out when he grabs me by the arm and shows me his best desperate face.

"Bex, are you sure you won't change your mind?"

Even Ollie's suddenly pitching in on Electric's side and applying the old peer pressure. "Yeah, come on Bex, just a couple of jobs, just to cadge a bit of holiday money together?"

"I've only just got back off my holidays if you hadn't noticed, and I'm well and truly rested up thank you very much," I tell them both, causing Electric to pucker his lips and apologise as menacingly as he can muster.

"Well then I'm sorry about this but you've left me no choice?" he shrugs, pulling out his mobile and dialling a number scrawled on the back of a fag packet.

"No choice about what?" I enquire. "Who are you phoning? If it's the Samaritans, don't listen to them. Stepping off tall buildings can actually work for some people."

"Yeah, hello, it's me. He's here with us now," Electric tells the person he's just phoned all surreptitiously before handing it to me. "Here, he wants to speak to you."

"Hello, Osama Bin Laden's office? How can I help you?" I ask the phone.

"You can start by giving me the computers you owe me?" a voice on the other end of the line tells me.

"Oh yeah, and who the fuck is this?" I ask, stuffed if I'm going to be brow-beaten into compensating Horace after I've already done two years for rearranging his office for him. But it ain't Horace on the phone. And it ain't Doris either.

"This, Adrian, is Omit fucking Hassan," the voice informs me, "and I don't appreciate your use of language."

I look accusingly at Electric, but the bastard just chews his lip and shows me his palms in response.

"Now, I repeat, where are my computers?" Omit asks again, this time a little more assertively.

"Er... we didn't get 'em. We got caught. We just did two years for 'em," I tell him, extremely unhappy to find myself on first-name terms with Tatley's number one nutbox.

"That was not what I asked. I asked you where my computers were. I placed an order with your friend two years ago. But that order was never filled and I lost business - and face - because of it. Which means you are in my debt. And I will collect, one way or the other. You have one day," he assures me, then the line goes dead.

"You miserable fucking rat! What d'you drag us into it with the Hassans for?" I fist-wave under Electric's nose.

"To water my end down of course," he explains all matter-of-fact. "I ain't facing those lunatics alone."

"And how much exactly do 'we' owe them?"

"Your end's three grand, but if we do a couple of jobs for them, then they say we'll be all square," he says, like that makes everything okay. Or would even happen. Something tells me the Hassans didn't dish out temp jobs, only permanent contracts. "What do you reckon?" Electric smiles enthusiastically.

I don't know whether to strangle him, happy-slap the shit out of him or ask him to drive us back to prison. In the event, I simply nick his fags and put some distance between us.

"Arsehole!" I shout, jumping from the van and storming off home.

Ollie stays long enough to assure Electric that he'll have a word with me and points out that the air freshener hanging from his rear view mirror is not actually an air freshener.

"It's actually a toilet cleaner," Ollie tells him.

"Is it?" Electric says, squinting at the block of Harpic dangling from his windscreen mirror. "Oh. Still, smells nice, don't it?"

2. Johnny on the spot

Ollie catches up with me just as I'm turning onto my front path.

"I tell you, the pair of you. As if I ain't got enough on my plate already," I fume when he falls in step with me.

"Why, what's up?" he says, causing me to pull up sharply and glare at him.

"You know what, it's so nice never having to worry about what I say getting spread all around town."

"Uh?" Ollie uhs.

"Mel," I remind him. "I wasn't looking forward to facing her five minutes ago, and that was before I had to ask her to lend us a few grand. This is really going to be some sweet fucking home coming this is."

I turn and continue on my way but Ollie just stays where he is.

"Oh well look, if you think she's going to be funny, perhaps it'd be best if you went and saw her yourself..." he tries, but I just go back and grab him by the lapel.

"Oh no, you're coming with me. If I'm having to step into the firing line, then I want you there with me to soak up a few plates," I tell him in no uncertain terms. This is one of my tried and tested strategies to surviving Mel's worst rages. See, if there's one thing that winds her up even more than me, it's Ollie asking her if everything's okay when she's flinging our stuff around the flat. Oh yes, Electric's not the only one who likes to water his end down whenever possible.

I try my key in the door but it won't make mates with the lock. It's then that I notice the gleaming new barrel.

"Don't tell me she's had the locks changed," I mutter.

"Okay," Ollie agrees.

"Hang on, did you know about this?" I say.

"No," Ollie stares.

"Are you sure?" I press.

"Of course. How could I? No one even mentioned nothing about it to me while I was inside, not Belinda, my mum, dad, Keith, Rollo, Dan or no one," he tells me, boxing me in the chops with this revelation.

"Did you get all them visits while you were inside?" I squawk, scarcely believing it after feeling like I'd just returned from the far side of Neptune.

"Yeah," Ollie confirms, then really goes for it. "I tell ya, your dad's a laugh, in' he?"

"My dad visited you too?"

"Yeah, but only a couple of times," he shrugs. "And only because he didn't want to entrust my birthday cake to the post, not after your mum had baked it herself and everything."

I don't know what to say. I'm dumbstruck. My miserable fucking family had abandoned me in my hour of need and deliberately tended to my best-mate, almost certainly because they knew it would eventually get back to me. I tell you, what a load of cunts. I tell you another thing an' all, the day I got a letter from the hospital pleading with me for a chunk of my bone marrow was the day I sent them a bag of Winalot.

I'm just about to put these thoughts and feelings into a stream of four-lettered abuse when the door's yanked open and a strange and angry Johnny stares out at me.

"What's this? What are you doing?" Johnny demands.

"Finding out who my friends are," I tell him, before facilitating the formal introductions. "Anyway, who the fuck are you?"

"I live here," Johnny tells me.

"That's funny, 'cos I could've sworn I did," I reply.

"Go on, clear off the pair of you," he barks, before discovering his door won't close over my foot.

"Slow your horses mate, where's Mel? I need to speak to her," I say, but Johnny just scrunches up his face.

"Mel? I don't know no one called Mel," he tells me.

"Yes you do," I nudge. "Blonde hair? Pissed off-looking? Nice arse? She lives here for fuck's sake."

"Well she doesn't live here no more," he informs us.

Ollie decides to have a go.

"We're looking for Mel," he says, in case Johnny hasn't tumbled this yet.

"Well then your quest goes on, doesn't it?" Johnny responds, finally kicking my foot off his threshold and slamming the door in our faces.

"Someone got out of the wrong side of bed this morning," Ollie tells me.

"Yeah, my fucking bed," I point out, then start ringing the doorbell. Johnny reappears.

"What now?"

"Er look, I think there's been some sort of mix up," I tell him, realising we'll get further with diplomacy than indignation. "We've er… been away… er… back packing," I decide.

"Very horizon-broadening of you," Johnny says, before trying to slam the door on us again.

"Oi you fucker!" I object.

"Oi yourself. You touch my door again and I'll call the law on you," he threatens, words I could really do without hearing on my first morning of freedom.

"What's up with you? I just want to talk a sec," I struggle, but Johnny's having none of it.

"No, this is a scam, I know it," he says, his brow a tangle of fear and mistrust. "If you've been away backpacking where's your backpacks?"

"I took it off, it got heavy," I tell him, fighting to keep the door open.

"Where's your suntan then?" the suspicious bastard persists.

"I ain't applying for a grant off Hackney council here mate, I just want to know where my stuff is," I say, and this finally catches his attention.

"Hold on, are you 'Shit Bag'?" he asks.

"You what?"

"There's a box in the garage with a few bits and bobs that's been left for someone called 'Shit Bag'," he says and I reluctantly confirm that I am in all likelihood the same.

"Yes, I believe that'll be me," I sigh.

"Oh. Come on then. It's in here."

*

I guess I couldn't blame Johnny for his suspicions, such are the perils of the unexpected knock. Most of us can't even survive a bath these days without some cunt in Nigeria ringing us up to tell us we've qualified for two free French doors and a trip to the Oscars with Elton John. All we've got to do is confirm our bank details and PIN number please?

And the man at the front door is even worse because while we're completing his survey on gullibility, half his mates are testing the findings via our back garden fence. Yes, you really have to keep your wits about you at all times, and us Brits are easier to catch out than most. You try scoring a few bank account details off some of our spaghetti-sucking cousins across the moat and see how many digits you get. Oh yes, we're easy marks alright, the ingrained British disposition makes us so, but we're wising up. It won't be long before the greeting "Good morning sir, and how are you?" gets redefined in the Oxford English Dictionary as fighting talk.

Still, old Johnny had survived his brush with stranger danger today and cleared a shelf in his garage to boot, which must've given him something to think about.

I'm doing a little thinking of my own back at Ollie's while I'm going through a box marked "*to be collected by 'Shit Bag', Spring 2009*", not least of all, where are all my pants? I should've had about ten pairs in here. I used to before I went down, so where are they now? Okay, yeah sure, Johnny would've had a rifle through my box to check out if there was anything worth choring, but I would've thought my grunters would've been safe enough.

Which left only one other explanation.

"Hey, you've got *Friends* on video," Belinda squeaks with delight when she looks in the box and sees my collection of home-recorded tapes. Yep, Mel remembered to leave those alright.

"Blimey, is that all the stuff you've got after four years of living together?" Ollie gawps. "Didn't have much, did you?"

"Will you stop trying to cheer me up, it isn't working," I tell him.

"So Mel never said nothing to you about going away?" Belinda asks.

"No. The last time I heard from her she said she was recording some stuff off the telly for me but there was no mention of her splitting town."

"Perhaps she'd just had enough of you," Belinda speculates.

"Yeah, perhaps that was it," I grimace.

"Well it ain't easy going out with a prisoner you know," Belinda explains. "Just seeing each other for a few hours a week, and even then, just for walks around the prison gardens or the odd day-release picnic by the seaside."

"The what?" I splutter.

Ollie looks at me as if I've just discovered remote controls after years of poking the telly with a couple of broom handles sellotaped together.

"Picnics by the sea. Didn't you have none then?" he asks.

"No I fucking didn't. But it sounds like you had one great big long one," I suggest.

"Hey it was still prison Bex," he reminds me. "It was still four walls and nothing but a telly and a PlayStation for company when that big old door shut at night."

"You had a PlayStation in your cell?"

"Yeah, but only a PlayStation 2. Not the new one. Didn't you have nothing like that then?"

"No, funnily enough I didn't," I fume.

"What did you have in your cell then?"

"A sex offender called Colin - who walked in his sleep," I tell him.

Ollie mulls this over. "Oh well, it's not like he could get very far I guess."

"He didn't need to, not with me in the next bunk," I recall with a shudder. Oh yes, ghosts and ghoulies hold no fear for me any more, not after a couple of years of Colin trying to go bump in the night.

"Well look, if you need a place to stop, you can always kip down on our couch until you get somewhere of your own," Ollie says, which looks like the best offer I'm likely to get today. At least, it is until Belinda opens her gob.

"But don't go getting any ideas about sneaking into our bedroom at night and joining us in bed you bad bad man," she froths, all-but dropping her knickers onto my head.

Ollie's a little more insistent.

"Yeah, don't alright!" he warns me.

"Don't worry, I don't want to," I promise him in no uncertain terms. The last thing I need after losing a girlfriend and finding a sofa is to be anywhere near that keg of dynamite.

I go back to searching through my box but don't find what I'm looking for, which unnerves me for reasons you'll come to understand.

"What are you looking for?" Ollie spots.

"A key," I tell him.

"What key?" he inevitably asks.

"It's just a key."

"To what?" he won't let go, so I decide to tell him. After all, no harm in him knowing now.

"Look, do you know the one single thing that kept me going through all those days and nights I was inside?"

Ollie and Belinda both have a guess.

"The Friday beer allowance?" Ollie suggests.

"What?"

"Colin?" Belinda tries.

"No. It was my nest-egg. What I was going to start over again with when I got out."

"I didn't know you had a nest-egg," Ollie says.

"Of course you didn't. That's because it's a secret nest-egg. I didn't even tell Mel about it."

Belinda takes another guess. "Like a surprise?"

"Yeah, something like that. Anyway, I've got three grand squirreled away, which I can use to get the Hassans off my back if the worst comes to the worst, only it's in a safety deposit box, and I don't seem to have the key anymore."

"I didn't know you had a safety deposit box," Ollie then says, really going for it today.

"Again, that because it's a secret safety deposit box. No one knows about it, not even Mel. Which is just as well I reckon, though it does mean the key's probably still where I hid it two years ago."

Ollie's full of consternation that I've been keeping things from him, particularly things decorated with the Queen's head.

"But we don't have any secrets from each other," he objects.

"Correction Ol, you don't have any secrets from me because you've got a gob on you like a runaway train. I on the other hand have lots of secrets from you," I put him straight.

Ollie's eyes crease in my direction.

"What else you keeping from me then?"

I decide this conversation's best left unexplored.

"That's between me and Colin," I tell him.

*

Johnny's not best pleased to see us again after only a couple of hours and is suddenly convinced beyond all reasonable doubt that we're definitely out to fleece him.

"No. Go away. I've given you what you came for. You're not coming in, now fuck off away from my property or I'll call the police," he shouts, before slamming the door on us again, raising the drawbridge and putting a couple of gallons of lead on the stove.

I shout after him through the letterbox. "Come on mate, please, I'll totally make it worth your while," but this is all undone once Ollie joins me at the letterbox.

"It's just a little key to a secret safety deposit box that we..."

"Don't tell him that, you big brain clot," I push him away.

"What?"

"If there's one thing I need even less than losing my key, it's for someone to find it who knows what he's found, you big gimbo," I say, before heading off to formulate a plan.

3. Our brave boys in blue

Across town, Sergeant Atwell's having about as much success with his afternoon as we are with ours. A red-eyed greasy beanpole in market-bought sportswear and chocolate-wrapper bling stares at him from across the custody desk and repeats a single phrase over and over again with full co-operation.

"No speeky Inglish,"

"Name? I need, your name?" Atwell tries for the umpteenth time, pointing at the form between them and wiggling a pen in an effort to nudge the penny.

The prisoner smiles and nods enthusiastically. "No speeky Inglish," he reckons.

Weasel pokes his head into the exchange as he wanders by.

"Making new friends?" he asks.

"I just love Mondays I do," Atwell sighs wearily.

"What's the charge?"

"Shoplifting. Though I'll bet you a pound to a drachma that he's done more, but I can't look him up on the computer without a name?" Atwell explains. "Just - tell - us - your - name?"

The prisoner smiles and gleefully tells the pair of them; "No speeky Inglish. No speeky Inglish."

"Here look, don't worry about that, we don't need his name," Weasel assures Atwell, "just his DNA." Weasel produces a clear plastic bag with a jumper inside and carefully unseals it.

"What's that?" Atwell asks.

"It's the sweater worn by the Parkside Strangler. I've been looking for someone to dump this case on for ages. Should clear up my workload nicely," Weasel tells him, then holds open the bag in front of the prisoner and borrows his hand.

"You think the CPS'll buy it?" Atwell says, hesitantly.

"Yeah sure, why not? Especially if he confesses everything in his suicide note."

"Oh no, we ain't doing another one of those again are we?" Atwell objects. "The enquiry's still snooping into the circumstances of the last one, and that was only four months ago."

Weasel looks at the prisoner who's still smiling.

"Yeah, but they haven't found anything yet, and they ain't gonna, so we can get away with another one as long as it's just an illegal."

"Oh, alright," Atwell reluctantly shrugs, rooting through the cupboards for a dirty bed sheet. "But Bennett can find him this time. I ain't filling in all that paperwork again."

Weasel agrees, so Atwell starts knotting the sheet.

"Okay then young fella, if I can just get you to handle this," Weasel invites, dipping the prisoner's hand towards the open bag.

The smile drops from the prisoner's face in an instant.

"Oh your fucking bike you bent bastard. My name's Cobb, David Cobb and I wanna see my lawyer. I wanna see him now!"

"Sorry Strangler, but no speeky Inglish," Weasel tells him, then instructs a nearby PC who's examining the contents of his handkerchief as if it were the face of the Madonna to bung him in the cells for a bit of quiet time.

"Cheers Tom," chuckles Atwell.

"No problem. Livens up the day a bit, don't it."

"So, who's sweater is that really?" Atwell asks, dropping his eyes back towards Weasel's 'evidence' bag.

"Oh, it's mine. Just got it back from the dry cleaners. Look, they still haven't got those egg stains out," he frowns, before a thought occurs to him. "Anyway, I hear Bex got out today? Think I'll pop over and see him this afternoon, just to make sure he's keeping his nose clean," he nods knowingly.

"Oh really? That's bad timing. It'll mean you'll miss the crack raid on the Steve Bilko Estate," Atwell tells him. The Steve Bilko Estate was originally intended to be named in honour of South Africa anti-apartheid activist and martyr, Steve Biko, but Tatley's Lady Mayor had never heard of Mr Biko and subsequently did what all Lord and Lady Mayors the length and breadth of Britain do in such situations and referred to her own depositories of knowledge rather than admit ignorance. Thus, the typo was corrected on the plans, the signs were reordered and the Steve Bilko Estate was unveiled - despite our esteemed Lady Mayor's niggling suspicion that his first name was actually Ernest.

The name of the place aside, The Steve Bilko Estate was no laughing matter, especially for the coppers who patrolled it.

"Oh, does it?" Weasel exclaims, then shrugs. "Oh well, never mind. Can't be helped I guess."

Atwell's been in the job for more than twenty years though and can spot a nutmeg when he sees one of his colleague's shoulders dropping. "Yeah, nice try. They're all waiting for you upstairs so you'd better draw your stab vest and get up to the briefing room. Riot boys will be here in half an hour," he says, punching Weasel's pause button.

Weasel turns back to face Atwell when the phrase 'stab vest' stops jangling around his brain and he decides to appeal to his fellow-Sergeant's better nature. "Er… yeah, well, you know the score Frank. Not sure I'm particularly up for this one, if you know what I mean. All those excitable Kingston boys and reinforced doors and all that. Look, do us a favour and cover for us while I slip off will you? Be a drink in it for you."

The Custody Sergeant chews this over for a second. He remembers only too well his own time on the front line; the anticipation, the danger, the knot of fear that gripped his stomach and pre-warned him when an operation was destined to go bad. It's a sixth sense that all serving officers have and he sees these concerns in Weasel's face. Atwell then sees himself clearing out Weasel's locker of his effects, packing them away in a little brown box and sending them home to his family. He further sees himself hanging up his own coat in the now empty locker, and finally being able to trust his lunchbox to the top shelf, safe in the knowledge that this one doesn't have a heating pipe running behind it to cook his egg sandwiches and ferment his Ribena.

"Tom?" Atwell says.

"What?"

"No speeky Inglish."

4. A window of opportunity

Ollie is crouching behind a bush just up the road from my old flat, keeping watch for matey, when I return.

"Don't this bloke ever go out? Surely no one can have that much milk?" he says, looking at his watch.

"Still in there then?"

"Yeah, the big agoraphobic. Anyway, where have you been?" he asks.

"Getting us a little help," I say, distracting him long enough for the wrong arm of the law to tap him on the shoulder and shit him up.

"'ello 'ello 'ello, what's going on here then?"

Ollie leaps out of his boots and instinctively goes to leg it when he clocks the police uniform standing two feet behind him, but I catch hold of his arm and hang onto it long enough for him to focus on the face.

"What the ... oh Norris, you big nimrod," he finally realises.

"Evening all," Norris grins, bending his knees theatrically. "Nice to see you again. Welcome home."

"Thanks," Ollie says, catching his breath. "Every day away from you was like torture."

"I can well believe it," Norris nods. "As attested to in the postcard Bex sent us - very comical."

"What did it say?" Ollie asks.

"Wish you were here," I tell him. Was ever a truer word scribbled onto the back of a piece of prison-issued note paper?

Ollie finally relaxes enough to take in the full majesty of Norris's get-up. "Where d'you get the uniform?"

"Joke shop on the High Street," Norris confirms.

"Check it out, he's got a radio and everything," I say, pointing out the optional extras.

"Does it work?" Ollie asks.

"Oh yeah, here listen," Norris demonstrates and starts talking into his radio. "Calling all cars, calling all cars, be on the look-out for a couple of shifty-looking blokes hanging around Monteagle Lane. One thin, one fat, wearing bowler hats and carrying a piano," he chuckles, then squeezes his radio a couple of times to make it squeak like *HMS Bathtime*.

"That's brilliant," Ollie reckons, making me wonder if he's got a rubber bone somewhere that does the same thing.

"So you know what to say?" I double-check with Norris.

"Relax," he reassures me. "I've been dealing with the jam sandwich brigade long enough to know the sorts of noises they make on their silly days. Don't you chicken curry a ding-a-ling."

Norris scoots across the road and up to my former front door. He gives us a nod and so me and Ollie duck out of sight as he rings the bell.

"This has got to be the worst plan in the world, hasn't it?" Ollie ventures.

After a few seconds, the door is yanked open and Johnny appears waving a shovel.

"Right, you asked for it...." he barks, but drops the shovel the instant he sees Norris's uniform. "Oh, sorry officer, I was expecting someone else."

"Is that so, sir?" Norris raises an eyebrow. "We've been getting reports about a couple of conmen in the area. You wouldn't know anything about this would you?"

Johnny almost orgasms with vindication.

"I knew it. I knew they were up to something. You can always tell," he triumphantly celebrates.

"You certainly can sir. Gypos were they?" Norris nods knowingly, pulling out his notepad and pen in readiness.

"What? Er well, I don't know. Maybe," Johnny thinks, keen to be as co-operative as possible.

"Yeah, well we get a lot of 'em on our patch we do sir; gypos, paedos, asylum seekers, single mums, Big Issue vendors. Scum of the Earth they are. Send 'em all back, that's what we say, isn't it sir, hey?" Norris rallies.

Johnny's suddenly on shaky ground and while he doesn't want to commit whole-heartedly to the ethnic cleansing of Tatley, he does want to show the nice young Constable whose side he's on in order to earn a little preferential treatment and avoid transportation to the Outer Hebrides himself.

"Erm, yes well quite," he agrees about as much as he dares. "Is there anything I can help you with, officer?"

"Yes sir, I'm afraid I'm gonna have to ask you to come down to the station and give us a description of these diddies for our files," Norris informs him. "Don't worry sir, we'll get 'em and give 'em a right good hiding when we do."

"Do I have to come right now?" Johnny frowns.

"I'm afraid so sir. Crime waits for no man as they say, so be a good citizen and get your hat."

"But I don't have a hat," Johnny says, taking Norris literally.

"I see," Norris says, his eyes narrowing as he makes a note of this in his pad. "No - hat."

*

Me and Ollie stay out of sight while Norris leads Johnny away from the flat and off down the road towards his car.

"Of course, if it was up to us, we'd hang the lot of 'em, wouldn't we sir?" Norris is saying, as he passes our bush.

"Er... er... yes, I suppose," Johnny is concurring.

"Okay, come on. Let's be quick," I tell Ollie and we dart back the way they'd just come and shin up the drainpipe to my old kitchen balcony.

I run my fingers along the ledge just above the window and am relieved to find my old "spare key" still there. It's not actually a "key" at all to be honest, it's actually just a reshaped length of wire coat hanger that's been straightened out and bent into a little loop at the end. I feed the loop through the little circular air vent in the top right-hand corner of the kitchen window and start fishing about for the latch. It only takes a couple of goes before I've got the window open and am replacing my "key".

"That was pretty smart," Ollie applauds, looking suitably impressed.

"Yeah well, I always like know how to break into wherever I live, in case I ever get locked out or for when Mel changes the locks. It's happened before you know," I tell him as I climb through the window. "Why, don't you know how to break into your place then?"

"No, I just use my key. It's a bit easier really."

"But what if you lose your key?"

"I'd use my spare," he says, following me through.

"But what if you lose your spare?"

"I'd get Belinda to let us in."

"And if Belinda's not in?" I press, helping him down off the kitchen counter.

"Well I dunno," he shrugs. "Get you to let us in I expect. I mean, I'm assuming you've sussed out how to break into my place already by now."

"Yeah, I have as it happens," I confirm. "Fancy putting a cat-flap there of all places."

*

After ten minutes of circling the block, Norris and Johnny finally happen upon Norris's car parked on the far side of the playing fields.

"Sorry about the mystery tour sir, forgot where I parked," Norris apologises.

Johnny stares at the beaten-up old Ford Escort Estate in front of him and then at the police officer who's currently counting his way through an enormous knot of keys to find a likely match.

"Hold on, what's this?" Johnny objects.

"What?"

"Where's your police car?"

This is an interesting question and one that's only just occurred to Norris himself. He decides to offer up the first explanation he can think of rather than going all out to try to come up with something convincing.

"Oh er well, I'm with CID, we travel about in unmarked cars see."

"But you're in uniform?" Johnny points out.

Norris sees he's right and again goes with the first thing to wander into his brain. "It's me day off," he explains.

Johnny's face falls as a wave of realisation crashes over him. "I don't believe it, you're in it with them!" he gasps.

"Well I wouldn't say with them sir," Norris disagrees. "More just sort of just helping 'em out for money, if you know what I mean."

"Oh my God!" Johnny yelps, turning and running across the fields.

Norris watches impassively as Johnny sprints away hell for leather, sniffs a couple of times and calls after him; "It's alright, don't worry, they ain't paying me to go chasing after you or nothing."

But Johnny just keeps on going, past the slides, across the football pitch and back up the alleyway towards the estate. Norris congratulates himself on a job half-done, counts the fifty quid I've paid him and turns his thoughts to opportunism.

Memories of Bennett pulling him over this morning scratch the back of his head and he decides to test a theory he's been formulating. He stuffs the money into his top pocket, steps into the road and flags down the first car to come his way.

*

There are some things I love and some things I don't. And fishing my hand about into a toilet cistern for a key I can't find, falls into the latter. Forget that the water's clean, that poo can't get up into this bit or that germs are kept at bay by one of Electric's air-fresheners hanging in the water, I just don't like sticking my hand about in toilets. I think it probably goes back to when I was at school, and the big lads used to shove little lads' heads down the bogs and flush them for a giggle. I always hated getting toilet water on my hands back then too, but those kids weren't going to stick their own heads in the bog you know.

"What d'you put it in there for?" Ollie asks me at my elbow.

"So Mel wouldn't find it, of course."

"But what if Mel had to fiddle about with the toilet mechanics or something?" Ollie suggests.

"Joking ain't ya?" I scoff. "You show me a girl who fiddles around with toilet mechanics and I'll show you a plumber in drag."

"Well Belinda does," Ollie says proudly.

"Really?" I'm surprised.

"Yeah, but only when it needs a really big flush," he explains.

"Lovely," I frown. I pull my hand out of the freezing cold water and dry it on one of Johnny's towels. "Bollocks!"

"What's up?"

"It ain't there. My key ain't there. Someone's had it away."

I realise time's not on our side but I ain't leaving without my key. One way or another, it has to be in here somewhere. I theorise that Johnny might've found it and put it in a drawer for safe keeping. He's unlikely to have thrown it away. I mean, only an idiot throws away a key when he doesn't know what it's for, so it has to be in the flat somewhere. And as this is only a one-bedroom flat with maybe ten drawers spread between three rooms, so it shouldn't take too long to go through them all. "Come on, let's have a look around."

*

Back across the estate, Special Constable Norris is reeling off a list of offences to a confused and apologetic young housewife who can't believe that she and her VW Passat have caused so much mayhem in the last fifteen minutes.

"… and there, see that there, you turned without indicating and that's an offence an' all see - dangerous driving or something, which all adds up to a tidy little ban for you madam," he bobs.

"But I've only been to the shops and back. I couldn't possibly have done half the things you've said," the housewife protests.

"Oh so you admit the other half then do you?" Norris pounces. "Well then, I'm afraid I'm gonna have to arrest you for endangering other road-users, resisting arrest and for drink driving."

Norris pulls out his plastic handcuffs and invites the housewife to step out of the vehicle and spread 'em, but at the last moment he looks around, leans in a little closer and offers her a chink of light.

"Unless," he unlesses, "you'd like to make it worth my while, huh?"

"Drink driving?" she still doesn't understand. "But don't I have to blow into something for that?"

PC Norris considers her counter-offer. "Well, you can if you want to but I'd prefer the cash to be honest, luv."

*

Ollie is talking to me from across the room but it's all going in one ear and out the other. Not that it matters, Ollie rarely imparts any information that you'll need later in life. And he only has a limited number of stories too, so if you ever miss one, you know it'll come around again within a couple of months. His anecdotes are the conversational equivalent of Robbie Williams' records; nobody ever asks for them, nobody ever listens to them, but you still can't get away from them, no matter where you fucking go.

"Yeah yeah yeah," I nod, as I paw through the drawers of Johnny's desk.

"I mean they say it tastes like real butter but does it fuck…" the background noise was saying before falling conspicuously silent.

I turn to check that Ollie's batteries haven't just dropped out, but see to my dismay Johnny standing in the doorway, staring at us with consternation.

Nobody moves for about three or four seconds. It's like one of those

208

stand-offs that always seem to drag on a bit too long in Clint Eastwood movies and for the briefest of moments I wonder if we've got away with it, but all too inevitably, Johnny dashes into the hallway and returns with his spade.

"Oh shit!" I yell, as he hurtles towards me swinging the spade around his head.

I grab the nearest thing at hand to shield myself with and brace myself for the imminent clang - but it never comes.

Instead, Johnny pulls up short and stares at me in horror.

"Oh no, wait, please, not that!" he hollers, so I look over at Ollie to see what he's done to save our lives, but typically Ollie hasn't done anything except try to climb back out of the window.

It's then that I notice what I've snatched up to defend myself with.

"Please, not my computer, please. Don't break it," Johnny pleads.

Ironic ain't it? A whole heap of computers had got me into this bother in the first place but now a computer's finally come to my rescue.

I raise Johnny's computer even higher above my head and aim it at the floor.

"Drop the spade or I'll drop your computer."

"No wait, you don't understand. It's got my book on it. I've been writing it for five years. Please don't hurt my computer or I'll lose it all," Johnny frantically begs.

Ollie climbs back down off the window sill. "Oh yeah, what's it about?"

"Uh?" Johnny stares at him.

"Your book? What's it about?" Ollie repeats.

"You had to ask," I sigh.

"Well it's about a guy who finds a trail of secret codes in Rembrandt's paintings that leads him to a discover a terrible secret and the location of a big treasure," he tells us a little too enthusiastically.

My eyebrows come together for a quick huddle. "Sounds oddly familiar," they conclude.

"No, no, this isn't like *The Da Vinci Code*. This is totally different," Johnny assures us. "I've researched it and everything. This is one-hundred per cent original."

"Yeah, I can see," I say, glancing over at the tattered and dog-eared copy of Dan Brown's bestseller on a shelf nearby, though I admit Johnny could've just been doing what Mary Whitehouse spent a lifetime doing when she used to read every dirty mag under the sun in order to safeguard the rest of us from them. Mel's uncle Vic did much the same thing, only on a slightly smaller scale. And in the privacy of his garage.

"Really? So are there really secret codes in Rembrandt's paintings?" Ollie coos.

"Well, some might argue that there are," Johnny teases knowingly.

This isn't good enough for Ollie though, who's not one for letting unspoken nods go unspoken. "Really?"

"Could be," Johnny nods again.

"No, seriously though, are there?" Ollie continues to press.

Johnny tries a couple more times to deflect the question but Ollie's having none of it and he's finally forced to come clean.

"No, not really," Johnny admits.

"Well then what's the point?" Ollie can't grasp.

"Yes thank you, but if we can just get back to matter in hand please, Ol," I remind him.

"I'm just saying it sounds rubbish though," Ollie persists.

"It does indeed sound rubbish," I agree, much to Johnny's indignation, "but I'm actually far more interested in our own little treasure hunt, starting with that key of mine."

A flicker of recognition flashes across Johnny's eyes as they dart towards the bedroom.

"And there it is, you do know what I'm talking about," I suddenly see. Johnny chews his lip as he weighs his options.

"I mean it," I tell him, lifting his computer above my head again and aiming it at the window.

"No wait!"

*

Norris has had quite a day. He's made fifty quid from me, ninety quid from three passing motorists and discovered a nice little lucrative sideline into the bargain. At this rate, the cheques he's left with the costume shop man for both hire and deposit of his police uniform might not even bounce. Well, they might not have if they hadn't been signed by Noddy and issued by The Bank Of Toy Town, which was the costume shop man's own fault for not paying close-enough attention while Norris was doing his Derren Brown double-switch with the old multiple cheques trick.

Norris is just waving off his latest sponsor and telling them to mind how they go when the roar of an approaching van him tells him another sucker is tearing up the Queen's highways and towards him.

He turns, raising his arm to signal the van to stop, but puts it back down again a bit sharpish when he sees who's driving.

Unfortunately for Norris, he's not sharpish enough.

The mini-bus screeches to a halt next to Norris and the dozen occupants all look out at him - each wearing a similar uniform to his.

"Got the call then did you?" the anxious Inspector in the front says. "Good, hop in then."

"Do what?" Norris gawps.

"The call for all units. You did get it then didn't you?" the Inspector barks impatiently.

"Er, no. Me radio's up the sink-hole," Norris tells him.

"Oh well look, it's all kicking off on the Steve Bilko Estate. Hurry up and get in. We need every man Jack available to help try and restore order before it turns into a full scale riot," the Inspector explains.

Norris blinks at him a couple of time.

"Yeah, about that..." he starts to say but the Inspector's in no mood to debate the issue with some snot-nose Constable.

"GET IN NOW!" he booms in Norris's face and the side door of the mini-bus is thrown back.

Before he can think, he's inside the bus and surrounded on all sides by day-glo jackets, peaked hats and determined scowls.

As the bus pulls away, Norris takes a tumble against one particularly angry-looking Sergeant in riot gear and neck tattoos who looks like he's been waiting for this all year long.

"What was that?" the Sergeant asks the mini-bus.

"What?" another copper responds.

"I thought I heard some little kiddy's toy squeaking."

Norris picks himself up and hurries into the back, dumping his arse into an empty seat away from the confused Sergeant.

"Has everyone got their stab vests on?" the Inspector calls back from the front.

Norris isn't sure he's heard right.

"Their what?" he asks as every radio on the bus suddenly erupts with anxious calls for urgent reinforcements.

Every radio, that is, except his.

Norris starts frantically looking around the back of the mini-bus for an emergency exit he can drop out of and it's only now that he clocks the copper in the next seat, staring at him with absolute incredulity etched across his face.

Norris stares back for about a dozen heartbeats before eventually finding his voice.

"Afternoon Sergeant," he reluctantly shrugs.

"Afternoon Norris," Weasel gawps.

*

Johnny digs out my key and hands it over on the understanding that he'll break my head if I break his computer. I have no intention of doing any such thing, I've got what I came for and now I just want to leave.

I circumnavigate Johnny at arm's length and back out of the front door, keeping Johnny's computer between me and his twitching gardening implement at all times.

"Give my computer back you bastard," he snarls, his eyes red and full of murder.

"Just stay back," I warn him. "I mean it, I'll drop it if you come any closer."

"You do that and you're a dead man, you hear me Shit Bag?" he wields the spade, matching me step-for-step up the front garden path and towards the street.

"Loud and clear fruitloop," I confirm. "I've got what I wanted and now I'm off, and I'll never darken your door again."

"Then give me my FUCKING COMPUTER BACK!" he bellows like King Kong barking at Fay Wray's over-familiar boyfriend.

"I've already said, not until you drop the spade," I remind him.

Johnny snarls like a man possessed and brandishes his shovel menacingly, really not wanting to trust me, but our Clint Eastwood stand-off has escalated into the Cuban missile crisis and neither of us will win if this thing goes bad. Eventually, after half a minute or so of soul searching, Johnny comes to accept this fact and reluctantly takes a leap of faith.

"Okay," he snivels, tossing his spade behind him. "But you'd better not try anything funny or I'll find you. I mean it. That's my life's work you've got there."

There's a pond on the front lawn and I have to admit I'm sorely tempted (just for a laugh), but I decide to be mature about this and live up to my side. After all, I have changed you know. I have gone straight - apparently.

Slowly, and very very gently, I start to set the computer down. Johnny tries to make a dash towards me, so I raise it up again and ward him back. I want a clear twenty feet between us before I'm willing to relinquish my Microsoft body armour.

Johnny reluctantly backs away again and this time I manage to set the computer down and jump clear before he's able to fall upon me.

Me and Ollie leg it up the road as Johnny snatches up his beloved computer and cradles it with tears of relief. He can't believe he came so close to losing everything he's ever worked for and suddenly he's desperate to get it back into the relative safety of his flat. He gathers up his precious hard drive and hurries back towards his front door, but unfortunately Johnny doesn't see the spade that's been carelessly discarded across his driveway just behind him and his feet come a cropper on the handle.

"Jesus," he screams as he trips and launches his computer against the side of his garage. The white plastic body doesn't stand a chance and disintegrates on contact with the brickwork, spewing its silver and green guts out across the cold hard concrete.

"Oh God NO!!!" Johnny gasps one last time, before fainting face first into a pile of silicone scrap.

Three thousand miles away, at the New York International Book Fair, publishers and literature scholars from around the globe manage to somehow carry on.

5. I might've known

Roland doesn't like his job. It's not a bad job as jobs go, but anything that forces Roland out of bed in the morning and into a Polo T-shirt is, by definition, "a load of shit".

The girl he's dealing with is painfully effervescent and enthusiastic, as new members often are, but none of it is rubbing off on Roland, who stinks of booze and has a blinding headache.

Roland swipes her Visa across his computer, files her form in the overflowing 'Miscellaneous' drawer of a big filing cabinet behind him and laminates her membership card.

"Okay, there you go, Ruth," Roland says, reading the name on the card before handing it to her. "That entitles you to use the gym weekends and week days after 6pm and the pool anytime Monday to Thursday. If you want to upgrade to a Gold membership, which is another tenner a month, you can come and go as you please. I'll even give you the keys and you can lock up at night if you like."

Ruth's enthusiastic grin cracks a little.

"Really?" she asks.

"No not really," Roland sighs, sinking into his seat to take the weight off his feet after these recent exertions. "So, if you want to go and get changed, I'll give you your induction and show you how to use the exercise machines in a bit."

"You?" Ruth gawks in surprise.

"Yes, me," Roland confirms. "I'm the gym's professional instructor."

Ruth doesn't want to be rude, but she's just paid out over a hundred pounds to join this gym, so she feels she has the right to ask the odd forthright question if it she suspects she's not getting value for money. And looking at Roland, who, and let's be frank here, isn't in the best of shape and even has to take a breather after rolling fags, isn't exactly the gym's greatest advertisement for physical fitness.

"You're a professional instructor?" Ruth tippy-toes.

Roland looks up from his Ginsters. "Of course," he glares. "Do I look like I hang around here when I ain't getting paid?"

"Oh, right, er okay," Ruth frowns. "Er, where do I get changed?"

Roland's had enough of this already and there's still four hours to go.

"Out in the car park," he tells her.

"The car park?"

"For fuck's sake," he mumbles under his breath, struggling to get his pasty inside him while it's still warm. He nods towards the corridor. "The women's changing rooms of course."

"Oh, right, yes, sorry," Ruth fizzes apologetically, jiggling her head in an effort to demonstrate that she's a bit ditsy and that this is apparently cute. "See you in ten minutes then?"

Roland nods and watches Ruth head off in the direction of the changing rooms, then quickly piles the rest of the pasty into his gob and closes his eyes for five minutes. When he reopens them, me and Ollie are shaking him awake and asking him if he's alright.

"What the fuck..." he gabbers, before leaning forward, coughing violently into the bin and rubbing his eyes.

"Hey Rollo, you alright?"

"Bex!" he beams when his eyes finally focus. He leaps from his chair, dashes around the desk and smothers me in a big bear-hug. "Ah mate, welcome home, how the fuck are you?"

"I'm fine Rollo. All the better for seeing you," I tell him. For a moment I worry that it's going to take all of my guile escaping Roland's loving arms, but this problem solves itself the moment he clocks Ollie.

"Big Guy!" he erupts, dropping me in an instant and transferring the full weight of his affections to Ollie.

"Yeah, alright Rollo, I only saw you last week," Ollie objects, doing all he can to keep Roland at arm's length.

"Oh yeah, great weren't it," Roland remembers. "Toasting Ol getting out we was. It was a real touching celebration, weren't it Big Guy?"

"That so," I comment. "I would've personally just had a few drinks, but each to their own I guess."

"Anyway Bex, what can I do you for?" Roland says. "You wanna free trial?"

"No thanks Rollo, last time I had one of those I got my membership card stamped for four years. No, actually I'm just here to make a withdrawal."

Roland looks about and nods knowingly. "Oh right, yeah sure you are. Follow me," he winks, leading me and Ollie out of reception and into the men's changing rooms.

"What are we doing here, Bex?" Ollie asks me.

"My safety deposit box," I tell him, approaching a bank of lockers.

"There you go," Roland says, banging the furthest locker to the left, "safe and sound. Ain't been opened in two years."

"Cheers Rollo. You put the custard in custodian, you know that?" I thank him, slapping him on the back. "Very much appreciated."

Roland tells me it wasn't a problem, then ambles back to the coal face.

"Nice safety deposit box," Ollie smirks.

"Well, it's cheaper than a real one isn't it. And you get your fifty pee back," I tell him, sticking my key in the lock, opening the door and fishing my finger about in the coin-catch to illustrate. "At least, you do if someone hasn't replaced it with an old Escudo bit," I notice with concern when I examine the coin.

Considerably worse than that, my nest egg's also gone. In its place is a small hand-written envelope addressed to "Shit Bag".

"It's for you," Ollie notices.

I recognise the hand-writing immediately and tear into the envelope with a sense of dread. "No no no no no!"

The note is indeed from Mel.

"Dear Shit Bag, I've taken your money to cover the back-rent you owed me and I've moved back to Leeds. If you try to find me, contact me or even send me a Christmas card (which would be a first), I'll tell the police everything I know about every single burglary you've ever committed. I have dozens of details and copious (it means lots) amounts of evidence. I never want to see or hear from you ever again. I mean this. Faint heart may never have won fair maiden, but if you come anywhere near Yorkshire, I will fuck you up big time. Lots of hate, Mel. - ps. I fucked Roland just before I left town (he was quite surprised about it). I want you to think about this as often as possible."

"Blimey," Ollie huffs in surprise. "You owed her three grand in back rent?"

"Thank you Ollie, I knew I could rely on you to see the big picture."

"So, what are you gonna do?"

I think on this for several seconds and decide upon two courses of action.

"Well, first off I'd better apologise to Rollo for inadvertently giving him Chlamydia. And then secondly I guess I'll have to go with plan B."

"What's plan B?" Ollie asks.

I reach into the locker and feel about the metal door rim before producing a second key. This key opens the locker beside this one, so I tell Ollie to take a step to the right and slip the key in the door.

"Pawn my tools," I tell him. I've got about a grand's worth of drills, glass cutters, diamond bits and other assorted high-spec gadgetry I can turn into folding money which might be enough to get the Hassans off my back. Or buy myself some time at the very least.

But when I open this locker I find haven't got these things either. Just another note from Mel.

"Your tools are in the duck pond, which is the best place for them. If I was you, I'd get a new bank - M," I read. "What a slag!"

I drop the note on the floor and walk out. Behind me, Ollie fishes his finger into the second locker's coin catch and calls after me.

"Hold on Bex, don't you want your... zloty?"

I tell you, there's none so capable of cuntiness as a woman scorned, or so they say. Okay, I'll be the first to admit that I wasn't the best boyfriend a girl could've ever hoped for. But then relationships are hard work aren't they? They're all chocolates and flowers and "how was your day dear?" and this is a lot to keep on top of. Especially if you're a bit like me and don't give a flying squirrel about any of this stuff at the best of times. Don't get me wrong, I loved Mel to bits, I really did, but just because you love someone to bits, that shouldn't necessarily mean you have to spend every waking moment worshipping their feet or striving to live up to their lofty standards when your own are a bit too much like hard work most days, should it? I mean seriously, it's too much.

Particularly for someone who's instinctively selfish like me.

And that's no bad thing, by the way - being selfish. Lots of very successful people are selfish - city traders, business men (and ladies), politicians, footballers, multi-national conglomerates - and they all seem to do alright for themselves. Only selfishness for these blokes is called "ruthlessness" and regarded as a quality, but you work late into the night and hardly see your old lady when you ain't got an office to hang out in and suddenly you're just a twat. And drunk again! And where's my Post Office book?

I tell you, it's a good job she has finally left because I've just about had enough of that attitude of hers.

Ollie catches up with me outside and gives me my zloty.

"Here, when she had your money away, why didn't she just leave your key in your box? I mean, she obviously found it," Ollie asks.

"What, and make things easy for me? Oh no, she's up there somewhere, sitting on a cloud laughing her head off at me," I say.

"Cloud? What are you talking about, she ain't dead?"

"Ollie please, don't spoil it for me, hey. I've had a hard day."

Ollie says he understands and pulls out his mobile. "So, shall we give Electric a bell then? Tell him we'll do a couple of jobs if he wants?"

"Better still, give me that," I insist, grabbing Ollie's mobile out of his hand and finding Electric's fag packet in my pocket. I dial the Hassan's number scribbled on it and see if I can't make a better deal for myself than the one Electric's proposing in exchange for a few choice bits of information about our mutual friend. However, when the phone's picked up at the other end, I suddenly discover there's no need.

I hang up, give Ollie back his phone and tell him to follow me.

"Hold on Bex, what's going on? What did he say?" Ollie asks as we head for Electric's place of business. "Bex, where are we going?"

"We're going to see Omit Hassan," I tell him, but Ollie pulls up sharply at the prospect. "Come on," I grab him, my confidence rejuvenated. "We'll be fine."

6. Meaty negotiations

Electric's junk shop is situated on the corner of a little parade of shops. There's a newsagent's, a sub-Post Office, a hairdressers, a kebab shop and two separate mini-marts that stock fresh fruit and veg but sell nothing but booze. Electric's place represents the odd dusty little shop that every parade seems to have, that never does any business but stays open regardless.

Me and Ollie walk straight past it and into the kebab shop.

"Hello boys, how can I help you?" the young Turk behind the counter smiles, as he sharpens his kebab knife with a theatrical flourish.

"Omit Hassan?" I ask, and the smile slips from his face momentarily.

"Er no my friend. I don't know no one by that name," he says, when he regains his composure.

Ollie's staring at us all confused and asks me what's going on.

"Ask him," I tell Ollie, but the opportunity's lost when the phone behind the young kebabist starts to ring.

"Hold on boys, one second," he urges us, before answering the phone. "Hello, Abbra-Kebabbra?"

I raise Ollie's mobile to my ear and speak to the Turk without taking my eyes from his.

"Hello my friend, yes Bex here," I tell him. "I've decided not to bother getting you your computers or sorting you out with that three grand. Instead I think I'm gonna drop the real Hassan family a note to let them know someone's using Omit's name. How does that sound to you?" I suggest, drilling my eyes into a face that's now whiter than mine.

For the benefit of those of you who might be related to Ollie, I should take a moment to explain that this kebab-technician is of course not Omit Hassan, any more than I'm Tony Soprano. He is just a Turkish restaurateur who has a passion for radio drama and who's silly enough to make crank calls from his own landline.

'Omit' - as I think we might as well call him - drops the phone back into its cradle and rushes towards the door to stop us from leaving.

"No wait, please don't. It was Karel's idea," he frantically explains - Karel being Electric's real name. "He said it was very big joke on his good friend. Please, I didn't mean no harm. What can I do? What can I do?" he implores.

I hate to see a man so reduced to such a pitiful state so I throw him a bone.

"Well, as Omit Hassan might say if he were here now, you are in my debt mate, and I do intend to collect - one way or the other."

'Omit' ponders this for a moment and asks if we'd like a kebab. "On the house, of course?" he urges.

217

This sounds like a splendid idea, so I relent.

"Yes I would now that you come to mention it," I accept. "King-size doner, extra meat, onions and chilli sauce."

'Omit' clatters about behind his counter toasting a pitta and carving great gouges out of the elephant's leg that's roasting in the window.

"Here, I'll get Belinda to show you how to work that thing with the flush tomorrow," Ollie tells me. "Sounds like you're gonna be needing it."

'Omit' looks to me anxiously and asks if there's anything else I want.

"No. Just that," I reassure him. "Every Friday night - for the rest of my life."

"Well that should knock a few years off of it at least," Ollie reckons, but I ain't done ordering yet and tap the counter to get 'Omit's' attention again.

"Twice."

*

We leave with two enormous, steaming hot doners and walk up the road. Ollie's already bitten his fingers twice trying to wolf it into his face at break-neck speed, so I tell him to leave it alone and give it to me.

"Why?" he asks cautiously.

"Because I want to use it for a demonstration," I tell him.

"What sort of demonstration?" he asks, not liking the sound of it one little bit and supremely reluctant to lose his dinner after only a couple of plunges.

"Look, it's alright, you'll get it back," I promise, but Ollie smells a rat (as well as several runaway cats obviously) and I'm forced to tickle his belly and tell him all sorts of lies before I eventually manage to prise it away from him.

"Come on, this way," I tell him, steering him along the parade and into Electric's shop on the corner. The little bell above the door tinkles to summon Electric from the back and a moment later he appears through his beaded curtains.

"How do boys, didn't take you long…" he starts confidently, only to fall silent when he spots the kebabs I'm holding in each hand. "Ah, now, hang on…"

"Hello mate," I greet him, then shake the kebabs violently, spinning them around my head and sending greasy hot sloppy meat in all directions over absolutely everything - walls, doors and windows, heaters, tellies, teapots and tat, nothing escapes. Electric even gets a faceful of mince when I set his countertop fan on full speed and feed the last few shreds through it to see how it performs.

"See you next Friday," I promise him, before tossing the wrappers into his waste paper bin (for irony's sake) and leaving.

As I pull open the door, I admire Electric's "NO FOOD OR DRINK" sign hanging in the door and smile to myself.

"Sod it!" Electric grumbles in my wake.

Ollie catches up with me as I march towards the pub and points out that I'd said I only wanted to borrow his dinner.

"And so I did," I point out. "You know where it is if you still want it."

"You're such a wanker," Ollie grumbles.

"It's been said before," I shrug. "And I'm sure it'll be said again."

"So that's it then? You really are out of the game for good?" Ollie harangues.

I check my stride and turn to Ollie. "Listen mate, whether I'm in or whether I'm out, I'll make that decision if you don't fucking mind. Not you, not Electric, not Weasel, and certainly not Rory Bremner in the kebab shop. If Mel couldn't get us to do what she wanted when she had tits and a gob for incentives, what chance d'you think you lot have?" I tell him. "I am, and always have been, my own governor."

"Hey, I ain't telling you what to do. I was actually just thinking about myself, you know," Ollie objects, making about as much sense as usual.

"Get away," I gasp in mock-shock.

To be honest, I don't know if Ollie was in cahoots with Electric to get us back to work, but either way, he was putting peer pressure on us all the same. Whether his motivations were black or whether they were white, he was still trying to press my buttons and that's never the cleverest idea in the world. Family, teachers, girlfriends and friends have been trying to get me to jump through hoops for as long as I can remember and if there's one thing that'll get me folding my arms and lighting a fag, it's the sound of a whip cracking behind me. Which is probably why I turned out the way I am. If I'd been left to my own devices when I was a kid I'd probably be a doctor or the manager of Dixons by now I reckon.

"You seem a bit angry," Ollie mind-reads.

"Oh do I? I wonder why."

"Are you pissed off that Mel's nicked your money?" he asks.

I frown and think on this. "No, not really," I finally conclude.

"Then what's up?"

As reluctant as I am to bare my own private misery to the bone without the benefit of studio lighting, cameramen, an agitated audience and a smug presenter to throw a chair at, I try to make Ollie see what a rough day I've had nevertheless.

"Look Ol, in spite of all our ups and downs, I can't believe Mel's actually gone and left me. I just can't get my head around it. We may have argued seven days a week and twice at Christmas, but at the end of the day I still loved her. She was... she was my life. My love."

"I know mate. I know," Ollie sympathises.

"Do you?"

"Yeah, she was your soul mate."

"More than that," I tell him. "She was everything to me. Everything."

Ollie nods sadly. "So, do you want me to ask Belinda to set you up with one of her mates then?"

"Yeah alright," I readily enthuse, wondering what we're waiting for. "Does she still knock around with that little slag with the pierced tits and wobbly arse, because I've always wanted a go on her?"

Before Ollie can remind me that this is actually his step-sister (I always forget) the sound of running footsteps coming from the far end of the street distracts us both.

We turn just in time to see Norris haring around the corner holding onto his police hat and sprinting towards us just as fast as his legs can carry him.

"Hey look, it's Norris," Ollie spots. "Here Norris, where d'you get to, you big skiver?"

"Sorry, can't stop," Norris apologises as he passes by in a blur.

A second set of footsteps turns our heads again and we now see Weasel rounding the corner and charging after Norris with grim determination etched across his face.

"Alright Sergeant, how's it going?" I ask, as he passes by as well.

"Not good," he calls over his shoulder without breaking stride.

I'm just about to chuckle with delight when a dozen more angry footsteps suddenly explode out of nowhere and we look back down the road to see an enormous knot of nutty Steve Bilko Yardies charging towards us with bin lids in their hands and murder in their eyes.

"Kill the pigs! KILL THE FUCKING PIGS!" they scream, baring their teeth when they clock us for a couple of hobnobbing copper's mates.

"Holy shit!" we shriek as one.

Me and Ollie peg it for our lives after Norris and Weasel - the fucking no-warning cunts - up the road, round the bend and into the streets of Tatley.

It's funny, I might not have Mel any more, a job, money or a place to call my own, but I never seem short of things to leg it from. I guess it's all part and parcel of life's rich tapestry, but I do sometimes wonder why this should be.

Just as I can't help but wonder what I'll be legging it from tomorrow. Whatever it is, I'm sure it'll catch me up in the end.

Things usually do, you know.

Well, no one can outrun themselves.

For the cast, crew
and viewers
with thanks

Cast (regulars)

Bex	Tom Brooke
Ollie	Fraser Ayres
Mel	Jessica Harris
Belinda	Chereen Buckley
Norris	Darren Tighe
Weasel	Gary Beadle
Electric	David Bradley
Roland	Andrew Buckley
Sgt Atwell	Ian Bartholomew
PC Bennett	Robin King
Charlie	Roger Sloman
Keith	Mark Burdis

The Warehouse Job

Bob Shaw	Lloyd McGuire
Customer	Dominic Coleman
Mrs Bob	Caroline Parker
Dan at Bar	Danny King

The Jackets Job

Alice (elderly witness)	Joan Linder
Number Four	Oliver Ford
Number Two	Richard Glover

The Teapot Job

Mr Cooper	John Normington
School Receptionist	Abi Eniola

The Footballer Job

Claude Delacroix	Dhafer L'Abidine
Wayne Crockett	Corey J Smith
Jackie (young biddy)	Faye Rusling
Newsagent	Stephen K Amos
Hopeful Clubber	Danny Glover
Mr Andrews	Steve Steen

The Office Job

Horace	Geoffrey McGivern
Doris	Selina Cadell
Security Guard	Jim Field Smith
Glamorous Date	Shirley Cheriton
Frumpy Date	Denise Mack
Lecherous Date	Sue Vincent
Speed Date Organiser	Philippa Fordham

"Thieves Like Us"

THE WAREHOUSE JOB
(first screened on BBC Three January 22nd, 2007)

THE ALARM JOB
(first screened on BBC Three January 29th, 2007)

THE TEAPOT JOB
(first screened on BBC Three February 5th, 2007)

THE JACKETS JOB
(first screened on BBC Three February 12th, 2007)

THE FOOTBALLER JOB
(first screened on BBC Three February 19th, 2007)

THE OFFICE JOB
(first screened on BBC Three February 26th, 2007)

THE KEY JOB
(never filmed)

Produced by Pete Thornton
Directed by Ben Kellett

Special thanks to **Micheál Jacob** for making the series possible and for giving kind permission for the publication of this book.

by the same author

books
The Burglar Diaries
The Bank Robber Diaries
The Hitman Diaries
The Pornographer Diaries
Milo's Marauders
Milo's Run
School for Scumbags
Blue Collar

television
Thieves Like Us

stage
The Pornographer Diaries: the play

Danny King was born in Slough in 1969 and later grew up in Tatley... sorry, Yateley. He left school at sixteen and went to work on building sites, in supermarkets, offices and for the Royal Mail.

In 1988 he was convicted of Burglary and Going Equipped, and in 1989 Taking & Driving Away and Resisting Arrest.

Ten years later he wrote a book loosely inspired by these criminal experiences called *The Burglar Diaries*, which was published by Serpent's Tail in 2001.

Then in 2006 he adapted it into the BBC Three sitcom *Thieves Like Us*, from which this book was lifted.

Danny now lives in Chichester with his wife Jeannie and son Charlie and hasn't stolen a thing for almost twenty years - except half the gags in this book.

Lightning Source UK Ltd.
Milton Keynes UK
14 July 2010

157004UK00002B/42/P